A DANGEROUS MAGIC

A DANGEROUS MAGIC

Frances Lynch

ST. MARTIN'S PRESS   NEW YORK

Library of Congress Cataloging in Publication Data

Lynch, Frances, 1930-
  A dangerous magic.

  I. Title.
PZ4.L9873Dan   1978   [PR6062.Y58]   813'.5'4
ISBN 0-312-18218-X   77-17766

Other books by Frances Lynch

Twice Ten Thousand Miles
The Fine and Handsome Captain
Stranger at the Wedding

You have but to know an object by
its proper name for it to lose its
dangerous magic.
                    Elias Canetti

PART I

1

It's no use at all, sitting down to write one's memoirs, and then trying to fudge them. One must be prepared to be utterly truthful. Of course, the truth is often painful—both to oneself and to those others, possibly near and dear to one, whom it may affect. But truthfulness is still absolutely essential. Otherwise the whole enterprise becomes a singular waste of everybody's time.

Especially when, as in my own case, one has reached the age of fifty-seven—if one's mirror is to be believed, *seventy*-seven at least—and has decided it's high time the record be set straight on any number of important particulars. Not, you understand, simply in order that one's soul may be purged but rather so that justice, no matter how long-delayed, may finally be done.

The lie I have lived has gone on long enough. The purpose of these memoirs is that it should be ended, once and for all.

I was twenty-nine when I consented in church to become the wife of Sir James Aubrey Tantallon. Up to that time my life had been rackety and some would say ill-spent. Certainly it had been the despair of my poor parents, while they lived. And equally certainly, for Sir James to give his name and high social position to a young woman only recently come from twice nightly performances on the stage of Edinburgh's Empire Theatre was both brave and extra-ordinarily generous. Even today, in these enlightened Edwardian times, I fear that the variety theatre is still hardly considered a respectable calling.

That I subsequently showed myself worthy of his gener-osity and courage is neither here nor there. I shall be grateful for it, and for the twenty-five long and happy years that he gave me, for the rest of my life.

Mind you, I wouldn't want it thought that I'm at all ashamed of my former occupation. My fame had been worked for honestly and well. Thanks to my dear friend and mentor, the great illusionist, Professor Henri Salvador, I was already at the top of my profession. The Incredible Madame Otranta had performed, as the saying goes, before all the crowned heads of Europe. But this was, needless to say, scarcely a recommendation when I was later striving for social acceptance as the wife of a member of Queen Victoria's most intimate circle.

My efforts were not helped, naturally enough, by the various improbable stories then going about as to my origins and early childhood. I was *not*, as the news-sheets would severally have me, a mysterious orphan, raised by the kindly holy men of Tibet. Neither did I come of gypsy stock, fleeing from an Andorran blood-feud. Nor yet was I the unacknowledged offspring of the Russian Ambassador to the Court of Spain, nor even the seventh daughter of a romantically dispossessed Polish nobleman.

Not that any of these exotic beginnings, devised in fact either by Professor Salvador or our more imaginative theatrical entrepreneurs for purely commercial reasons, were openly referred to. But they lurked in the background nevertheless, and took a great deal of living down.

The Queen herself, of course, God rest her, had her own problems. Not the least of these being. . . . But I run ahead of myself. The agreeable gentleman who has consented to publish these memoirs would, I feel sure, much prefer me to keep any revelations concerning the poor late Queen until their proper place in my narrative. . . .

*　　　*　　　*

The letter from her great-aunt's publisher arrived one morning in late August, a letter that was to prove momentous, concerning as it did the vexed question of the old lady's memoirs. All the same, young Bridie Tantallon came running down the stairs and across the dingy oilcloth of Mrs. Bartlett's hall in such a hurry that she might easily have missed it propped up between the chipped Jubilee mug and the pink pot-dog present from Brighton on the middle shelf of Mrs. Bartlett's coat-and-umbrella stand.

She'd given up expecting letters. Indeed, in the months following her father's death and her subsequent move from their pleasant rooms in Maida Vale, near Lord's Cricket Ground, she had given up expecting very much of anything at all—except the doubtful, twentieth-century pleasures of being an independent young woman, with the poverty and loneliness that this seemed to involve. She would, therefore, very probably not have seen the letter at all, had she not paused anxiously to reassure herself in the umbrella-stand's lozenge-shaped mirror that her hair had at least survived the four flights down from her tiny parlour-bedroom without escaping entirely from its multitude of pins and tortoiseshell fastenings.

Her haste was on account of being on her way to yet another interview—this time with the Black Diamond Shipping Company in Horseferry Lane—and, although she had little hope that it would come to anything (there were, by all accounts, already a full seven thousand girls in London quite as expert on the typewriter as she, and nobody seemed remotely inclined to increase that number to seven thousand and one) she was nevertheless determined to be punctual. And to create at least a passable first impression.

Having satisfied herself that her heavy coils of auburn hair were still more or less where they ought to be, and jammed her brisk straw boater firmly down on top, she was about to turn quickly away when the letter caught her eye. She picked it up. The envelope was clearly addressed to her, and type-written—which suggested a business communication. A spon-taneous offer of employment? Sad experience caused her very much to doubt it. A bill then, perhaps. She hesitated a moment, then stuffed the letter into her handbag and hurried out through the shabby front door, thankfully leaving behind her the unappealing odour of boiled cabbage and moth-balls that permeated every corner of Mrs. Bartlett's seedy establishment.

She contained her curiosity about the letter until she had boarded the omnibus taking her down to the City, climbed the precipitous stairs and installed herself safely upon one of the wooden seats of its upper deck. Then she took out the letter and opened it.

It was, she saw at once, from Mr. Pugh-Hennessy, the man who had been her father's publisher, the owner of a small but prosperous publishing house situated in a narrow terraced house on Floral Street. His letter was short, and to the point. " I would be very grateful," Mr. Pugh-Hennessy wrote, " if you could visit me at your earliest convenience here in my offices in Covent Garden. The matter will, I believe, be to our mutual advantage. It concerns the memoirs of your great-aunt, Lady Otranta Tantallon. If you could see your way to sparing me an hour or so of your valuable time, I would esteem it a great favour."

Her valuable time. . . . Bridie smiled a little sadly to herself. Since her father's death her time had not been in the least valuable. And anyway, if Mr. Pugh-Hennessy wanted a little of it, who was she to grudge him? He was, after all, the nearest she had to a friend—they had known each other almost for as long as she could remember, ever since he had first consented to publish her father's books. These were, as she now knew, musical biographies and critical works of a virtually unsaleable kind. Mr. Pugh-Hennessy's loyalty and faith in Professor Tantallon had seen Bridie and her father through many lean months, and it was he who had sorted out the Professor's affairs after his sudden death.

She did not make friends easily, had no close relatives, and the special circumstances of her life had hardly encouraged her to maintain a wide social circle. Her mother had died when she was twelve, of influenza, leaving her the sole companion and helpmeet of her dear father, who himself had suffered, poor soul, from a progressive affliction of the eyes that had cruelly brought him total blindness for the last several years of his life. She regretted not a single one of the days spent by his side—his courage and unfailing good spirits had been a source of constant inspiration to her—but the sad fact was that they had left her now, at nineteen, quite without friends of her own age and far too shy to be able to go out quickly and make some.

She read the letter again, holding it as still as she could against the wind and the omnibus's thunderous jolting. Lady Otranta's *memoirs*? What on earth could Mr. Pugh-Hennessy possibly expect her to know about Lady Otranta? In all her life, she and her great-aunt had never even corresponded, let alone met. In fact, the two sides of the family, hers and Lady Otranta's, had positively not been on speaking terms these thirty-odd years.

All the same, if Mr. Pugh-Hennessy wanted to see her, she'd go. He had, after all, suggested that the visit might be to their mutual advantage. And she could certainly do with a nice bit of mutual advantage. The only question that remained, therefore, was exactly when she should visit him—now, at once, or later, after her morning's interview?

She stared again at the letter in her hand. Interviews terrified her. It was silly, she knew, but they absolutely terrified her. Warty men with cigars and bursting waistcoats, who stared at her as if she was something the cat had brought in. And besides, dear, kind old Mr. Pugh-Hennessy, who wasn't in the least warty, had asked her to come at her 'earliest convenience'. So surely it wouldn't be civil to keep him waiting?

Somehow the summons from the Black Diamond Shipping Company found its way overboard, to drift down onto the crowded pavements of the Tottenham Court Road. She herself left the omnibus rather more decorously, at a stop in the Strand, and made her way briskly towards Covent Garden.

A simple enough decision, she had thought. An understandable decision, even a reasonable decision. However, less than a week later she found herself regretting it with almost hysterical intensity. For, as a direct result, she was by then irrevocably committed to the Flying Scotsman and well on her way up to Castle Tantallon. That was, of course, her great-aunt's home near Kincardine, on the shores of the Firth of Forth, across the water from Leith and the ancient, black-stoned city of Edinburgh.

She still didn't quite know how it had happened. Distractedly she peered out of her first-class carriage window. How fast the train was going—no wonder it was called the Flying Scotsman! When she'd left Euston at ten that morning it had seemed that she would never *really* arrive, that the journey would safely go on for ever. Yet now, with the next stop York, it was already almost half over.

If only, oh, if only she'd done the sensible thing. If only she'd gone off first to the nice shipping company, and got herself a nice position, and been able afterwards to say to Mr. Pugh-Hennessy, firmly and in all honesty, that she really couldn't do what he wanted of her because she had a prior commitment—with the nice warty man at the Black Diamond Shipping Company.

She'd protested, of course. Much as she would in ordinary circumstances have welcomed the chance of a break, any break, from her lonely and penurious existence under Mrs Bartlett's roof, the prospect he offered was simply too alarming. But, without that prior commitment, she just hadn't had a leg to stand on.

"Lady Otranta won't *eat* you, my dear. After all, you *are* a member of the family. And she *has* written to say she'll have you. So you *truly* don't have a thing to worry about."

No doubt he'd meant well enough. From his point of view there probably wasn't anything very much to be afraid of.

Bridie shivered slightly. By nightfall she'd be at the castle. By nightfall she'd be face-to-face with the fearsome Lady Otranta.

She'd tried to explain things to him. She tried to tell him how bad she was at dealing with people she didn't know, how even the simplest conversation with strangers threw her into a ridiculous panic. But Mr. Pugh-Hennessy had scarcely listened. His mind was quite made up—it must be she and none other who went up to Castle Tantallon. He'd commissioned memoirs from Lady Tantallon, and now the old lady was apparently unwilling to go through with them. Bridie was just the person to go up and help her. Reason with her. Persuade her.

Again, as she sat dismally watching the golden harvest fields of the Midlands hurry by, Bridie shivered. Help her? Help an old lady with memoirs she probably had some very good reason for not writing after all? Reason with her? Persuade her to begin them? The idea was preposterous. Horrifying, even. Why her? Of all people, why *her*?

It wasn't as if she'd given in easily.

"We've never been exactly close," she told Mr. Pugh-Hennessy. "My father's side of the family and hers. Why, my grandfather was to be her brother-in-law, and he refused even to go to the wedding."

"But that's an *ancient* quarrel, an *ancient* quarrel. . . ." Mr. Pugh-Hennessy paused to insert a little finger in one ear and rattle it vigorously. Clearly he considered the matter already settled. "I tell you, my dear, this is the *twentieth century*. Family differences are a thing of the past, entirely. Don't you think?"

"It's not what *I* think, Mr. Pugh-Hennessy. It's what Lady Otranta may—"

"Over and done with. *Quite* over and done with." He hoisted himself with some effort to his feet and moved away to the open window. He was a fusty person, tall and thin, with steeply-sloped eyebrows, a profusion of dark, greying hair, and the very latest in lugubrious false teeth. "Believe me, child, in polite society today the question of Lady Tantallon's—ah—*unorthodox* beginnings is long forgotten. She has redeemed them entirely. She is undoubtedly a *most* remarkable woman. Don't you think? And she has some . . . er . . . remarkable things to tell. . . . Otherwise you may be *sure* that I would never have commissioned the book in the first place."

He flashed her his rather over-furnished smile. "I have no doubt at all that the two of you will get on together excellently."

Suddenly the view from Bridie's compartment window was obscured as the train entered a cutting and thick white smoke funnelled down beside the carriage. She turned from the window and closed her eyes. So polite society had quite forgotten the matter of her great-aunt's beginnings, had it? Was the family quarrel also forgotten? Certainly not by her father, while he had lived. For him everything about the good lady had been faintly ridiculous, if not downright disgraceful. Why, even her name was an outrage: *The Incredible Madame Otranta*, indeed! A complete fabrication, of course—she could hear his voice even now—just the sort of thing some little conjuror's assistant might come up with, a wretched young woman who actually earned her living telling fortunes and being sawn in half twice-nightly. She'd been born in a slum—he had it on good authority—and her name was almost certainly Mavis or Aggie or some such. Calling herself the celebrated mentalist, Madame Otranta, indeed!

In the circumstances, Bridie thought, it was hardly surprising that her side of the family had opposed Sir James's remarriage so bitterly, and the first Lady Tantallon scarcely ten months departed this life. Twentieth century or not, she wondered, could such a quarrel really be so quickly forgotten?

Not that Bridie herself cared a fig for the Lady Otranta's origins. Times were undoubtedly changing, and she knew that even families as old as the Tantallons must change with them. And besides, on her marriage the second Lady Tantallon had clearly risen to the occasion. Within a very few years she had become accepted in the strait-laced circles of Scottish society and even in that of the old Queen. And her elder son, from what Mr. Pugh-Hennessy had said, was now a worthy successor to his father's title and estates.

On the other hand, the old lady's nature, her evident eccentricity and fearsomeness, concerned Bridie very much indeed. The prospect of being faced with that, on top of a houseful—nay, a *castleful*—of total strangers, with two sons, a step-daughter, and heaven knows what else, terrified her quite out of her wits.

And in any case, the forgetting of family quarrels was not a one-sided activity. However broad-minded Bridie herself might feel, and however cordial her great-aunt's invitation might have been, it was perfectly possible that the rest of the family would view the matter less than agreeably.

The note of the train's wheels changed as it rattled out of the cutting. Bridie opened her eyes, saw distant mill chimneys across a wooded valley. If only Mr. Pugh-Hennessy had been willing to listen to her.

" But won't Lady Tantallon think it strange," she'd insisted, " that I should visit her now, simply upon a matter of business, when in all my life I have never before gone anywhere near her?"

" Strange? Why *strange*?" In moments of agitation Mr. Pugh-Hennessy's teeth whistled like a broken-winded cab horse. " I cannot see what's *strange* about it. You had your father to look after. A *blind* man—you could hardly be expected to leave him to his own devices. Don't you think? Not to mention the *invaluable* assistance you gave him in his work. The research, the hours of painstaking dictation . . . he'd have been *lost* without you." And to this last she could say nothing, for in fact it was true.

Assuming the matter now closed, Mr. Pugh-Hennessy turned away and fixed his attention upon the busy roadway below. But still Bridie lingered in his gloomy book-lined office, urgently racking her brains for an argument that might make him change his mind.

It wasn't, she supposed, worth pointing out that her father's blindness had only come upon him in the last few years of his life. And the rift in the Tantallon family dated from long before she had been born, a good thirty years, to the time of her grandfather, Sir James's younger brother.

Mr. Pugh-Hennessy's office overlooked Floral Street, from where the sounds and smells of nearby Covent Garden market rose powerfully in the heavy summer air: iron-shod cart wheels and horses' hooves clattering on the cobbles, the incomprehensible cries of the costermongers, the occasional sharp backfire of a passing motor car, the sickly aroma of well-strawed manure and vegetables rotting in the gutter. Bridie had visited it often, in the company of her father. It was a rough place, but vivid and warm-hearted. She liked it.

She waited a moment longer, anxiously watching Mr. Pugh-Hennessy's dusty brown barathea back, her thoughts whirling, her fingers picking tensely at the seams of her skirt. Then, bravely she cleared her throat.

Mr. Pugh-Hennessy turned back into the room. Seeing her still there, he frowned irritably and flapped his long bony hands at her. " Run along now, child. Run *along*. . . . Mr. Thwaite will see to all your travel arrangements."

" But—"

" What is it? Is it your wages? See Mr. Thwaite about those also. He knows my mind—I'm sure you won't find the firm *ungenerous*. . . ."

"Of course not, Mr. Pugh-Hennessy." She took a deep breath. " But . . . but I still believe you would be better advised to send someone with a little more—" she hesitated, for the word that came to her mind was *courage*—" someone with a little more experience. By your account, sir, Lady Otranta is a somewhat difficult person, and I—"

" Difficult? Of course she's *difficult*. Most old people are difficult. I'm difficult meself." He patted at his velvet coat lapels in vague self-deprecation. " Though I grant you that at least if I were handsomely commissioned to write my memoirs I'd try a bit harder to get the job *over* and *done* with."

He returned to his desk and began to rummage among the papers on its littered surface. Several thick folders slid unheeded to the floor spilling their contents across the carpet. "An outline she sent us. Promising the most *astounding* revelations. And her life was remarkable enough in all conscience. An *excellent* outline—I have it here somewhere. . . ." His telephone lurched on its stand and would have fallen if Bridie had not darted forward and caught it. The old man sighed, and gave up the search.

" An *excellent* outline, you understand, and then nothing. Not a *word*." He drummed with his fingers. " And that was *four* months ago. Since then, nothing but excuses. Interminable letters full of *ridiculous* excuses. Ask Mr. Thwaite—he'll show them to you. First that outline, and then not another *word*. Of course she's difficult."

18

Suddenly he was still, his head still bent, eyes peering up at her through the tangled hedges of his sloping brows. " That is precisely why I'm sending *you*, my child, and not one of the fellows upstairs." He watched her earnestly for a moment longer, then relaxed. " It's not as if you were simply one of these brassy new typist creatures. Your work with your father has given you *literary* skills as well. Don't you think? And besides, with the Lady Tantallons of this world it's breeding that counts. *Breeding*. And you have it."

He came round the end of his desk, took her by the arm and led her firmly to the door. " You see—I have faith in you. I'm *sure* you won't fail me. So run along now to Mr. Thwaite, there's a good child." He opened the door and thrust her through. " You'll do a good job, Bridie. I *know* you will."

It was pleasant that he thought so well of her. The nice golden haze occasioned by his flattery lasted her perhaps four paces away down the narrow corridor outside his office. Then it faded, to be replaced by the hard, cold reality of her situation. If Lady Tantallon was refusing to complete her memoirs she presumably had some very good reasons for doing so. And who was she, Bridie, to make the old lady change her mind?

Panic-stricken, Bridie turned. But Mr. Pugh-Hennessy's office door was closed now, its chipped brown panels blank and forbidding. She dared not question their awful finality.

The train lurched, and began to slacken speed. Brought back to the present, Bridie saw that the countryside had been left behind and she was looking down upon a jumble of smoky grey rooftops, with the tall tower of a cathedral rising massively in its midst. York Minster. A moment later the train entered the station and stopped with a juddering of brakes.

Steam billowed up past her carriage window. Through it she watched absently as people hurried to and fro on the platform, women in light summer clothes, little boys in sailor suits, men jaunty beneath tilted straw boaters, porters struggling with laden barrows. Briefly her attention was caught by a bearded figure in a kilt. His hair was wild, and of a fiery ginger. For a moment it seemed that he was gazing intently in her direction. Their eyes met for an instant, then the steam thickened, obscuring her view. And when next it drifted away the man in the kilt was nowhere to be seen.

It was his kilt, of course, that had attracted her notice. Perhaps she had stared impolitely. And perhaps the man had noticed. In a sudden agony of embarrassment Bridie let the fringed velvet curtain fall across the window and turned towards the compartment's interior. She should not have stared so! If she was going to stay in a Scottish castle the sooner she got used to seeing men in kilts the better.

Outside in the corridor people sidled past. Each time one of them stopped to peer in at her she held her breath. For most of the journey she had had the compartment to herself, for which she was profoundly grateful. Now, alas, the door was suddenly opened and an elderly manufacturing gentleman with an over-large rose in his buttonhole leaned in.

"Will these seats be taken?" he asked, with a lilting Scottish burr.

Speechless with shyness, she shook her head.

He entered, followed by a motherly person in blue bombazine, clearly his wife. They talked together softly, settled themselves at the far end of the compartment, then turned and regarded her with frank and friendly curiosity. She lowered her gaze.

"It's a grand day, is it not?" the gentleman's wife suggested.

"Yes," Bridie agreed, still looking at the floor and blushing deeply.

"I see from the label on your box you're for Edinburgh. It's a fair flower of a city. D'ye know it?"

"No," Bridie admitted, earnestly studying the lower edge of the empty seat opposite her.

"Do ye no? Och, you're in for a fine treat, I'm thinking. Is she no, Angus?"

"Aye, she is that, my dear." The manufacturing gentleman rubbed his hands with great heartiness. "The fairest city in all the land. A veritable corn-u-copia of riches."

To which Bridie could find no reply whatsoever, except to

shuffle her feet and wish that the red plush seat would open and swallow her.

At that moment, mercifully, the guard's whistle shrilled close by her ear, the train jerked violently, and they were on their way again. Enabled by this distraction to pretend an absorbed interest in the passing scene, Bridie turned to the window, hitched the curtain back again, and watched with blank unseeing eyes as the city of York disappeared into the summery haze behind her.

She knew it was foolish to be so shy. Ridiculous, even. But that was the way she was. Her father had understood her difficulty, even if all he'd been able to do was to pat her hand and tell her consolingly that she'd just have to wait patiently till she grew out of it. Well, here she was, nineteen years of age, and still waiting. She knew she wasn't silly, or empty-headed. She had done well at her school—until her mother's death had forced her to leave—and her education thereafter had been well taken care of by her father. Conversation with him had never presented the slightest difficulty. But strangers, and the modern 'small talk' expected of young women now that King Edward was on the throne left her blushing and wordless. In her life with her father she had had so little opportunity to accustom herself to either.

Out of the corner of her eye she observed the manufacturing gentleman and his wife to be now engaged in some quiet private conversation of their own. Surreptitiously she stretched her legs and relaxed. Even though Mr. Pugh-Hennessy had insisted upon sending her all this way, it was still generous of him to treat her to a first class ticket. Or generous perhaps of Mr. Thwaites—for apparently nobody in the office was really certain as to which of the two men actually ran the establishment, Mr. Benedict Pugh-Hennessy behind his fine mahogany desk on his fine Turkey carpet, or Mr. Thwaites in his musty, paper-strewn cubbyhole, sandwiched inconveniently between the rowdy messenger boys on one side and the jangling, crankhandled telephone switchboard on the other.

Except that it couldn't have been Mr. Thwaites, since it was generally accepted that he'd never been guilty of anything as human as a generous impulse, not in all his fifty-seven years of service to the company. So that it must indeed be Mr. Pugh-Hennessy whom she had to thank for the gracious manner of her journey, for the plump upholstery of the seats, and for the promise of an excellent lunch in the clerestory-windowed first class dining carriage.

Lunch. The thought prompted her unobtrusively to consult the little gold fob-watch, that had been her mother's, pinned to the tucks of her blouse. The time was a few minutes before two—doubtless the steward would soon be along to announce the second sitting. His announcement of the first sitting had disappeared along the corridor so quickly, long before she'd had a chance even to understand properly what he was saying.

And besides, back at Mrs. Bartlett's she'd got into the habit of lunching late. Late and alone, of course, at a respectable Lyons eating house round the corner in Campden Town. This helped her to stave off the evening's pangs of hunger until seven or eight, when two slices of bread and margarine eaten secretly—Mrs. Bartlett didn't approve of the consumption of food in her parlour bedrooms—would tide her over till morning.

Parlour bedrooms—what visions of grandeur the phrase conjured up. And, in general, how drab was the reality thus concealed. A reality with which Bridie was well acquainted, in her searches through the less fashionable areas of London for accommodation in keeping with her extremely meagre means. They had never been wealthy, her father and she—although the dearest of men, it had to be admitted that he had never fully mastered the knack of making money, nor of retaining it once it had been made. But since his death unfortunately she had found herself not only quite alone in the world, but also virtually destitute. The small regular income he had derived from various learned journalistic contributions had naturally ended, leaving her with the proceeds of the sale of their Maida Vale furnishings, together with shares yielding no more than some thirty pounds per annum.

Parlour bedrooms, therefore—from Battersea to Shepherds Bush to Campden Town. And all equally dismal, with the same over-sized iron bedstead in the same undersized room, with the same threadbare carpet runner and the same rickety chiffonier-cum-writing-desk that served neither function even tolerably well, with the same gate-legged table beneath the same plum chenille tablecloth, and with the same collapsed armchair beside the same minute gas fire. Such surroundings, to say the very least, did little to lighten either the melancholy solitude of her life or the increasing anxiety as week followed week without her obtaining a decent place of employment.

So that really, if she was wise, she ought to be very grateful for the break in her dreary round that this journey to Scotland was providing. And that might even—should her mission, against all the odds, be successful—lead to some permanent position in Mr. Pugh-Hennessy's employ.

A movement caught her attention, out in the corridor beyond the manufacturing gentleman and his wife. A man was passing, a tall man in a Lovat green jacket. She could not see his face and yet she froze, staring as if mesmerised, for the jacket was of a shade she had seen before, and very recently. He stopped, lowered his head, looked in at her. Yes, it was the man from the platform at York, the man in the kilt, the man with the beard and the fiery red hair.

Once again their eyes met, hers wide with embarrassment, and a hint of fear, his uncertain, narrowed a little, assessing her thoughtfully. Had he come expressly looking for her? Would her companions intervene if he opened the door? What could he possibly want with her?

She dragged her gaze away, stared fixedly at the seat opposite. The train tilted briefly, clattering over points. She held her breath. And when she turned to the corridor again, the man was gone.

She felt suddenly very foolish. The man in the kilt had boarded the train only a few miles back—now he was walking along the corridor looking for a seat, nothing more. And anyway, what would it have mattered if he *had* come in? There was nothing, she told herself crossly, absolutely nothing at all for her always to be so afraid of.

She thought again of her father. Even after his sight had

failed him completely he'd refused to be afraid. Every day he'd gone out about the city, tapping with his stick, visiting the shops, walking in Kensington Gardens, and always coming home with tales of the interesting people he'd met.

"The world out there is for living in," he'd told her repeatedly. "And the people, they're for talking to, for getting to know. Oh, there's good and bad, I grant you. But even the bad, if you give them the chance, will find some spark of goodness in themselves. At least, that's the principle I've always worked upon."

And he'd been right. Even though, just now and then, he'd met rogues who had cheated him. And even though his steadfast determination to be fully a part of the exciting world outside had led him in his blindness finally to a wretched death beneath the hooves of a panic-stricken dray horse. Even then he'd been right. The world *was* for living in. And people *were* for talking to, for getting to know.

If only, if only she didn't find it all so *difficult*.

Just then the dining car attendant approached, announcing the second sitting for luncheon. Her companions rose at once, opened the door, stopped him, and obtained tickets. Seeing how it was done, Bridie obtained a ticket for herself also. Then she lingered, waiting until they had gone off down the corridor. The attendant, a bright little monkey of a man in a vivid red waistcoat, jerked his head encouragingly.

"They're serving now, miss. Any time you care to go along."

Still she lingered, anxious that the manufacturing gentleman and his wife should not suggest sharing a table with her. The attendant glanced in, saw her luggage on the rack, her floppy straw hat with the pink daisies, her portmanteaux, her domed leather hat-box, the travelling container for her Royal Barlock typewriter, and mistook her uncertainty.

"Safe as houses, miss," he said. "This here is the Midland and Scottish, miss. Not like some of the others as I wouldn't care to mention."

She thanked him, waited till he was gone, then stood a moment to tidy herself in the bevelled mirror above the seats, flanked on either side by sepia photographs of Scottish glens. A reasonable face, she decided. Too square perhaps for real beauty, but with sufficient sort of nose, eyes of a passably unusual golden-brown, well-shaped eyebrows, not too thick, and a mouth that was really quite adequate when it smiled. Nothing to be unduly ashamed of. Her hair though—anxiously she licked her palms and pushed ineffectually at its heavy auburn coils. Somehow it just would not get used to the idea of being *up*—always it seemed on the point of betraying her, of escaping the myriad pins she stuck randomly into it and cascading down about her shoulders. She frowned at it, patted it once more by way of last-minute encouragement, put on her hat and went out into the corridor, a long-legged slim figure looking considerably more determined than it felt.

The dining car had ornate plush chairs with buttoned backs, and cut-glass panels set into the mahogany partitions. The manufacturing gentleman and his wife were installed at a table opposite two young men in gaily striped blazers whom they had already engaged in conversation. Bridie waited nervously by the door till an attendant came and showed her to a table for two. He held the chair for her, and she sat down.

" Madam is travelling alone?"

She nodded.

" Then she would perhaps prefer to take her luncheon undisturbed?"

She nodded again.

At once the chair opposite her was lifted and borne away. Once again she blessed Mr. Pugh-Hennessy for his generosity. Oh, the delights of first class travel!

She ordered her meal: onion soup, to be followed by fillet of sole and then roast duck *á l'orange*. Then, with an excitement she hadn't felt since her father had taken her to the Savoy after the triumphant publication of his biography of Felix Mendelssohn-Bartholdy, she finished by ordering the *bombe glacé*. Briefly she wondered where all that book's royalties had gone. Mostly on doctors' fees, she thought sadly. And even then they hadn't been able to save his failing eyesight.

But then the soup arrived and, by the time she was halfway through her fish, even the prospect of her coming meeting with the formidable Lady Otranta seemed no longer quite so daunting.

Suddenly, a shadow fell across the table. She looked up expecting to see the waiter, and found herself gazing into a pair of piercing blue eyes deepset beneath beetling ginger eyebrows above a positive entanglement of ginger beard. Her fork clattered noisily onto her plate. It was he again, the man in the kilt and the green Lovat jacket. And this time he was obviously confronting her.

He bowed stiffly. She saw now that he was older than she had at first thought, the red of his hair and beard streaked liberally with grey. " Mistress Bridie Tantallon?" he enquired.

She licked her lips nervously. " I think you have the advantage of me, Mr.—"

" Duncan Symonds." He bowed again and held out his hand. She shook it timidly—" I serve your great-aunt, you see," he went on, " I'm the factor on the Tantallon estate."

She just managed a smile, feeling the colour rise to her cheeks. " Oh yes?"

" I've been in York on business. We supply timber to a furniture manufactory there. It was Sir Andrew's idea that I keep an eye open for you on the train."

She retrieved her fork. Sir Andrew—that would be her great-aunt's elder son. " That . . . that was very kind of him," she stammered. " But I really—"

" He was feared that I might not know you. But he needna have fashed hisself. The Tantallon features are no easily mistaken. And you have them, Miss Bridie. You have them to perfection."

She was not certain whether or not this constituted a compliment. Her father, whom she presumed she must resemble, had always seemed to her—for all that she loved him most dearly—too rugged of feature for real handsomeness. That she might so easily be identified as his daughter was a new thought, and not altogether a comfortable one.

" To perfection," Mr. Symonds repeated. " I knew it the

moment I first set eyes on you in York. You noticed my interest then, I'm thinking."

So he was admitting that he had stared at her. And with no hint of an apology either. She found his directness disconcerting, yet oddly in no way disagreeable.

" If I didna approach you at once," he continued, " it was because I chose to make gey certain. So I checkit in the other first class carriages. And there wasna a body as came anywheres near you."

Again the possible compliment. Yet still with no shade of impertinence. Paternal, rather. " You . . . you knew I'd be travelling first class, then?" she queried.

He nodded. " It was a' laid out in yon Pugh-Hennessy's letter. And Sir Andrew had a fair suspicion his telegram wouldna meet with much of a reception."

" Telegram? What telegram was that?"

Mr. Symonds smiled quizzically down at her and stroked his beard. "Aye . . . weel, I'm no honestly surprised your employer kept it from you."

That could hardly be said to have answered her question. But before Bridie could press him further, Mr. Symonds had caught the sleeve of a passing waiter.

" I'd take it kindly if you'd bring us another chair, laddie. Miss Tantallon and I have important matters to discuss, y'ken."

His confidence astounded her. Inviting himself to her table as if they were old friends. And yet . . . well, it was done so openly, and with such cheerful innocence, that when the waiter turned a questioning eye in her direction she helplessly nodded her agreement.

The chair was brought and Mr. Symonds seated himself opposite her, disposing his kilt expertly as he did so. Then he waved away the waiter who would have had him order something to eat—he himself had lunched, so he told her, before leaving York—and, resting his elbows on the table and his bearded chin upon his knuckles, gazed affably across at her.

" I've no put you off your food, I hope. It's plain fare we have at the castle, so I'd make the most of it."

27

He watched her keenly as she fumbled with her knife and fork, captured a small piece of fish, conveyed it to her mouth, chewed, swallowed.

Seeing her awkwardness he clucked sympathetically. "I'll warrant it's as cold now as a herring on a marble slab," he said. Then he raised his voice the merest shade. "Miss Tantallon will have her next course now, an' it's convenient," he announced.

And at once, almost like magic, her plate was whisked away, and the duck appeared in front of her, and she was accepting French beans and golden-brown potatoes from a silver chafing dish. And the extraordinary thing was that she, who would usually rather have died than have such attention drawn to her, now found herself almost enjoying the unquestioned sense of friendly importance Mr. Duncan Symonds gave her.

"Are you no taking wine wi' the duck?" he murmured. "There's a Barsac they have on these trains as I've heard is passing drinkable." He leaned slightly closer. "And if you had a wee half bottle I'm no saying as I wouldna join you in a glass."

And, to her own astonishment, "I'll have half of a bottle of your Barsac, please," she heard herself saying. "And would you please bring two glasses?"

When the wine was brought it was he, reassuringly, who tasted it and approved. She tried to remember the capacity in which he had said he served her great-aunt. *Factor*—was that the word? She'd no idea what it meant, but he was certainly unlike any other servant she'd ever heard of.

"I'm thinking this is your first visit to the Lowlands," he observed, watching her across the top of his glass.

She nodded. "I've never been to Scotland at all. And I'm much looking forward to it."

Her own words surprised her. Certainly she hadn't been looking forward to her visit half an hour before.

"Aye . . . weel, you'll be seeing us at our best the now. It gets gey dismal come October."

"I'm sorry to hear that." She frowned. Already the year

was into the first week of September. "Surely Mr. Pugh-Hennessy explained that I'd be with you for five or six weeks at least? Lady Otranta's memoirs, you know—there's a great deal of work to be done on them."

For a moment he didn't answer. Then, "The heather's mostly past its best," he said heavily. "But we'll find you a sprig of the white if we're canny. It's for good luck, y'ken, the white is."

It was his second avoidance. Possibly he was trying to tell her something. But just then the train began to slow, distracting her attention. For the first time in miles she turned to the window. They had come unnoticed to a sombre city, mile after mile of soot-caked rooftops beside a murky river, and over all a heavy pall of smoke which dulled the brightness of the day to a sickly yellow. Soon station boards were announcing Newcastle.

"Mercifully it's a short stop, this one," Mr. Symonds told her, half-rising to close the window above their table. "If you're wise you'll hold onto your breath till we're on our way again."

He seated himself and began to tell her about the city: the fine ships that were made there, and pottery fit for the King's table.

He sighed. "It's a sadness," he said, "that the price for a' that must be so much filth and squalor."

His bitterness surprised her, and he a man she'd thought composed of wry smiles and easy confidence. She ate her food quietly, and tried not to notice the acrid fumes that passed for fresh air in this busy city.

It was however, as her companion had said, only a short stop. In no time at all they were on the move again, the roofs and towering chimneys quickly left behind.

She looked across the table. "You said it was Sir Andrew's idea that you should try to find me on the train. What for, exactly?"

He settled himself calmly in his seat. "Mebbe I should tell you something of Castle Tantallon," he said. "It was built some sixty years ago, y'ken, about the time when the old

Queen, God rest her, was discovering the wonders of the Highlands. Sir James was appointed steward of her estates near Stirling. He built the castle and marrit himself the first Lady Tantallon. The Lady Margaret was daughter to the provost of Edinburgh, and—"

But Bridie was tired of not receiving direct answers to her questions. " Is this why my cousin asked you to meet me? So that you could acquaint me with the family history?"

The corners of Mr. Symonds' eyes crinkled unconcernedly. " I'd say Sir Andrew was in fact your *second* cousin—though I'll grant you that's neither here nor there. The original Castle Tantallon, y'ken, lies away to the east. It's been a ruin these hundreds of years. Sir Jamie's idea it was to build a—"

" But you still have not answered my question, Mr. Symonds." She waited, suddenly horrified by her boldness. She couldn't imagine what had possessed her. Could it really be that scarcely an hour in the company of this forthright gentleman had made her so totally forget all her habitual shyness?

Mr. Symonds, however, seemed in no way put out by her tart reminder. " I'm thinking Sir Andrew's instructions are no longer of muckle importance," he said, scratching the side of his nose in amused perplexity.

She took a deep breath. " I'd like to hear them all the same," she insisted.

" Aye . . . weel, I was afraid you might." He finished his wine and placed the empty glass carefully upon the white damask tablecloth. " The fact is, Miss Bridie, I was to put it to you —in the kindest fashion, mind—that you'd be far better staying the night in Edinburgh and taking the morning train back down to London. That Castle Tantallon was, in short, no place for you."

Bridie stared at him incredulously. " But that's absurd ! Mr. Pugh-Hennessy made all the arrangements. I have Lady Otranta's personal invitation."

" Sir Andrew kens that weel. He also understands your employer's difficulty concerning the memoirs. That is why he was feart that his telegram might have little effect. So he askit me to—"

"Telegram?" Bridie was angry now. "That's the second time you've mentioned a telegram. What exactly was in this telegram?"

Mr. Symonds spread his hands. "Words . . . just words. And if yon Pugh-Hennessy didna show them to you, I reckon he must have had his reasons."

Yon Pugh-Hennessy, indeed! "May I take it you don't approve of my employer?"

"Don't approve?" Mr. Symonds laughed. "I know nothing of the man. Save that he has a fancy Sassenach name I can scarce get my tongue around."

Bridie felt she was being distracted from her main purpose. She tapped her fingers on the rim of her glass. "If your instructions were to send me back to London," she said, "how is it that you've been so reluctant to carry them out?"

"On account of I've never been a man to waste my time." Suddenly her companion was serious. "One look at you told me you were a Tantallon to the verra tips of your fingers. Not that it surprised me, y'ken." He paused, thoughtfully pushing at the tablecloth with the prongs of a fork. "So I'll just ask you this: now that I've told you Sir Andrew doesna want you at the castle, are you likely to be away at once, back down to London?"

"Certainly not!"

Slowly his seriousness dissolved into the broadest of smiles. "Then you've answered your own question," he said.

"But how could I go back?" Bridie insisted crossly. "I have my employer to think of. And besides, Lady Otranta is relying on me to—" She broke off. She must be mad. Wasn't this just the excuse she'd been looking for? Not to have to go to the castle? Not to have to face her alarming great-aunt? And yet . . . well, the letter from Lady Otranta that Mr. Pugh-Hennessy had shown her had been disjointed, but not unwelcoming. And she, Bridie Tantallon, was hardly one to shirk her duty at the very first hint of opposition. "And besides," she repeated, glaring obstinately across at Mr. Symonds, "Lady Otranta is relying on me to help her with the writing of her memoirs."

Mr. Symonds rubbed his hands. " You see? It isna only the Tantallon face you've been gifted wi'. You have their spirit too. Their determination." He tilted his head. " And their blind, pig-headed obstinacy as well, I wouldna be surprised."

His complacency infuriated her. " How dare you!" she said.

Abruptly his smile faded. He straightened his back. " You'll find we dare much, we Scots," he said with calm dignity. " Both for ourselves and for those we serve."

Silenced utterly, Bridie lowered her gaze. For a time neither of them moved. Then her companion relaxed, leaned forward and put his hand gently on her arm. " There now, Miss Bridie. I fear I've preachit at you, which was never my intention. We've a terrible weakness for the pulpit, we Scots. Aye, and we're unco' proud, too. Can you forgive me?"

Her heart was touched by the warm simplicity of his words. She lifted her eyes. Of course she could forgive him. For in truth there was nothing to forgive.

" Don't let us talk of forgiveness, Mr. Symonds. Let us say instead that we understand each other a little better now."

He nodded. Then he lifted the wine bottle and poured its small remaining contents equally into their two glasses. " To your stay at Castle Tantallon," he said, lifting his glass. " And may it be a happy one."

She joined him gladly in the toast. Briefly there was silence between them. The train clattered on through the sunny countryside. Then the attendant came and removed her plate. When he was gone she cleared her throat.

" Though I really don't see that my stay can be happy if Sir Andrew is so determined to make me unwelcome," she said softly.

" Och, *that* . . ." He waved the suggestion away. " I'm no saying that he doesna have his reasons, mind. But once you're at the castle he's no a man to deny you a decent hospitality."

She was relieved to hear it. All the same, " These reasons of his—what are they exactly?"

For once, however, Mr. Symonds appeared in some difficulty. "That's . . . weel, that's something I'd rather you found out for yourself, Miss Bridie. It may be that they're nobbut a fret about next to nothing. In which case you'd be better not knowing. I'd just have you mindful of this, though—she's a remarkable old wummun, the Lady Otranta. I'd do anything in the world for her. Anything at a'."

With that unsatisfactory reply Bridie was obliged to content herself, for Mr. Symonds now turned to the window and spoke firmly of the distant prospect. The ridge of the Pennines, so it appeared: the ancient highway between North and South. Her pudding arrived, the *bombe glacé*, dark and enticing beneath a glaze of liqueur, with a crisp sugar violet placed elegantly upon the top of its chocolate-coated sphere. And, unlike many anticipated pleasures, it fully lived up to her expectation.

They came to Morpeth, then on through hills and wooded valleys, with glimpses of mirror-smooth water and four-square granite cottages. Gradually Mr. Symonds began to talk again about the people she would meet at her destination. He was always carefully circumspect and loyal, she noticed, and never more noticeably so than when speaking of Lady Otranta's elder son, Sir Andrew. From this she was able to deduce his secret disapproval.

"He works himself into the ground, that laddie. Out in a' weathers. Forestry, sheep-herding, the saw-mills—I've never seen a man more eager to learn. And he's no afraid to get his hands dirty. Next month he'll be there with the rest of us, juicing the sheep. It's no his fault if—"

"Juicing the sheep?" Bridie laughed. "What on earth is that?"

"It's a dip the shepherds use to keep the poor beasts healthy. Tobacco and soapy water boiled up in a cauldron. Aye, it's no the laird's fault if the men think him a wee bit interferin'."

And not only the men, Bridie decided. "And what of his brother?" she asked.

"Young Mr. Robert?" Duncan Symonds stroked his beard thoughtfully. "He's a second son a' ower, if y'ken what I'm saying. But he'll find his place in the world soon enough. You'll get on with him fine, I'm thinking. And there's nothing his mother asks of him as is ever too much bother."

This was clearly more than could be said for the older Sir Andrew. But they had to break off then, for the dining car attendant was hovering with the bill. Bridie reached for the sovereigns Mr. Pugh-Hennessy had given her, only to be respectfully forestalled by her companion. " The Tantallons of Tantallon may be Scots, Miss Bridie, but they're no ower tight-fistit. Sir Andrew gi'ed me the most precise instructions."

But that, she thought, was when he'd believed she might be persuaded to return at once to London. Nevertheless, she didn't argue. Mr. Pugh-Hennessy would doubtless be delighted to be spared the price of such a sybaritic luncheon.

The bill paid, Mr. Symonds accepted her invitation to return with her to her compartment, and together they went back along the corridor. She was relieved to find the manufacturing gentleman and his wife sleeping soundly in their corners, and neither stirred as she and Mr. Symonds stepped cautiously over their out-stretched legs and settled themselves by the window.

Bridie waited a moment. " There's an older half-sister, isn't there?" she then asked. " And not married, I understand?"

Mr. Symonds frowned and hesitated. " Weel now, she's the strange one, yon Mistress Melissa. Nearing thirty, aye, and still no marrit, and no for want of suitors either. But she goes her own way and she keeps her own counsel." He lifted one hand and scratched the side of his nose in what was becoming a familiar gesture. " It's a dainty wee name she has, but I wouldna say as it suited her. They sent her away to a Sassenach schule, y'ken, and she came back home wi' the queerest notions. She's aye gadding about on one of them bicycles—and she's a great one for what she calls 'the rational dress'. Yon baggy trouser things. Not at a' what old Sir James would have approved of, I'm thinking." He brightened. " But she's a good-hearted body, and you'll get on fine wi' her. So dinna fash yoursen on that account."

In Mr. Symonds' book it seemed that everyone got on fine with everyone. He and her father, Bridie decided, would have had a lot in common.

"And what of Lady Otranta?" she asked, as casually as she was able.

At which Mr. Symonds sat forward, his hands laid purposefully on his thick, muscular knees. "My lady is a remarkable wummun," he said with some emphasis. "A remarkable wummun—I'd do anything in the world for her. And so would every man on the estate. Anything at a'."

Bridie remembered his having said something very similar only a few moments before, when Lady Otranta's name was mentioned. *A remarkable wummun*—and spoken so fiercely that it was almost as if he were challenging her to contradict him. It had to be admitted that the words themselves told her very little. And yet, possibly, by what they left unsaid, they told her a great deal.

After a short pause Mr. Symonds relaxed. "And then there's old Peggy. Herself is the one you'll be needing to be on good terms with. They're as close as twa corbies, her and my lady."

"Peggy?" This was the first time Bridie had heard of any such person. "Who's Peggy?"

"A fair old tyrant, if you want the truth, Miss Bridie. Workit for my lady back in her theatre days, old Peggy did. Dresser, I believe the word is. Back when my lady was a famous *artiste*." He gave the word its French pronunciation. "Before her and Sir James was marrit, y'ken."

"And she still looks after Lady Otranta?"

"Looks after? Aye, you could say that. And more. For I swear there's no a person within fifty miles of the castle as doesna go in fear of her." He smiled again. "My lady included."

Listening to him now, much of Bridie's former apprehension returned. Certainly what she had learnt of the castle's occupants was hardly reassuring. Mr. Duncan Symonds, with his charming directness and good humour, might have disarmed her completely—but what of the others? What, in particular, of her second cousin, Sir Andrew, who had tried so hard to prevent her coming? Was it not enough to be travelling to meet all these strange, threatening people, without having also his inexplicable animosity to contend with?

She was quiet for a time, staring disconsolately out of the window. Suddenly a thought came to her. "Mr. Symonds— you told me that you were employed by Lady Otranta."

"Aye. The estate needs a manager, y'ken."

Manager—so at least the unfamiliar word *factor* was now explained. And something of her companion's easy confidence also. "If your employer is Lady Otranta," Bridie insisted, "then how can it be that Sir Andrew would send you on a mission so completely contrary to his mother's wishes?"

It was a question that verged on the impertinent. If she had feared that Mr. Symonds might take offence at it, however, she was quite mistaken.

"That's no a verra great problem," he said, folding his arms and regarding her imperturbably. "First point—it's no for a man in my position to take sides in every wee family difference that may come along. And second point—as I've told you already, I kenned weel that you'd no be a true Tantallon if you took heed of a single word I said." He smiled. "So where was the harm in it?"

Mr. Symonds paused. He was, she saw now, a man of rare shrewdness and diplomacy. "And I'd say you're a fair bit wiser for the chance of this wee talk it's given us," he concluded. "If I've helpit you, I'm glad. For it's no an easy household you'll be going into, I'm thinking."

She nodded slowly. For all his kindness, the picture Duncan Symonds painted was hardly reassuring. On top of all her other forebodings, she had discovered that she was entering a divided family, unwanted by at least one of its members. Briefly she felt a surge of resentment against Mr. Pugh-Hennessy for having concealed from her the matter of Andrew Tantallon's telegram. Her anger didn't last, however. He was, after all, a businessman and her employer. For him it was his investment in Lady Otranta's memoirs that counted, and in that she could hardly blame him.

36

No, in her present situation she could only be profoundly grateful that the amiable Scotsman opposite her seemed willing to give her his support and friendship. Clearly she was going to need both in the difficult weeks that lay ahead.

2

I must begin at the beginning, then, not with the late Queen's troubles but with a brief account of my true origins.

It is possible, of course, that the reality of my birth would have been as shocking to the royal circle I had recently entered as were the more exotic versions then in circulation. I was born, you see, in a humble red-brick villa at the better end of Dulwich, which is a southern suburb of London. And my parents, although honest and industrious, weren't in the least exceptional, my father being a senior accounting clerk in the City and my mother coming of sturdy Hampshire farming stock.

It might perhaps be said in their favour, however, that they shared the standards of the nobility sufficiently for the career I chose to be a source of real distress to them— distress that I'm sorry to say was never eased by pride in my later successes, since they were both of them killed shortly after my eighteenth birthday, instantly, in a gas main explosion that brought down several adjoining houses in our street.

The day of their deaths remains vividly in my mind. The news was brought to me by an earnest young constable just as I was about to go on at the Chiswick Empire. At that time I had not yet met Professor Salvador. Instead I was manipulating cages of singing birds for a certain aged Doctor Melodious, having moved on from my first employer, a Captain Sawbright, for whose troupe of child acrobats I had held paper-covered hoops and shouted the occasional " Hup there!" by way of apparent encouragement. The principal improvement in working for Doctor Melodious was that he paid me three and sixpence a week, all found, against Captain Sawbright's half-a-crown.

I took the young constable's news bravely, and went on all the same. My parents might be dead, but Doctor Melodious was not. Not yet. Not quite. And he needed me.

A sensible enough reaction. But hardly an appealing one. Yet I was showing, I see now, the sturdy heartlessness that was to stand me in good stead in my future life. There would be times not far distant when an iron will and a brisk lack of sentiment were all that lay between me and disaster, when the life and happiness of the man I loved rested in the balance and it was up to me alone to act, and act decisively. . . .

* * *

" Wait 'ere, please, miss. Madame Otranta will see you in a minute."

Old Peggy followed these grand words with a disparaging sniff, then turned and shuffled from the room, closing the door firmly behind her. Lady Otranta's intimidating personal servant was a short and immensely fat old woman, encased in a huge brown tent-like garment the front of which—as befitted that of an ex-theatrical dresser—was liberally equipped with useful rows of pins, spare lengths of ribbon and dangling elastic, and a large pair of dressmaker's scissors which were suspended from a cord about her neck. On her head she wore a grubby white cap that only indifferently concealed her almost total lack of hair. Her hands were grubby also, and the carpet slippers on her feet bulged with the most mountainous array of bunions Bridie had ever seen.

Bridie looked about her, selected a chair by one of the narrow windows, and sat down to wait. The room she had been shown to by an elderly manservant called Meredith, somewhat toothless but with impressive Dundreary whiskers, was small and octagonal in shape, presumably set into one of the pointed turrets she had seen at the corners of the castle's main block. This much she had been able to glimpse of Castle Tantallon and very little else, for the motor car bringing her and Mr. Symonds from the steamship landing stage at Kincardine—a buttercup yellow Argyll he drove most expertly

39

—had scarcely left the surrounding pine trees before it was clattering over a massive drawbridge and entering the castle's inner courtyard.

From the deep slit of a window she could see little except treetops and the distant silvery waters of the Firth of Forth. The crossing by paddle-steamer from Leith had been charming, and quite uneventful. Nevertheless, she'd been glad of Duncan Symonds' company, for the tramway ride before it had been a positive torment. The journey from Edinburgh's Waverly station to the Albert Dock at Leith must have been five miles at the most. But five miles of such a lurching, clattering progress, along cobbled streets thronged with little honking motor taxis, and crammed with such a mass of cheerful, inquisitive people, all talking at the tops of their voices—and to *her*, all too often—in a language that couldn't possibly be English and yet (according to Mr. Symonds) most certainly was, that it had seemed far longer than all the four hundred up from London put together.

Scotland, it seemed, was a country where even total strangers spoke to you and asked you your business. It was all very nice and companionable, she supposed. But without Mr. Symonds to answer for her she wouldn't have known where to put herself.

" It's the wee thing's first time north of the border, y'ken. She's on a visit to her great-auntie, ower in Kincardine."

If Mr. Symonds had said the words once, he'd said them a dozen times. By the time they'd reached the Albert Dock she was sure half of Edinburgh must know she was going to Kincardine to see her great-aunt.

How foreign it all was! And what a rush and scramble there'd been, just to get together her luggage and find a porter. Why, she'd hardly even had a chance to peer up at Edinburgh Castle standing among tall, continental-looking houses high in the midst of the city before she'd been bundled into the tramcar and rattled off down Prince's Street, past insistent gaudy hoardings advertising *Balmoral Soap: the Scottish soap for Scottish folk.*

Foreign. And smelling so strongly of breweries. So different from the final beautiful miles of the train journey, with Mr. Symonds leaning discreetly beside her at the carriage window, explaining the passing scene to her : the Eildon Hills, beloved of Sir Walter Scott for their unrivalled views of the countryside, then the River Teviot far below them, and soon the peaceful ruins of Melrose Abbey. Here all was noise and bustle, and row upon row of black stone houses.

On the steamer she'd been able to escape to the relative quiet of the first class promenade. She'd leant on the rail, a light sea breeze ruffling her hair, and watched the garish pleasure gardens of Portobello fade slowly into the evening mists astern. A banner proclaimed Monsieur Bleriot's monoplane on show there, fresh from its Channel crossing. That, now, must be the very best way to travel, alone in the silent spaces of the air.

" You know," she'd said, turning to Mr. Symonds where he stood quietly beside her and settling the straw hat with the pink daisies more firmly upon her head, " I'd always thought the Scots were supposed to be dour, reserved people."

He'd smiled. " Aye, well, yon's your Highlander, dour as the crags he comes from. Your Lowlander, now—he's a different kettle of fish altogether."

And now, here she was, within moments of meeting her great-aunt, who was neither Highlander nor Lowlander but— if Mr. Pugh-Hennessy were to be believed—a woman supremely and impressively *herself*.

Seldom had Bridie felt so alone and vulnerable. Abandoned by Mr. Symonds at the castle door—he had the car to deal with and his own quarters to go to, he said—she had been welcomed, to her profound confusion, by none other than the man who had tried his best to stop her coming at all, Sir Andrew Tantallon himself.

He had come towards her down the wide staircase and across the stone-flagged entrance hall, limping slightly, his hand outstretched. He wore a high-lapelled dark green jacket over narrow tartan trousers. He was tall and lean, with neatly-cut hair and moustaches of a surprising silvery fairness, and piercing blue eyes that looked down at her from deep sockets, dark-rimmed either from sickness or from some deep anxiety. His features were weather-beaten, his shoulders broad. He was clearly an outdoor man, someone at home out on the wild hillsides surrounding Castle Tantallon, yet he had an easy grace and most courteous manner.

To her astonished relief he greeted her warmly, and seemed, indeed, unsurprised to see her, as though his efforts to prevent her arrival had been no more than a figment of Duncan Symonds' imagination.

"My dear cousin—you've got here safely. I'm so glad. I trust the journey wasn't too arduous?" His accent was slight, but unmistakably Scots.

She removed her gloves and shook his offered hand. "Not at all, thank you. The fact is, you see, I was. . . ."

She'd been on the point of saying how pleasantly Mr. Symonds had helped her pass the time. Second thoughts, however, told her that mention of his name might raise the awkward question of the unfulfilled task Sir Andrew had placed upon him. So she tailed off, and fiddled embarrassedly with the string of her purse.

The hall around them was huge and dank, and dismally lined with suits of armour. A massive pipe organ stood against the wall beneath the curve of the stone staircase.

"I'm delighted to hear it." Sir Andrew appeared not to notice her confusion. "Well, Meredith will show you to your room, and take you afterwards to my mother's quarters. She's sure to be expecting you." He frowned briefly, as if in some doubt. Then his brow cleared. "Of course she's expecting you. Of course she is."

He limped a pace or two away, then turned. "Forgive me, cousin. I must speak with the kitchen." He took out his watch and consulted it elaborately. "There was, you understand, no great certainty as to whether you would arrive in time for dinner."

His words were bland enough. But the meaning they cloaked —as both he and Bridie well knew—was rather less pleasant: there had been no great certainty as to whether she would arrive at all.

He bowed then and went away quickly, down the echoing length of the entrance hall and through a green baize door at the far end. All his movements, Bridie saw, were strangely jerky and ill-controlled, as if he were suffering under some great inner tension. As the door closed behind him she heard him at once begin to give urgent instructions to the servants beyond. How different was the life of these Tantallons from her own simple, solitary existence down in London, in a parlour-bedroom just off Campden Hill.

The ancient butler, Meredith, conducted her wordlessly up the stairs and around a stone-vaulted gallery to her room, carrying with him the smaller of her portmanteaux. He seemed so frail, and leaned so heavily upon the iron banister, that she would have taken the case from him, had not a certain obstinate proudness in his bearing warned her otherwise.

The gallery was hung with stags' heads and a formidable array of weapons, cudgels and spears and barbaric leather shields. Her room, when finally they came to its black-studded door, was hardly more welcoming. In the centre of the floor, surrounded by deerskin rugs, stood a vast four-poster bed with intricate tapestry hangings. A wash-stand, a book-case packed with faded leather volumes, a throne-like chair and a wardrobe as large as a small room completed the furnishings. A single gigantic oaken candlestick stood by the bed, and the sunset striking in through the leaded panes of the deeply-mullioned windows cast a menacing crimson light on the walls and low beamed ceiling.

The room, in fact, was so grotesquely gloomy that, had Bridie herself been in better heart, she might well have found it, and the entire fake castle surrounding it, positively comical. As things were, however, her spirits, already low, plummeted still further.

Still without speaking, Meredith put down her case, sighed, and went away. Wretchedly she listened to his departing footsteps. She would have called him back, just for someone to talk to, had not the utter silence of the place laid itself like a leaden weight upon her tongue. After he had gone she wandered uneasily for a moment, then braced herself, removed her hat and, crossing to the wash-stand, splashed ice-cold water upon her face. The shock revived her a little, and she dried herself vigorously upon the rough hand-towel provided.

So this was Castle Tantallon. She didn't know whether she should laugh or cry. Certainly she couldn't stay. Nothing on earth would make her. Not even the Tantallon pig-headedness Mr. Symonds had accused her of. She must go and tell Sir Andrèw at once of her decision. At least he, for one, would be delighted to hear it.

At that moment the old man Meredith returned, bringing the second of her cases. He put it down, wheezing faintly, then he lifted his head. " My lady will see ye now, Mistress Bridie," he said, his voice a gentle sing-song, the sibilants rustling like dry grass in a summer breeze.

But Bridie would not let herself be beguiled by it. " No," she said firmly. " No—first I must talk to Sir—"

" If they've told ye the old one's something to be afeared of, Mistress Bridie, that's nobbut their nonsense. She'll like ye fine."

" But—"

He took a pace forward and touched her arm. " Ye canna disappoint her. Och, she's talked of little else but your coming this week and more."

There was something in the softness of his appeal that was irresistible. Bridie hesitated, took a deep breath, and nodded her head. After all, there'd be plenty of time for her to talk about leaving later.

The whiskers on Meredith's face spread into a toothless smile. " I was sure ye'd see it. My lady's a puir lonely soul. Nobbut a puir lonely soul since Sir Jamie's going."

A puir lonely soul? Yet Duncan Symonds' description of her had been far prouder: *a remarkable wummun,* he called her. And Mr. Pugh-Hennessy had labelled her difficult, unreliable, even outrageous. Could all of these really be aspects of the same person?

Meredith had led her then, at his own snail-like pace, back along the gallery, through a narrow stone arch and on down a succession of echoing passages till finally they came to the small octagonal room, far more comfortably furnished than anything Bridie had so far seen in the castle, where she was now waiting. Old Peggy had been there, ready for her. She'd risen with surprising agility from the table at which she'd been sitting, bent over some enormous and unidentifiable piece of purple needlework.

"I take it you're the great-niece," she'd said with ill-disguised scorn. "You can call me Peggy. It's not a great favour, mind; everybody always 'as done, right from the top of the bill down to the perishing call-boys." She'd paused then, peering pugnaciously up at Bridie over the tops of her steel-rimmed spectacles. "And it don't mean you can go taking no liberties neither."

"Of c-course not," Bridie'd stammered in reply, for whatever the old woman might lack in inches she amply made up for in sheer self-confidence and strength of will.

And now, here Bridie was sitting nervously by the slim arrow-slit of a window, looking down across the pine trees to the silvery waters of the Firth of Forth, waiting for her final awesome summons to the presence of her great-aunt. Four hundred miles by train, a tramway journey, a steamer passage, and a ride in a snorting motor car—and all to see Lady Tantallon, Madame Otranta, the one-time famous mentalist. Suddenly the tension in Bridie snapped. She giggled. Certainly after all that the old lady had better be worthy of it!

*   *   *

I often wish that my father had lived long enough to see me settled. And I regret very much, now that it is too late, the pain that my running away from home must have caused him.

He was a simple man, I think, and good-hearted. I doubt if either his marriage to my mother or his work in the City brought him much satisfaction. Mostly in his leisure time he took refuge in reading: in particular the works of Horace Walpole and Mr. Dickens. Oddly enough, it is this addiction of his that I have to thank for the uniqueness of my name: it derives from the title of his favourite Walpole book, *The Castle of Otranto,* and is, in spite of what I know has often been suggested to the contrary, the name actually given to me at my baptism. Poor man! Had he only guessed how well it would look in later years on the play-bills, he would certainly have bowed to my mother's wishes and called me something less romantic, like Mavis or Aggie. He was a Methodist, you see, with a very poor opinion of things theatrical.

But I was as headstrong and obstinate then as I suppose I must admit to being today. And I was determined that my life was not going to be ruled by the expectations of others. I had my own way to go. And I would go my way, no matter what. . . .

*   *   *

" Madame Otranta will see you now, miss."

At last, and after far longer than the promised minute, fat old Peggy had reappeared portentously in the doorway.

" And jus' you see you watch your p's and q's, mind!"

Bridie nodded meekly. She'd heard of p's and q's before, from the querulous middle-aged gentlewoman who had taught her typing and shorthand. Timidly she walked through the door Peggy held open for her, into the room beyond.

" Your great-niece, Madame," Peggy intoned majestically behind her. " Jus' arrived up from London." So saying, she closed the door, firmly shutting herself out and Bridie uncompromisingly in.

For a moment Bridie stood quite motionless, spellbound. The room, curtained and dimly lit with flickering candles, was in dramatic contrast to the rest of the castle. It was, for one thing, unbearably hot. Also, its air was heavily laden with the smoke from sticks that smouldered aromatically in oriental vases. Thick Chinese carpets lay upon the floor, cluttered with the ornate, shadowy shapes of such quantities of furniture and other less explicable objects that Bridie hardly dared move an inch for fear of knocking into something. Opposite the windows a huge log fire burned beneath a fringed and much-mirrored overmantel. While to one side of the fire—and Bridie started involuntarily when she saw it—sat the figure of a

46

swarthy turbaned Turk, his back to her, hunched forward over what appeared to be a chess-board.

" Come forward, child, so that I can see you."

Her great-aunt, Bridie saw now, was on the far side of the fire, dressed entirely in black and sitting upon a high-backed chair upholstered in that same sombre hue, so that principally only her pale hands and face were visible, floating as if disembodied in the shadows.

" No, child—on second thoughts it would undoubtedly be better if you went and drew the curtains."

Obediently Bridie moved with care towards the nearest window. Her great-aunt's voice was husky, yet possessed of an unmistakable magnetism. Now it took on a slightly ironic note.

"Usually when visitors come I humour that abominable old Peggy creature in the matter of these absurd theatricals. They are so dear to her heart, you see. And besides, candlelight is kind to a woman such as myself, no longer in . . . shall we say the first flower of her beauty?"

A faint dry laugh disturbed the still, incense-laden air.

" But you, my child, are no ordinary visitor. It is better that we should see each other as we are, and know the worst, and the best, from the very outset."

Bridie fumbled for a moment with the cord of the curtains, then pulled upon it so that they parted with a rustle of rich brocade. At once the room was flooded with pale evening light.

" Excellent, child. Now the other window."

Only when the second pair of curtains was drawn and no further excuse to avert her gaze remained, did Bridie turn to face her great-aunt. What she saw then across the crowded room was a pale, gaunt woman, bright areas of rouge lying uneasily upon painfully haggard cheeks beneath an elaborate coiffure of hair improbably black, bolt upright, regarding her intently through jet-framed lorgnettes. An eccentric figure, but at the same time a powerful one. A long silence ensued, broken only by the soft shifting of the logs in the hearth.

Suddenly her great-aunt let the eye-glasses fall. " Well,

child?" she demanded, "Is the spectacle much what you expected?"

Blushing deeply, Bridie lowered her gaze and shuffled her feet on the thick dusty pile of the carpet.

"Well? Has the cat got your tongue, then?" The old lady drummed fingers on the arm of her chair. "Your employer warned me in his letter that you might be shy. Nevertheless, I—"

"I—I did not come expecting anything in particular," Bridie blurted. "I'm sorry if I seemed to stare, Great-aunt. But the castle . . . this room . . . everything here is so very strange to me."

"So." The word was sarcastically spoken. For a moment longer Lady Otranta watched her forbiddingly. Then she turned slowly away, held one claw-like hand out to the warmth of the fire beside her. "Bridie, Bridie my dear," she said, her voice suddenly gentle and very weary, "have you never wondered, my dear, why it is that the old like to torture the young?" she paused. "Might it not be because the old are jealous? Jealous of youth, of its courage and beauty?"

She sighed then. Her shoulders sagged. She lay back in the chair and closed her eyes.

Bridie took an anxious step forward, then stopped, her attention abruptly drawn away to the hard, unblinking stare of the dark-skinned Turk sitting across the fireplace from her great-aunt. The light from the windows glinted in his eyes as if in two cold, hard jewels. Bridie stood transfixed, her great-aunt momentarily forgotten.

Then, all at once, she relaxed. The man, she realised, had not moved a single muscle since she had entered the room. "Why he's a dummy!" she cried, in sudden absurd relief.

Lady Otranta opened her eyes. "Az Rah?" she said. "A *dummy*? I tell you, my child, in his time poor Az Rah has defeated the finest chess players in all the courts of Europe."

Though Bridie had never seen the illusion, she had heard of it many times. "Was it you," she asked, fascinated now, her shyness quite forgotten, "who hid inside him and controlled his movements?"

"Lord 'a mercy, how knowing the young have become these days." Her great-aunt sat up straight again. "Use your eyes, child. Where would there be space within poor Az Rah for such as myself?"

He was indeed exceedingly small and slender, hunched over a cabinet the doors of which stood open to reveal an obscure array of cogs and levers.

"A dwarf, then?" Bridie suggested. "Or a young child, even?"

The old lady rose unsteadily and, leaning heavily upon an ebony stick, stooped to place a fresh pine log upon the fire. "Tell me, my child," she said, "what room my son has put you in to sleep?"

The sudden change of subject surprised Bridie into frankness. "Room? To be honest, Great-aunt, not a nice room at all. A huge draughty cave of a place, with a big four-poster bed, and—"

"I was afraid he might." Lady Otranta clicked her tongue irritably. "I imagine he thinks to make you so uncomfortable you will not stay. But he is mistaken if he believes I will be too . . . too busy to realise what he is doing. You see, he does not want you here. He even sent a telegram, so I am told, to prevent your coming."

Bridie nodded, wondering briefly what it was that Lady Otranta had stopped herself from saying. "I know about the telegram," she said. "Mr. Symonds met me on the train and told me."

"Ah yes, my faithful Duncan. I'm glad he found you. What a dear, good man he is."

Bridie hesitated. "Great-aunt, why does your son not want me here?" she asked.

Stiffly the old lady walked to one of the candles, wetted her finger and thumb, and extinguished it between them. "You must ask him that yourself, my dear," she said, very softly. "Though I expect that you will discover for yourself soon enough that I am not . . . I am not always as you now see me."

She went slowly round the room, from candle to candle,

extinguishing each one in turn. In an embarrassed, uncomprehending silence Bridie watched her, taking in only dimly the extraordinary items of furniture between which she moved. As well as various innocent-seeming chairs and tables there were cabinets clearly theatrical in purpose, and a strange crystal casket upon spindly legs, and a screen from which knives projected in the outline of a human body. Not as she was now? What could the old lady mean?

Lady Otranta completed her circuit. "On the subject of your room," she said, her voice now firm again, "I shall speak to the disgusting Peggy about it. You shall have quarters in my own part of the castle. Those old four-posters were never comfortable. I used to tell my Jamie he'd been swindled by the man he bought them from." She sighed. "This whole castle, come to that, a wearisome place, built simply to humour the old Queen, God rest her. She had a fancy, you see, for what she thought of as *Scottish* architecture."

The old lady cleared her throat dryly. "Though where we'd have accommodated Her Majesty had she ever paid us a visit, I really cannot imagine. She liked her comforts, that one did."

Bridie couldn't help smiling. It was truly the most curious conversation, and not at all what she'd expected. "You knew Queen Victoria quite well, I believe."

Thoughtfully Lady Otranta placed a cone of silver cardboard over a wine bottle standing on a side table. When she lifted the cone again the wine bottle was gone, replaced by a vase of paper flowers. "I knew the Queen as well as anyone could—who wasn't a servant that is," she murmured, half to herself.

The trick had been simple enough, the flowers concealed within the shell of the fake bottle which was lifted off inside the cone. But the old lady's reply to Bridie's question remained the most baffling enigma.

For a moment Lady Otranta stared blankly at the cone still in her hand. Then she laid it down. "All this," she said, gesturing around her, "the maestro left to me when he died. The great Professor Salvador . . . and he really was great, you know. The young ones—Maskelyne, Devant—they're nothing beside him. And he left me all his secrets." She sighed again. "You'll think me foolish to have kept them."

"Not at all, Great-aunt."

"But so I am. Old and foolish." Then she brightened. "But now, child, we shall sit down and you shall tell me about your father." She paused, tapping her crudely painted cheek with the frame of her folded lorgnettes. "He never forgave me for marrying dear Jamie, of course. Neither did your grandfather. My true crime, you see, child, was that I made a success of it. And that's the hardest thing in the world to forgive."

She frowned, then seated herself and indicated a nearby chair for Bridie. "I want you to know, my dear, that I never returned their disfavour. Why should I, when I was getting so much the best of the bargain? Wealth, happiness, twenty-five years of the best marriage any woman could hope for . . .?" She tailed off, smiling sadly as she shook her head. "But you were going to tell me about your father. I understand he was blind, poor man, in his later years. You must tell me everything, unless, of course, it will pain you to speak of him?"

"Not to you, Great-aunt."

Certainly Bridie's memories of her father were still sharp and full of the pain of loss. But there was about the old lady a warm understanding and an originality of mind that overcame all the girl's uncertainties. "Oh, how I wish you could have known him," she cried. "You'd have loved him as I did, I know you would. Oh, how I wish this silly family quarrel had never been!"

"Quarrel? What quarrel was that?" Solemnly Lady Otranta lifted one hand and snapped her fingers. "There—it is gone, my child. Disappeared completely. Indeed, I rather think it never was."

She laughed then, and Bridie with her. And eagerly, forgetting her shyness, unmindful even of the outlandish trappings of the room in which they were seated and the baleful, glassy stare of their Turkish companion, Bridie poured out her story.

Her mother's sudden death, many years before, of influenza;

her father's thoughtful care, his personal attention to her education; the simple, contented manner of their life together, sharing everything, especially, as she grew older, his joy in music and her small but useful talent at the piano; his books on the lives of the great composers; her struggles to acquire skills that would be of use to him, the shorthand of Mr. Pitman and a considerable dexterity upon the typewriter; his failing eyesight, the doctors, the ugly, useless treatments they inflicted him with; his later blindness, his indomitable spirit, his tragic death in the mire of a London street.

She spoke of it all as she had never been able to before, not even to kindly old Mr. Pugh-Hennessy. Her great-aunt listened attentively by her side, and seemed to understand even the things that were left unspoken.

When the story was finally done Lady Otranta sat for a time in thoughtful silence. " Clearly, child, you are a determined and courageous person," she said at last. " And not least because it cannot have been easy for you to come here alone, simply at the whim of that wretched Mr. Pugh-Hennessy."

She sighed. " He's an impatient man, your employer. He does not, nay, *will* not, understand my problems, the difficulties that surround me."

Bridie waited, awkward now, not knowing how to reply. Suddenly the old lady leaned forward and took her hand. "You must not be disheartened, my dear, if your work here with me does not progress as rapidly as you would wish. You must remember that we all, in our own ways, have our crosses to bear."

She smiled then, with false brightness. Her grip on Bridie's hand tightened as she used it to pull herself laboriously to her feet. " There now, child, it is almost time for dinner. You just go and make yourself ready. Andrew carries on his father's ways; we change for dinner even here in the barbaric north. And, Bridie, ask that dreadful old Peggy creature to come in to me, will you? She's as crotchety as a Musselburgh fishwife, but if I talk to her nicely she'll see that you get your things moved after dinner to more comfortable quarters. A room in the family part of the castle, I think."

Bridie thanked her, then rose and made her way cautiously out of the room in the last of the fading light of evening. She found old Peggy, a lamp lighted now, still bent over her purple needlework. The light was golden, delightfully old-fashioned, so different from Mrs. Bartlett's single hissing gas mantle. She passed on her great-aunt's message.

" Huh!" Peggy got up, peered suspiciously over her spectacles, her bright black eyes sly above the prodigious curves of her cheeks. " A word from *Madame* and I'm supposed to come running. Is that it?" She paused, then jerked her head in the direction of the next room. " You bin a long time in there. On her best behaviour, was she?"

" I . . . I don't know what you mean. Lady Otranta was very kind to me."

The old servant stood foursquare upon her bunioned feet, hands on her hips, looking Bridie up and down. " Ho yes—*Madame* can be kindness itself when she's a mind to. . . . But jus' you remember, my pet—things ain't always sunshine here, not by a long chalk. And when they ain't, well, it's old Peggy as gets to bear the brunt of 'em, like as not."

Bridie retreated to the opposite door. " I—I'm sure my great-aunt would be quite lost without you," she muttered awkwardly.

" Lost, you say?" Peggy sniffed. " She's that all right—with or without me. I does my best, mind, though I can't think why. Precious little thanks I gets from *Madame* for all my trouble."

Anxious to avoid further such confidences, Bridie smiled noncommittally and made good her escape. Besides, it seemed to her highly probable that Lady Otranta and Peggy were in fact a thoroughly devoted old couple—the more they abused each other the more they needed—and loved—each other.

As Bridie approached the vaulted gallery, the sound of the organ came to her, echoing confusedly down the bare flagged passage. Somebody was playing Bach, a complicated fugue, and playing it with enthusiasm even if not with total accuracy. When she emerged from the final archway, the music burst over her in a thundering, tumultuous flood of sound.

Intrigued, she went to the gallery rail and peered down into the shadowy spaces of the entrance hall.

The candles flanking the organ console had been lighted, and seated at the keyboard was a man she took at first, from his head of silver-blond hair, to be her cousin Andrew. Then, abruptly, as if her presence above him had caught his eye, the music stopped in mid-phrase, its echoes dying slowly between the cold stone walls and the burnished suits of armour, and he turned to look up at her.

The candlelight showed the Tantallon features, the square brow above deep eye-sockets, the straight nose, the angular jaw-line, but somehow softened, blurred a little, with a mouth wider and more sensual. The face too, unlike Sir Andrew's, was clean-shaven, and the hair far longer and more unruly than she was sure he would have thought suitable. The whole figure, also, was slighter than his. This, then, must be the younger brother, Robert.

" Well, well, well—here's the brave little cousin newly up from the big city!" he cried. His fingers broke into a few deafening bars of *My old man said follow the van*, which he merged skilfully into the funeral march from *Saul*. Then he stopped. " Forgive me," he said. " I'm supposed to be the artistic member of the family. The name's Robert. And you'll be Bridie."

She nodded, suddenly overcome with shyness again.

" Welcome to Castle Tantallon, Bridie. You play the organ yourself, so they tell me."

" A little," she conceded faintly, then doubted if she had been heard. " A little," she repeated, speaking a great deal more loudly.

" That's the way, cousin Bridie. We all have to speak up to make ourselves heard in this ghastly mausoleum of a place. But you play more than a little, my dear, if my spies are to be believed."

If there was one thing Bridie hated, it was to be patronised. " By ' your spies ' I presume you mean Mr. Pugh-Hennessy," she said primly, descending the staircase towards him with all the dignity she could muster.

54

Robert swivelled on the organ bench to face her. " Pugh-Hennessy?" he repeated, mimicking her tone. " Now, isn't that the hoitiest-toitiest name you could possibly imagine? *Pugh-Hennessy . . . Puuuugh-Hennnnesssy. . . .*"

He pursed his lips and raised his eyebrows, looking so ridiculous that she couldn't help but laugh. At which his mood changed abruptly and he became exaggeratedly solemn. " Now *that*, dear cousin Bridie, is *it*. Laughter. The only way to make life at Castle Tantallon even remotely bearable."

As she reached the bottom of the stairs he rose from the bench and came to her side. She saw now that, although not as tall as his brother, he was still a good half-a-head taller than herself.

" It certainly doesn't seem to be a very cheerful place," she admitted.

"And thereby hangs a tale, little coz." He stooped and, after looking conspiratorially to left and right, took her arm and led her away to a corner. " You've been closeted with our honoured Mama," he murmured in her ear. " Tell me now, how was the Incredible Madame Otranta? Drunk, of course. But doubtless, in your honour, not yet entirely incapacitated?"

" *Drunk?*" Angrily Bridie recoiled from him, horribly shocked. Suddenly his joking had gone much too far. " Of course she wasn't . . . d-drunk." She had difficulty with a word so distasteful to her tongue.

And just as suddenly her companion had shed his flippancy and was looking at her with genuine sadness. " Well, that makes a nice change, at any rate. But I'm afraid there's no ' of course' about it. That's what the joss-sticks are for—to cover the powerful reek of spirits." He sighed. " It's the great Tantallon secret. I thought the whole world knew it. Mama drinks." He broke off. " Doesn't it sound awful, put like that?"

Appalled, Bridie simply stared at him. What could she possibly say?

He paused, then smiled ruefully and shrugged his shoulders. " Well, I suppose it really *is* awful, if you think about it. Which we don't, mostly. . . . If only it made her happy, I wouldn't mind so much. You know, I'd always thought of people who drink as *happy* people. But not poor Mama. And not my brother either—you've seen for yourself what it's doing to good, honest Andy."

Still Bridie was without words. Until, incongruously, her cousin burst out laughing, leaned towards her, and kissed her lightly upon the forehead. " That is why," he said, " I do my best to keep the flag flying, my dear. And now, heaven be praised, I've got you here to help me."

Help him? Instinctively Bridie pulled away, her mind vigorously rejecting the truth of what he had told her. She refused to believe it, not of the intelligent, dignified old woman she had just left. He must be lying to her for some unimaginable reason. He must be.

And yet. . . . Sentences began to return unbidden to her thoughts, remarks she had failed at the time to understand. Old Peggy: *On her best behaviour, was she?* Lady Otranta herself: *I am not always as you see me now. . . . we all, in our own ways have our crosses to bear.* And even Duncan Symonds's defensive: *She's a remarkable wummun*—as if in his loyalty challenging any man to contradict him.

Explained also were her aunt's rambling letters, and her unwillingness, her apparent inability, to get on with her memoirs. Oh, the poor, poor woman!

But with her pity came also the realisation of the size of the task Mr. Pugh-Hennessy had set her. The odds against which she had to struggle. It was no wonder, indeed, that Sir Andrew had wished to keep her from the castle.

Through all this silent agonising her cousin Robert had stood motionless, watching her face intently. He must, however, have sensed her initial drawing away. " I wasn't serious about your helping me," he said coldly. " I wouldn't even want you to. It's nothing to do with you. After all, she's not *your* mother."

He turned then, and went slowly away, across the flagstones and up the wide staircase. On the gallery he paused, leaned over, his cheerfulness regained. " They'll be beating the dinner gong in five minutes or so," he called down. "And I warn you, brother Andrew's a great one for punctuality. So I wouldn't blot your copybook with him—not on your first evening."

Bridie looked up at him, his wryly smiling face deathly pale in the shifting candlelight. "Thank you for the warning," she said. Briefly she hesitated. "And I'd like to help you. If I can. And if you would really like me to."

3

A^s *for my mother, she was—unlike my poor father— neither simple nor goodhearted.* That's the plain truth. She wore enormous hats, and bullied our wretched cook-general unmercifully, and was obsessed with a determination that I should 'better' myself. By which she meant, of course, that I should marry a man my social superior.

To be honest, I'm glad she didn't live to see me Lady Tantallon—it would have given her such horrible pleasure, and for all the wrong reasons. I loved my Jamie very much, you see, and love was a word I swear I never heard pass her lips.

The first stage of her plan for my betterment had been a young ladies' academy overlooking Dulwich Park and run by the Misses Abernethy. There I learnt my letters, some genteel needlework and water-colouring, the multiplication tables and, later, a smattering of the elder Miss Abernethy's own particular version of the French language. (When I tried this out in my adult years on Professor Henri Salvador he claimed that I might just as well have been addressing him in purest Hottentot. The multiplication tables, on the other hand, as these memoirs will show, turned out to be of the greatest use to us both.)

The second stage of her plan involved my introduction into high society, which in Dulwich meant tea parties with the wife of the local sanitary inspector and visits to the sort of improving lectures that wisely provided lemonade and fish-paste sandwiches as an additional attraction.

I was sixteen and a half when I ran away. I had never actually been inside a theatre, of course, but I had learned enough from the play-bills on the walls of the Dulwich Town Hall to know exactly what I wanted to do with my life. I was going on the stage. I was going to be a famous actress.

Ironically enough, it wasn't until twelve years later, when I had left the theatre for good, that I achieved this last ambition. The stage then was the stage of life, and my audience none other than the Queen of England. She mostly took not the slightest notice of my performance, being far more concerned with the doings of that egregious Scotsman, her servant, John Brown.

But I hasten too quickly. My path to such Olympian heights was not easy. And there were lessons to be learned on every step of the way. Lessons in courage and determination. Lessons in deviousness also. . . .

*　　*　　*

Dinner at Castle Tantallon was served in a hall of impressively baronial proportions. Faded banners fringed with gold hung from a ceiling so high as to be almost invisible in the sickly light thrown by an insufficient number of candelabra set at intervals along the rugged, black-oak table. A veritable petrified forest of antlers decorated the walls, and to one side of the empty, tomb-like fireplace stood an enormous stuffed bear, bald in mostly unmentionable places and spreading his arms in a leering, unsavoury welcome. While at a short distance behind the chair at the head of the table, mounted upon a gilded easel, was a massively-framed portrait of the late Sir James Tantallon, clad in full Scottish ceremonial dress, silver-haired beneath a threatening, thunderous sky.

Amused at first by so much laborious grandeur, Bridie soon became uneasy, seeing how the old man put them all to shame. Of all the people assembled around one end of the table's long perspective, only he, and possibly her great-aunt, his widow, had stature enough, sheer presence enough, to be equal to the room and its monumental appointments. The strange thing about Lady Otranta was that, although still dressed from head to foot in her rustling blacks, and her haggard face still painted crudely, almost like a doll's, she managed nevertheless to radiate a sort of inner strength, an unquenchable vigour, so that the room was ridiculous no longer, but a fitting frame for her restless, indomitable spirit.

At least, that is, for the earlier part of the meal. But then the wine, which Bridie was distressed to see she drank in large quantities, began to take effect.

For the rest, even her elder son Sir Andrew, tall as he was, and undeniably handsome, appeared muted, dwarfed by his surroundings, and by his mother. While Robert, in spite of a constant brave flow of nonsensical conversation, seemed really to add up to little more than a frightened boy, whistling impertinently in the caverns of his ancestral home.

And what of Melissa, their half-sister? She had come in late, and had suffered Sir Andrew's mild reproach unrepentantly, muttering something improbable about a broken chain on her bicycle. Then she'd turned to Bridie and briskly introduced herself. That done, she'd seated herself opposite and set to work on her food. She was clearly a sturdy young woman, and purposeful. And her face, although brown-eyed and not at all of the Tantallon cast, being oval, with a longish nose and drooping eyebrows beneath fine black hair pulled back in an uncompromising bun, was open and humorous and decidedly attractive, for all its air of strenuous commonsense. A young woman with no lack of suitors, so Duncan Symonds had said. And Bridie wasn't surprised.

What, finally, of Bridie herself? Just up from the largest city in the world, the capital of all the Empire—did she sparkle with worldly sophistication? Did she dazzle all eyes with the latest in Bond Street fashions? She had to admit that she did not. In point of fact, her blue cotton frock with the pie-frill collar and the little puff sleeves was ready-to-wear off the racks of Swan & Edgar's, and, for all it fitted her trim young figure becomingly enough, was, from its long journey in the smaller of the two portmanteaux, badly crumpled. And, as for conversation, well, if her cousins hadn't winkled on at her with topics no doubt carefully chosen for their interest to a young woman-about-town, she doubted if she'd have opened her mouth the whole meal. Such indeed was the paralysis of mind into which her situation had thrown her that her contributions in reply were shamefully inadequate, and a great source of private disappointment to her.

"Mrs. Pankhurst, Melissa? Yes, I went to one of her meetings. She was shouted down, however."

And later: "Mr. Churchill? There are so many, Robert—which one is he?"

And, later still: "No thank you, Andrew. No more of the rhubarb flummery, thank you."

All in all, therefore, she was not showing herself to be the most scintillating of companions. Neither was she being of much help to Robert in his efforts to "keep the flag flying".

It should perhaps be said in passing that her refusal of the flummery had been not so much because she was full, as on account of its—and indeed the entire meal's—depressingly spartan nature. She knew she'd been warned by Mr. Symonds to expect plain fare at the castle—but would that often mean, as it had this evening, three courses all of which were principally *oatmeal*? Oatmeal soup, lightly flavoured with celery, followed by a brown oatmeal concoction called haggis, and with a mixture of oatmeal and unsweetened rhubarb to finish. Admittedly this last was topped with excellent cream, but that, however, curdled instantly and almost audibly upon contact with its acidic companion. What further permutations of the Scotsman's staple food, she wondered, were in store?

Her cousins Robert and Melissa, she noticed, hardened no doubt, put all away with seeming gusto. And if Andrew ate almost as sparingly as she, this was certainly on account of his anxious preoccupation with his mother at the head of the table who ate scarcely at all, but drank wine copiously, in silent, grim determination.

Pathetic were the manoeuvrings that took place between mother and son. Repeatedly Andrew contrived unobtrusively to move the old lady's glass beyond her reach only for her to lean firmly forward and retrieve it. Until finally she turned on him, with a flush to her cheeks that was more than mere rouge, and loudly demanded, "Can it be, son Andrew, that you are trying to tell me something?"

At which he was obliged to retreat in embarrassed confusion. "Certainly not, Mama. Whatever made you think such a thing?"

While his brother and half-sister, further down the table, engaged her, Bridie, in brighter conversation than ever.

The butler, too, did his loyal best to support Andrew, but with no greater success. "Are you blind as well as senile, Meredith? Can you not see that my glass is in need of replenishment?"

Her son and step-daughter, further down the table, meanwhile talked frantically of Balfour and George Bernard Shaw.

Bridie could have wept. Never before had she so longed for a meal to end. Yet the end, when it came, took her completely by surprise. They had only just embarked upon the cheese when Lady Otranta suddenly rose from her chair and stood, swaying very slightly, her hands gripping the table's massive edge.

"We are forgetting our manners, Andrew," she said, enunciating each word with exaggerated precision. "There is a guest here this evening. We must open a bottle of the Boy with which to toast your cousin."

"Champagne, Mama?" Her son caught the butler's eye and shook his head minutely. "If you say so, Mama."

"Certainly I say so." The old lady staggered, and momentarily closed her eyes. "I . . . I fear I am not very well. Another time, perhaps . . . If my niece will forgive me I think it would be better after all if I went to my room." Making a great effort, she straightened her back. "Will you kindly ring for Peggy to assist me?"

Upon which the fat old dresser appeared with such promptness that Bridie could only suppose she had been ready and waiting behind the door, and led her mistress away. The brothers stood in silence, watching them go. When she was almost out of the room, Lady Otranta paused, threw off Peggy's supporting hand and turned, leaning heavily upon her stick.

"Bridie, my dear. . . ." She hesitated, frowning as if she had momentarily forgotten what it was she intended to say. "Bridie, my dear, may I commend you to your Bible? 'Judge not, that ye be not judged.' Hmmm? There's much truth in it."

She swayed then, and would have fallen had not Peggy taken her firmly by the arm. And together, precariously, the two old women vanished from sight, the door swinging slowly shut behind them with a click that resounded painfully in the sudden hush that had fallen upon the dining room.

For a long moment no one moved or spoke.

" Well, at least she managed without help this time," Robert murmured at last, seating himself with elaborate nonchalance. " A distinct improvement on certain other occasions I could mention."

While Bridie, speechless, lowered her eyes to her plate, near to tears. For him, for her great-aunt, for them all.

Suddenly Andrew cleared his throat and moved to the head of the table, where his mother had been sitting. " You will understand now," he said, addressing Bridie, " why I tried to discourage you from coming here. I wanted to spare you, I wanted to spare us all. I tried to do what I thought was right, but I was . . . prevented."

It seemed like an accusation. Bridie flushed. " I came here to help," she replied hotly. " It seems now that my help is needed even more than I thought."

Her cousin frowned. " Poor Mama is . . ."

But he got no further, for there was a sudden commotion as Melissa scrambled to her feet. " If there's to be another family discussion," she cried, her voice hoarse and scarcely controlled, " leave me out of it! D'you hear, Andy? Leave me out of it." And, upsetting her chair, she stumbled away down the room and through the far door, banging it soundly behind her.

Robert clicked his tongue. " Poor 'Lissa," he said. " She does take these *contretemps* to heart so."

" And so do you, Robert," his brother admonished him sharply. " In your own way, if only you'd admit it."

The two men glared at each other. In the silence that fell again, briefly, Bridie was made powerfully aware of the bond that existed between them: Andrew standing stiffly in the place so recently vacated by his mother, head held high, the candlelight emphasising the rugged directness of his features; his brother Robert, leaning negligently back in his chair, one hand toying with crumbs upon his plate, his face mostly shadowed and uncertain, only his wry smile clear in all its studied, false indifference. As unlike as these two men were, they were still brothers. And they both cared deeply, in their own ways, as much for each other as for the pathetic, tragic old woman, Lady Otranta Tantallon, their mother.

Slowly Andrew relaxed. He seated himself, turned to Bridie. "You spoke of helping Mama," he said gently. "I wish I thought that were possible. But we have tried, all of us. Believe me, we have *tried*. We—we love her, you see."

He covered his eyes. "Even Dr. Macnab—it's a pretence really that he comes all the way from Edinburgh just to treat her for her arthritis—he has tried also. And I promise you he's not one of those old-fashioned, moralising quacks. He's known Mama for a long time—known her and loved her. Nobody, you see, who knew her in the old days could possibly fail to. Yet even he—"

He broke off then, his voice suddenly strangled in his throat, and turned away, finishing his sentence with a small, helpless gesture.

"Macnab's not a bad old stick," Robert affirmed, tactfully filling in for him. "He's got no time at all for most of the so-called 'cures' you hear about. There are powders one can put into wine for example—they may put a person off drinking for a while, but they're full of antimone and terribly dangerous."

Bridie leaned forward. "But might not someone like me, a complete outsider, stand a better chance of helping?" she said. "Could I not, for instance, perhaps get her interested again in her memoirs? Keep her busy? Take her mind off—"

"Those memoirs? Positively not." Andrew swung round on her, his sudden vehemence alarming. "Those wretched memoirs—I swear they're in some way at the root of all the trouble."

"What Andy means," Robert put in, much of his old flippancy now recovered, " is that right up until Mama started committing herself to paper she was as right as rain. Papa's death set her back, of course—it did us all. But she rallied splendidly, and was coming along like a house on fire."

Andrew nodded. " I blame myself, of course. When she suggested writing the story of her life, you see, I thought it was a good idea. It would give her something to do—as you said, an interest. And she'd had such an extraordinary life, its story would surely be one well worth telling . . . How was I to know?"

He sighed and looked down, absent-mindedly straightening a knife on the table in front of him. " I even gave her the name of the man she should contact in London, Pugh-Hennessy. His family had rented an estate up here once—not that he and Mama had ever met, you understand, but I thought the coincidence might take his fancy. And it did, it did . . . How was I to know? How was I to know what misery my encouragement would bring in its wake?"

He spread his arms wide, then lowered them in disgust at the futility of the question.

" But how," Bridie wrinkled her forehead, " how could just writing some memoirs bring about such a . . ." Her words needed no completion, so she gave them none.

Andrew paused, as if strangely reluctant to reply himself, and nodded across at his brother. And even Robert seemed embarrassed, for he rolled the crumbs to and fro on his plate with a new intensity.

" According to Macnab," he began, " —and he's right up to the minute, mind, well-read in all the latest continental developments—according to Macnab the writing of these memoirs has forced Mama to remember certain things best forgotten. Possibly it's making her face secret truths about herself that she'd . . . well, she'd managed to ignore for many years. And the poor old thing just can't take it. So she's turning to drink as the only way out."

Loudly his brother brought his hand down flat upon the table. " The idea's quite ridiculous, of course. What things? What secrets? A woman like Mama, conscientious, loving, virtuous—what secrets could she possibly have?"

Robert shrugged his shoulders. " Macnab says we all have secrets, even the most loving and virtuous of us."

Bridie was silent again at this new, unsettling thought. Unconsciously her eyes were drawn back to the portrait of old Sir James, windswept and inscrutable. If his widow had secrets, had she shared them with him? Had they both, seemingly so entrenched in their unassailable respectability, lived in a sense double lives? Possibly in daily danger of exposure? If they had, certainly the old man's craggy features admitted none of it.

" Anyway," Robert concluded, " if Mama does indeed have secrets, I vote that she be allowed to keep them. If she wants to go no further with her memoirs then that's her business. Convince her of that, and maybe we could all get back to normal again."

Possibly he was right. In which case, Bridie wondered, where did that place *her*? She remembered how warmly her great-aunt had seemed to welcome her coming, and understand her purpose. Could the memoirs be such a painful matter for her? Or might they not, once completed, act as a release, like the pouring out of her heart to a trusted confidante?

She gathered her thoughts. One thing was certain—her position in the Tantallon household, which she'd never thought would be easy, had turned out to be far more complicated than her worst fears could ever have imagined.

*   *   *

I called myself Lucy London. You won't have heard the name—it never made even the very smallest print at the bottom of the programme. Yet it seemed fetching enough at the time—and I needed *something* to hide behind, in case my parents sent the law after me.

It was three years before *Madame Otranta* was born. And *Lady Tantallon* eight years after that.

Sometimes, even after all these years, I wonder who I really am. Little Lucy London who couldn't dance and couldn't sing but tramped month after month from theatre

66

to theatre, trying to convince producers that she could do both? Or Madame Otranta, successfully deceiving willing audiences night after night with the oldest tricks in the business? Or Lady Tantallon, living perhaps the greatest lie of all?

Once these memoirs are done—if they are ever done—perhaps I shall know the answer.

When Lucy London first ran away from home she went to Bristol, to the Hippodrome and then the Theatre Royal. In neither case did she even get past the stage door keeper. They were a jaundiced lot, those men, and probably with good reason.

Thereafter Bath, Cheltenham, Gloucester, and up through the Midlands. Birmingham, Manchester, Stoke-on-Trent . . . and her tiny savings, dwindling all the time.

Mostly I remember the men. So bored. So tobacco-stained. So fat.

"You wouldn't have a nice line in fire-eating, would you?" they said.

Or, "You could always come back when we're hiring for the flying ballet."

Or even, "I might have something for you, duckie, if you hung around and saw me afterwards."

I tried that once. I was that innocent. But not for long. It was a hatpin that saved me—a large hatpin. With an amber head.

And then, one rain-drenched afternoon in Leeds, I was actually allowed inside a theatre. And I was introduced to Captain Sawbright.

It would be nice to say that he engaged me because he thought me talented. Or pretty. Or *something*. But that simply wasn't the case. I was given the job solely because I was there, and because the only available costume—which had previously been worn by a girl who had run off that day with the leader of the orchestra—fitted me perfectly.

I don't recall minding. A job was a job. And after three months on the road one wasn't too fussy. I've always been good at making the best of things. James was the grand exception. I never needed to make the best of him. Neither of him nor of my charming, handsome, *intolerable* children . . .

*   *   *

Next morning Bridie woke to leaden skies, and to the steady drip of rain on her window-sill from the stone coping above. As her great-aunt had promised, Bridie's things had been moved the previous night to a more domesticated part of the castle, and she had slept well, in a neat little chintz-covered bed, in a neat little chinzt-curtained room.

To her relief, her cousin Andrew had approved when he heard of the move.

" The fault was mine for pre-judging you," he told her frankly. " I thought you would have to be a very brassy, *London* sort of person, to push yourself in where you knew you weren't wanted. Hence the Baronial Bedroom, kept specially for unwanted guests."

He smiled shamefacedly, suddenly young and vulnerable, and infinitely appealing. " But I was quite wrong. You're not like that at all. You're just like one of us, really."

And there was nothing he could have said that would have pleased her more.

For a while she lay in bed, listening to the rain and remembering his words. Remembering also his face in the candlelight as he had spoken them, his smile warm and his eyes gentle for all the dark lines of worry that encircled them. A sudden wish had come over her then to smooth those lines away, and to still his hands that fussed constantly, nervously, hither and thither. A wish so powerful that her pulse quickened even at the memory of it.

And Robert it had been who had sensed her confusion and turned the conversation with some light remark she couldn't for the life of her recall. Robert, the brother who had a jest— good or bad—for every occasion. It would be comforting to think that his manner wasn't just a pose, that in truth nothing really mattered very much to him. But that simply wasn't so.

Robert was in need of help and reassurance just as much as his brother.

Bridie sighed, and threw back the bedclothes, and went to the window. Her room faced away from the water, towards a sodden wooded hillside up which a broad track wound between the trees until it disappeared gradually into dense white layers of low-lying mist. Nothing stirred in the still, dank air, not a blade of grass. Bridie shivered slightly, and turned back into the room.

Just as she was finishing at the wash-stand a knock upon the door heralded the arrival of breakfast, brought to her on a tray by the timid young chambermaid called Agnes whom Bridie had met the night before. Now, as then, the poor girl curtsied nervously and scuttled out again before Bridie could think of anything to say to her. How silly it was, Bridie thought, that the two of them should be so separated by their mutual shyness. If only she could explain to Agnes just how awkward it made her feel, being waited upon, she who had spent her whole life looking after herself, and her father too. If only she could tell the poor girl about her parlour bedroom at Mrs. Bartlett's. The truth of it was that they were both equally out of their element in the grim formalities of Castle Tantallon.

She ate her breakfast slowly, at a little table by the window —porridge, of course, and tea, and two bantams' eggs boiled as hard as little bullets—turning over in her mind all that she had learned since coming to the castle. Clearly she must talk to her great-aunt as soon as possible. Then there was Mr. Pugh-Hennessy down in London—if the old lady's memoirs were really to be abandoned then he must be told of it at once, and given reasons. But what reasons? The truth? That Lady Otranta was habitually too drunk to complete them? It was a cruel thing to say of any person.

Besides, Bridie wasn't even sure that it was so. And, even if it was, could it be the *whole* truth? What then of her great-aunt's unconquerable dignity, her intelligence, the sheer power of her personality? Could these really exist in someone totally a slave to her weaker nature?

69

Then again, there were her cousins to be considered. Melissa too—the quiet one, the half-sister, probably always keeping herself apart, thinking of herself as an outsider in the tight little Tantallon family—her views therefore might well be all the more revealing. Anyway, all three of them certainly had a right to some say in the message that was finally sent to Mr. Pugh-Hennessy.

But, first of all, Lady Otranta. Not an easy confrontation, after what Bridie had seen at the dinner table, but one that must be gone through with all the same. Her breakfast done, Bridie rose briskly from the table, paused in front of the mirror to confirm her businesslike appearance—plain white blouse with a small cameo brooch at the high neck, above a floor-length, dark grey woollen skirt—and then made her way purposefully in the direction of her great-aunt's room.

"What's this, then? Where ezzackly d'you reckon you're off to, Miss?" Once again old Peggy, like an irritable watchdog, was lurking by her mistress's door.

Bridie squared her shoulders. "Good morning, Peggy," she said, pleasantly but firmly. "I have important matters to discuss with my great-aunt."

"Not now, you 'aven't." Peggy sniffed indignantly. "Nobody discusses nothing with Madame—not before noon, they don't."

"But that's ridic—" Bridie stopped herself. Perhaps it wasn't so ridiculous, not if one remembered the night before. She lowered her voice. "Is my great-aunt still sleeping, then?"

Peggy folded her arms, ponderously rearranging the various dressmaker's necessities pinned to her enormous bosom. "'Ow should I know what she's doing? I'm not one for key-holes, me, not at my time of life."

"But—"

"Nobody's to disturb 'er, y'see." Peggy explained, unbending a little. "Not even me. Every morning it's the same —I takes in her breakfast around nine, and she swears at me a bit, and I pushes off again. Leaves her to it." Peggy disengaged one hand, tweaked at the ribbons of her cap. "I mean . . . it's only natural. I mean, when a person's not been well the night before she still needs her beauty sleep just the same as the rest of us."

Not been well—it seemed an evasion more humiliating even than the truth.

"You don't have to pretend with me," Bridie said briskly. "I saw my great-aunt. I know she was d . . . drunk—" in spite of her determination to speak boldly, Bridie's tongue tripped over the unfamiliar word. "And—"

"*Drunk?*" Peggy threw back her head and cackled raucously. "If you think that's drunk, you should just see Madame sometimes."

It almost certainly wasn't true, said simply to shock her. But Bridie hung her head. She knew she was being put in her place. And she realised suddenly how pompous she must have sounded. "I'll . . . I'll come back in the afternoon then," she muttered. "Perhaps we can work on the memoirs after lunch."

"After lunch? Frankly, miss, I doubts it. Oh, she was fine enough yesterday, I grant you. But that was something of an hexception—on your account, like, if you take my meaning." Suddenly the old woman leaned forward and clutched at Bridie's arm. "And besides, if you ask me, them memoirs is a lot of wicked nonsense."

Bridie stared at her, frankly curious. Surely old Peggy wasn't one to subscribe to Dr. Macnab's advanced theories. "Why wicked?" she asked.

"Well, I mean to say . . ." Peggy shrugged her fat shoulders evasively. "Well, there's some things as is better not told. Wouldn't you say so, miss? Wouldn't you say as there's some things as is better left to the himagination?"

What things? Did the old dresser know, or was she simply guessing? With a little more prompting, Bridie felt, she might be persuaded to be more explicit. "You may be right," she said guardedly. "But it really depends on what you mean by—"

At that moment, however, the door to her great-aunt's room opened and, to her great astonishment, Mr. Duncan Symonds came through, a business-like folder labelled *Accounts* tucked under his arm. He saw her, closed the door calmly behind him, then politely inclined his head.

"A verra good morning to you, Miss Bridie," he said.

"And the same to you, Mr. Symonds." Then, addressing him but staring hard at old Peggy, "And how did you find my great-aunt this morning?" she enquired heavily.

Mr. Symonds frowned. "And how should I be finding her Ladyship? A wee bit tired, y'ken, but. . . ." He sighed, and shifted his feet. "Weel, mebbe after the way she was last night you know full weel just how I found her. But the affairs of the estate have to go on, for a' that. And I need my instructions." He hesitated, cleared his throat. "I'm thinking I'd best be awa' about my business."

He walked round her, his gaze averted. At the far door he paused. "On the train now—mebbe I should have preparit you. But it's no an easy thing to say to a virtual stranger. And there was always the chance that the old one might surprise us a'. With yoursel' in the house, a new member o' the family and a'. . . . But it wasna to be."

He shook his head sadly, turned, and went slowly out of the room.

"*Always the chance.* . . ." Peggy snorted derisively. "He's got a hope—hasn't seen 'em, not like I have. You can't work the music halls the way I have and not see 'em. Drunks, I mean. Not a kipper's chance in hell, I'd say."

Her gloating acceptance of the old lady's condition infuriated Bridie. "You didn't tell me the truth," she accused. "You said nobody was allowed in to see my great-aunt before noon."

Peggy leaned forward again, venom suddenly in her eyes behind their thick spectacle lenses. "Not *him*—not Mr. Duncan flamin' Symonds. He's the flamin' hexception. A regular little John Brown, he is. Treats her like she was the old Queen. *And* she lets him. I tell you, it's history repeating itself, that's what it is."

She lowered her voice to a penetrating whisper. "And what I'd like to know is, where does that leave her oldest son? Where does that leave poor Sir Andrew? Out in the cold, that's where—just like Prince Edward. Out in the cold,

I tell you. Up the creek, and without a paddle."

Bridie was silent now. She had wondered about her cousin Andrew's position in the household. Now it was clear: he had none. Like the Prince of Wales, now King Edward, he was under the thumb of a mother who would give up none of her authority. And, like the old Queen who had had her faithful Scottish servant John Brown to dance attendance upon her, Lady Tantallon had Duncan Symonds. Bridie didn't blame Mr. Symonds—he was a decent, kindly man who certainly wouldn't take advantage of his position. But at least it was no wonder that back on the train he had betrayed a poor opinion of the new laird of Tantallon.

Yet there was a difference here also. History wasn't precisely repeating itself. The Prince, in his frustration, had turned to fast living, to women and gambling and alcohol. . . . Her great-aunt's words returned to her: *a bottle of the Boy.* It was Prince Edward's partiality for champagne and his frequent cries for the boy to bring him another bottle that had caused his friends to give it that nickname, whereas Andrew had stayed decently by his mother's side. And, according to Mr. Symonds himself, he worked himself into the ground, out in all weathers, helping the men, always eager to learn. She thought, too, of his touching concern for his mother. Indeed, the more she considered him, the more she knew he was worthy of her respect and admiration.

Old Peggy straightened her back. "Mind you," she wheezed, "I'm not saying anything I haven't already said to Madame a thousand times. Not that it makes no difference. But we understand each other, Madame and me."

Bridie looked at her, putting Andrew for the moment out of her mind. There was more, she thought, than just mutual understanding between Peggy and her great-aunt. There was mutual need. Two women, grown old together, sharing memories, sharing too the sad, inexorable changes that age brought with it. They needed each other. They might scorn each other, abuse each other, but there was need also. And with need, love.

"I'm sure you understand each other very well," Bridie

said gently. And then, with sudden insight, " And if anyone can help Lady Otranta, I know you can."

Peggy faltered. Suddenly all her arrogance disappeared, and her vast bulk seemed to diminish. Her sharp little eyes misted over. " If only she'd *listen*," she said. Tears ran down her fat cheeks. " If only she'd *listen* . . . but I just can't somehow get through to her. She's keeping somethink from me. I know she is. And after all these years . . ."

She tugged a grubby handkerchief from her sleeve and mopped her face, pushing her spectacles all askew. " The drink's nothing—we've always enjoyed a tipple, me and her. Why, the laughs we've had!" She groped blindly round for her chair and collapsed onto it, weeping openly. " But she could stop the drink any time she wanted—just like *that*. I know she could. Honest, miss, it's like as if somethink was driving her on. And she just won't listen . . ."

There was anger in her sorrow, frustration at events she could no longer control, no longer even begin to comprehend. Her sudden helplessness was pitiful. Bridie moved forward, put one arm round her shoulders, comforted her.

" Dear Peggy . . . we'll think of something. You'll see. It'll come out all right. We'll think of something."

Gradually the old woman's crying subsided. She blew her nose. Ashamed now of her show of emotion, she took off her glasses and dried them, then she reached for her needlework and tugged crossly at its shapeless folds. " Dratted thing," she muttered. " Eight and four-fifths yards of best shot taffeta, and you'd never think it . . ."

Softly then, Bridie left her, venting all her distress harmlessly upon the innocent purple mound of crumpled material. *We'll think of something*, she'd said. Easy words. And at the time she'd even believed them. Think of something . . . but what? Her great-aunt's problems were surely far too complicated for simple, *Peg's Paper* solutions.

She had been moving without conscious purpose. Now, finding herself upon the vaulted gallery, she started slowly down the stairs. A figure passed, scarcely noticed, in the hallway below. It stopped, turned back.

" Care for a walk?"

Bridie jumped. She hadn't expected to be addressed. The voice was Melissa's.

"You'll have to get used to walking—if you're here any time, that is. There's precious little else to do. Unless you ride a bicycle, of course."

"I have ridden one," Bridie replied, a little doubtfully, hurrying down the rest of the stairs and telling herself she should be pleased that Melissa, in her bluff way, was trying to be sociable. "But not very often."

"Never mind—we'll soon put you in the way of it. I'll get Duncan to provide one. There's a Rudge-Whitworth, not too old, in the stables. Now, how about that walk?"

"I . . . I'd like that very much." Bridie hesitated. "But isn't it raining?"

Melissa laughed, a short sharp bark that Bridie was going to find typical of her cousin. "This is Scotland, my dear. If we waited till it wasn't raining we'd scarcely move outside the front door." She moved to a tall lancet window by the entrance, and looked out. She was wearing a tailored coat and skirt made of heather-coloured tweed, a tam o'shanter rakishly pulled over her dark hair. "As a matter of fact, though, we're in luck. It seems to have blown over for the moment. We'd better make the most of it."

She opened the inside door to the massive porch, then paused. "You'll need a cloak, though. And what about your shoes?" She lifted her own skirt to reveal neat black galoshes. "Don't worry—we're sure to have something to fit you."

Along one wall of the porch, beside a sturdy elmwood boot-jack, there stood a low, bench-like cupboard containing a jumble of assorted weatherproof footwear. Melissa beckoned Bridie, seated her upon the cupboard, and expertly assessed her shoes.

"Fives, are they not? Excellent. The very thing. You can wear Mama's—Lord knows, she'll not be needing them." She rummaged, finally unearthing a pair of Wellington boots that fitted Bridie as if they had been made for her. "It's many months since Mama went out walking," Melissa explained briskly. " Her arthritis, you know. And the other thing, of course. . . . Come along then, if you're coming. This bright spell won't last for ever."

She handed Bridie a soft tweed cloak from a peg, then strode on ahead, out through the huge, iron-studded doors. Bridie followed her at a trot.

" I was wrong, actually, when I said there was nothing to do," her cousin called back over her shoulder. " I was forgetting the sheep-juicing. You couldn't have come at a better time, really."

Struggling into the cloak, Bridie caught up with her halfway across the courtyard. " You mean the sheep-dipping?" she said, remembering what Duncan Symonds had told her on the train. " But surely you and I . . . I mean, surely we aren't expected to—"

" Lord, no." Melissa laughed again, short and sharp. " That's strictly for the men—and good luck to 'em. But we have a bit of a do afterwards for everyone on the estate, not forgetting the local gentry, *noblesse oblige* and all that. It's the nearest we get to a harvest festival, not having a harvest, y'see. A feast, dancing, that sort of thing."

They were passing out under the main archway, down onto the heavy drawbridge.

" The preparations have started already," Melissa went on. " Invitations, ordering in the provisions . . . Have you brought anything to wear?"

Bridie, hurrying to keep up with long strides of her cousin was unprepared for such an abrupt question. " I—"

" It doesn't matter if you haven't. I expect we can fit you out. It's nothing very grand. Just a lot of hopping about. Can you dance a reel, then?"

In Bridie's life there had been little occasion for dancing, of whatever sort. She hesitated, feeling inadequate. " I—"

But Melissa didn't wait for an answer. " It doesn't matter if you can't," she said in her customary off-hand fashion.

" Thank you very much," Bridie said. " I—"

" There's time enough to put you in the way of it. The party's not for another ten days."

" Do you sing?" Melissa next demanded.

Puzzled, Bridie shook her head. " I'm afraid not. But I do play the—"

" Thank the Lord for that. I do, y'see, and that's quite enough caterwauling for one night. The thing is, we're all expected to do something. Andrew recites—mostly Sir Walter Scott. Robert, on the other hand. . . ."

They were out on the drawbridge by now, its massive planks wet and slippery beneath their feet. The moat lay below, a shallowly-dug channel somewhat clogged with rushes and weed, among which a pair of damp swans paddled disconsolately. All at once there came a loud, inarticulate cry of warning from the courtyard behind the main archway. Bridie turned and looked back. And what she saw stopped her dead in her tracks, utterly immobile, frozen idiotically, suicidally to the spot.

The family's motor car, the big yellow Argyll that had met her at the ferry, was bearing down on them, pilotless, wheels flashing, rolling in eerie silence ever faster down the courtyard's steady incline, lurching, the loose canvas of the driver's hood flapping wildly as it careered through the archway and out onto the drawbridge. Bridie knew she must run, yet still she stood there, paralysed by terror, directly in the vehicle's runaway path.

It was Melissa who broke the spell, her panic-stricken screams. Bridie dragged her gaze away from the motor car, now almost upon them, and saw her cousin sprawled upon the wet planks, scrambling, slipping, tearing frantically at the cumbersome folds of her skirt. In an instant Bridie was at her side, pulling her clear, while in a silent rush of gleaming paint and leatherwork the Argyll surged past them, towering overhead, close enough for Bridie to see the mud-flicked underside of its running-board, past them and down onto the rain-dark gravel of the drive.

It rolled on, slowing now, till it mounted the far grass verge and came to rest with a squeaking of branches, in the impenetrable thicket of rhododendrons beyond. And behind it, in the middle of the drawbridge, lying flattened, neatly bent in two, she saw with painful clarity one of her cousin's galoshes, the imprint of the motor car's tyre showing vividly across its shiny black rubber.

She was safe, and Melissa also. She leaned, gasping, on the drawbridge's low parapet. Footsteps approached at a run. Her senses were reeling, and gratefully she closed her eyes as a strong arm came round her shoulders.

" I shouted . . . I tried to warn you. . . . Thank God you're both safe."

It was Robert, his arm comforting about her. She gave way then, and drifted helplessly off into the soft, grey mists of unconsciousness.

4

When I first met Sir James Tantallon he was dying. He didn't know it, of course, and neither did I. I simply saw a tall, distinguished gentleman standing in the door of my dressing room, leaning lightly on a gold-mounted malacca cane. I suspected that he was ill, however, for he was painfully thin, and his fine patrician's face pale and haggard. But hardly *dying*. . . .

He'd spoken to me earlier that evening, he said, across the footlights. I'd been on the point of telling him the inscription inside his watch when he'd suddenly had to leave the auditorium. Perhaps I remembered.

I did remember. The inscription had been giving me a lot of trouble. Inscriptions always did—yet Professor Salvador refused to give them up. He'd stand down in the aisle, with the watch or whatever it was in his hand, and ask me question after question till I thought I would scream. So it had been a great relief to me when, on that particular occasion, I'd been spared the ordeal.

Henri was quite right to insist, however. It was on feats like that, you see, that my reputation as a mind-reader mostly depended. That and my trick of guessing dates and numbers, which I managed without his saying a single word.

Anyway, Sir James had come to apologise. He'd been taken with a sudden spasm of sickness, he said. He was subject to these fits. And he wanted me to know his departure had had nothing to do with my performance, which he'd found fascinating.

And so he should have too! It had taken us long enough to work up, the Professor and I. It was Henri who had rescued me from Doctor Melodious's miserable little birds.

Something about me had taken his fancy—I never discovered exactly what. But he'd needed a new assistant and there I'd been, all tights and unsuitable spangles, holding cases of yellow-painted sparrows for " In a Monastery Garden ".

He'd offered me fame—and five shillings a week—in exchange for a few simple mental exercises, and I'd leapt at the chance. I'd grown out of my ambition to be a great actress long since. Even the fame he offered me seemed scarcely important. It was the five shillings that attracted me—and never again to have to clean out a bird-cage.

God knows, if I'd guessed what he meant by 'a few simple mental exercises' I might have thought twice. They turned out to be a thousand times worse than anything the Misses Abernethy, for all their multiplication tables, had ever come up with. Still they sharpened my mind. And, while they were being painfully mastered, my body came in for some honing, too.

I was, for example, the legs of the girl he sawed in half twice nightly! I was a slender and supple young woman, yet the constrictions of the space into which I had to fold myself for that performance never ceased to amaze me. I was also expected to disappear from the stage in at least seven different ways, all of which needed near-miraculous agility.

It was all, I suppose, undignified. Just as the singing birds had been. But I am ashamed of neither. It was honest toil. And the time was to come when I would thank the Professor for this early training. When it would be all that stood between me and certain death. . . . I couldn't have known that then, of course. So I worked at my lessons, and longed for the day when I would put the gymnastics behind me and emerge seductive and sphinx-like, as Madame Otranta.

Nor was I wrong in this. For it was as Madame Otranta that James first saw me. And James fell in love with me, so he told me later, on that very first evening. . . .

*　　*　　*

Bridie remained unconscious for no more than a few seconds. Then she opened her eyes, discovered that she was sitting ungracefully propped up against the wet parapet of the wooden drawbridge, and scrambled at once indignantly to her feet. She wasn't the fainting sort, and she had no opinion at all of those who were.

Dizziness returned, however. Obstinately she clung to the wet parapet, her thoughts still confused, peering anxiously round through ill-focused eyes. Melissa sat on the ground a few feet away, nursing one ankle, while Robert leaned solicitously over her and murmured gentle words of encouragement. Beyond them she could see through the great stone archway to the castle courtyard, its cobbles gleaming blackly beneath the lowering sky.

Suddenly, in a flash, the entire horrific sequence of events came back to her—the runaway car, her paralysis, Melissa's cry of terror, their last-minute scramble to safety. She turned her head. Yes, the Argyll was still where she had last seen it, on the far side of the drive, leaning precariously, half buried in the rhododendrons.

Robert looked up. " You're all right then—thank God for that." His face was deathly pale, his eyes dark with shock. " What can I say? You . . . you saved 'Lissa's life." He shuddered. " It was like a nightmare. I saw it all—I was just coming across from the stables. I shouted—I ran as fast as I could —but I could do nothing. You saved 'Lissa's life."

Bridie felt embarrassed. " The stupid car went nowhere near us," she muttered. It wasn't true, but might save her his further gratitude.

" You're sure you're all right?"

She nodded. Melissa stood up slowly, leaning heavily on his arm, and hobbled to her side. " No great harm done then," she said gruffly. " I'm grateful, though. . . ." She broke off, shook her head angrily from side to side. " Oh, how I *detest* the sort of little ninny who always manages to fall over at just the crucial moment!"

Robert protested. " You couldn't help it, 'Lissa."

She turned on him. " Naturally I didn't do it on purpose, Robert. But for God's sake—I might have killed the pair of us."

Bridie moved away a pace. Both of her cousins were badly shaken, near to quarrelling in the aftermath of their panic. " I —I wonder how it happened," she said, hoping to direct their emotions elsewhere. " I mean, motor cars don't usually run away like that, do they?"

Robert gestured angrily. " The hand-brake must have slipped. I'm always telling Duncan he should leave wedges under the back wheels."

" Or better still," Melissa put in, " leave the wretched thing in gear."

None of this meant very much to Bridie. But she wasn't surprised to see that Melissa had made it her business to understand such things. She was that sort of person. And anyway, the diversion was having the desired effect.

" I shall get Mama to speak to Duncan severely," Robert said, frowning. " Not that it'll make the slightest difference," he added bitterly.

He left them then, and went to pick up Melissa's mutilated galosh from the middle of the drawbridge. He held it, staring down at it in horror for a long moment. Then he braced himself and flung it far into the air, so that it disappeared among the dripping branches of the encircling pine trees. It was as if he was ridding himself of the terrible possibilities it represented. He watched it go, then turned slowly back to them. When he spoke it was with a clear effort at his usual lightness of manner.

" No more walks for you two. We'd better get you both back into the castle *tout de suite*."

Bridie examined her skirt. There were long scuffs of mud on it, and on the cloak Melissa had lent her. " You see to Melissa," she said. " I can manage." Then she hesitated. " Shouldn't we do something about the car, though?"

Robert scowled. " I'll send Duncan. The whole thing's his fault, anyway."

He gave his arm to Melissa, whose ankle was obviously still paining her, and together the three of them slowly made their way up, in through the stone archway and across the cobbled courtyard. A short distance from the main entrance to the castle Robert left them and went on ahead. Bridie watched him approach a patch of dry cobbles away in the far corner of the courtyard, presumably where the Argyll had been parked, and stoop over it. She saw him touch two small objects on the ground, and stand for a moment staring at them thoughtfully. Then he came back to her and Melissa.

"The wedges are there, all right." His voice was hushed, uneasy, and he glanced anxiously round at the castle's high, blank windows. "I really don't see what can have happened. It's . . . it's almost as if they've been moved."

Melissa laughed, a sharp, unexpected sound that echoed unpleasantly between the high surrounding walls. "Moved on purpose, you mean?"

Robert glared at her. "It's hardly something anyone could do by accident," he snapped.

In the silence that followed Bridie felt the cold touch of a new terror. "But why?" she faltered.

It was a question nobody cared to answer. Again silence pinned them there beneath the dark, watchful eyes of the castle. To be broken at last by Melissa, brusquely cuffing her brother away.

"Lot of nonsense," she said. "The things could easily have slipped—the ground's wet enough. Besides—who'd want to frighten us like that?"

She laughed again, scornfully, and hobbled away in through the castle door. Her voice could be heard inside: "Meredith! *Meredith*—ah, there you are. Tell Duncan, will you—tell him his precious machine's gone galloping off down the drive all on its own."

Robert glanced sideways at Bridie, and tentatively took her hand. "'Lissa's quite right, of course. Trust me to dramatise things. You mustn't take any notice. The wedges slipped— they *must* have."

She managed a reassuring smile for him, and let him lead

her in after Melissa. In the doorway, however, she paused and glanced back over her shoulder. What she saw confirmed her worst suspicions. The ground where the wedges lay wasn't in the least wet or slippery. And it seemed to her that the motor car must have been aimed with great care—otherwise it would have crashed into one or other side of the archway.

She sat down just inside the door, slowly removed the boots she had borrowed, and put on her own shoes. It was impossible, surely, that anyone could seriously have wanted to harm her and Melissa. What then? A foolish joke—perhaps even Robert's own—that had gone terribly wrong? Or could it possibly have been . . . she paused in her silent struggle with her shoe buttons . . . could it possibly have been a warning, aimed at her alone? Connected, since there could presumably be no other reason, with her great-aunt's memoirs? A warning —with the clear implication that if she persisted in the task Mr. Pugh-Hennessy had set her there would be worse to follow. . . .

" Why so thoughtful, fair coz?"

She started, looked up and saw Robert smiling down at her. He had come to their rescue, had he not? But could she trust him? Could she trust anybody?

She shrugged. " You'd be thoughtful too, if your shoes had buttons like mine," she said lightly and stood up, dusting the mud off her skirt as best she could.

They retired to a small sitting room on the right of the entrance hall where Melissa was already resting, her painful ankle on a chair in front of her, and had coffee brought to them which Robert freely laced with brandy.

Melissa stirred her cup. " Where's Andrew got to?" she asked. " I'm surprised he didn't hear all the commotion."

Robert replaced the stopper in the brandy decanter. " He mentioned something about going up to the sawmill with Duncan. . . ." All at once a thought seemed to strike him. He hesitated, then put the decanter back on the table and shook his head, as if brushing an unwelcome idea away. " The big saw-blade had buckled," he said with some emphasis, as if to affirm the truth of the matter. " It's the second time this month. Andy wanted to see if there's something wrong with the alignment."

Bridie made no comment. From what she had seen of Sir Andrew she simply could not believe him capable of such a foolish, dangerous trick. And if Duncan Symonds was with him, then that exonerated both of them. Only one of the castle servants was left as a possible culprit. No—Robert had been quite right, the whole idea was ridiculous.

Shortly afterwards the rain came down torrentially, ruling out all further possibility of a walk that morning, even if Melissa's ankle would have allowed it. So they went to the library instead, a comfortable, leather-smelling place with a brisk log fire burning in the grate, and there her two cousins showed her some of its treasures—in particular two volumes of the diary Queen Victoria had published, calling them *Leaves*, with an inscription in them to old Sir James, written in the Queen's own hand. There had been, so Robert said, a third volume planned, dealing with Victoria's years with her trusted servant John Brown, but her advisers had warned her against its publication. Brown had been very unpopular with the Queen's English subjects at the time—she allowed him to be too familiar, they thought. And hinted at even harsher objections. So the manuscript was suppressed, and had never been heard of since.

Bridie did her best to appear impressed and interested, but secretly her thoughts were far more concerned with the impending interview with her great-aunt. After that she hoped she would know better where she stood. At last it was noon. Bridie excused herself from the library and went nervously upstairs to Lady Otranta's quarters.

This time the octagonal room was empty. Bridie crossed to her great-aunt's door and timidly knocked upon it. Peggy's voice, somewhat faint, called for her to go in. The room beyond was empty, but through yet another door on its far side Bridie could see into Lady Otranta's bedroom. She crossed the exotically cluttered sitting room, giving the silent, motionless Az Rah a discreetly wide berth, and went to stand at the foot of her great-aunt's magnificent bed. Like the rest of the bedroom furniture, it was done in red lacquer, in the Chinese manner, with intricate landscapes and golden dragons rioting over every possible surface.

"Well, child?" Lady Otranta was sitting forward while Peggy plumped up the pillows behind her. Her dead black hair hung down thick and straight on either side of her face, which was heavily powdered, with round, doll-like patches of carmine high up on her cheekbones. She peered at Bridie through narrowed eyes. "Well? Have you lost your tongue again?" she asked waspishly. "Or did you really only come in order to gape at me and screw your handkerchief up into a more than usually grubby little bundle?"

Bridie jumped, and stuffed her handkerchief hurriedly away in her sleeve. What a change this was from their previous afternoon's conversation. Devoutly she wished that the old lady could make up her mind whether to be nice or nasty.

"Good morning, Great-aunt," she began. "I hope I find you—"

"You find me very well indeed." Slightly, but unmistakably, Lady Otranta's words were slurred. "Or at least I will be, as soon as this fumbling nincompoop finishes whatever it is she thinks she's doing."

Bridie looked past her and saw old Peggy nod her head wretchedly in the direction of the bedside table, on which stood a tray with a glass and a half-empty whisky bottle.

Quickly Bridie shifted her gaze away. She didn't want to see. She didn't want to know. "I'm glad you're feeling well," she said brightly. "Because, you see, I'd very much like to talk to you about. . . ." She hesitated. Clearly now was hardly the best time for any sort of serious discussion. But if not now, when? She battled on. ". . . to talk to you about your memoirs. Mr. Pugh-Hennessy has asked me to—"

"That man!" Her great-aunt flung herself back on her pillows. "Doesn't he understand? Doesn't he know what it is to be a writer, an *artist*?"

Peggy had stepped back from the bed. "Now don't you go bullying the poor young lady. Ain't the gent down in London been dealing with writer folks every blessed day of his life? Don't you reckon he knows what he's doing?"

Bridie held her breath, waiting for the inevitable blast of Lady Otranta's scorn. None came. Instead, the old lady sagged down in the bed and closed her fever-bright eyes. "Dear Peggy," she murmured, "whatever would I do without you to remind me of my manners?"

"Huh!" The fat old dresser reached down for her charge's skeletal hand and squeezed it briefly. Then she moved to Bridie's side. "Madame'll behave herself now, I reckon," she said, making no attempt to lower her voice. "And if she don't, just you call me. I'll only be in the next room."

Her words were brusque enough. Only her eyes, just before she turned and lumbered slowly away, pleaded with Bridie to try to understand, and not to judge her great-aunt too harshly.

Lady Otranta waited until she heard the bedroom door close. Then she sat up and opened her eyes. "You see now what I have to put up with, my dear." She paused, tweaked at the sleeves of her glaringly crimson silk nightdress. "What we both have to put up with. . . . But enough of all that." She patted the bed close beside her. "Come and sit here, child, where I can see you, and tell me all about your Mr. Pugh-Hennessy."

Bridie seated herself where she was bidden. A dusty scent of attar of roses came from the old lady, strongly overlaid with raw spirits. *We understands each other*, old Peggy had claimed. And clearly she'd spoken no more than the truth. Also, however—and this was more to the point—Lady Otranta had some glimmerings of understanding of herself.

Bridie folded her hands in her lap and began. "Mr. Pugh-Hennessy is very concerned that you should complete your memoirs, Great-aunt. He believes they will attract a great deal of interest."

"He also has a not inconsiderable sum of money already invested," put in her great-aunt.

"That too," Bridie conceded. "But all the same, if you truly do not wish to proceed any further with—"

"Not proceed any further?" Lady Otranta raised her eyebrows. "You've been listening to my son Andrew, I see. The boy's a fool. Of course I want to proceed further. I've started the memoirs, and I intend to finish 'em." She gave Bridie a sly glance. "But in my own time."

Bridie's heart sank. How she wished that Mr. Pugh-Hennessy might have been there himself to say those things which had to be said. "But Great-aunt, already a full three months have passed since the commission, and—"

"I've . . . not been well." The old lady fussed with the edge of her sheet. "My . . . my arthritis. You ask the boys—Dr. Macnab from Edinburgh attends me regularly."

Bridie wondered if she were being given a way out. "Then might it not be better," she said gently, "if Mr. Pugh-Hennessy cancelled the contract? If you are unwell, then I'm sure he'd understand."

"No!" Her great-aunt clutched painfully at her arm. "No. The memoirs shall be written. I promise you that. They shall be written. And soon. . . ."

Confused and embarrassed, Bridie looked away. Inexorably her eyes were drawn to the half-empty bottle on the bedside table, a silent, bitter reminder that the old lady's promise, no matter how sincerely meant, was unlikely to be fulfilled. She resolved on one last attempt to make her great-aunt see reason.

"Both your sons," she said, "believe that this writing distresses you. It worries them a great deal to see you so . . . so upset."

"Let us call things by their proper names, child." Lady Otranta lifted her head. "It worries the boys to see their mother *drinking*. And well it might. Do you not think, Bridie my dear, that it worries me also?"

The words were wrung from her painfully, as if in a sudden moment of total, agonising self-awareness. Then, slowly, she leaned forward and hid her face in her hands. "If you only knew, child . . . if you only knew how beset I am. . . ."

Instinctively Bridie reached out and put her arm round the old lady's shoulders, pathetically thin beneath the gaudy night-dress. "Then you must let me help you," she whispered.

"That's what I'm here for. Together we can surely—"

But her great-aunt interrupted her, moaning and shaking her head wretchedly from side to side. "If you only knew, child. If you only knew. . . ."

Bridie tried again. "Then why don't you tell me?"

Suddenly Lady Otranta was still. She lowered her hands from her face. Her breathing calmed and she relaxed, resting in Bridie's gentle embrace. For a long time the room was silent, save for the hasty ticking of the ormolu clock upon the mantel and the occasional flurry of rain against the window panes.

Then she raised her head. "Don't leave us," she begged. "Don't leave us and go back to London. Perhaps I *shall* tell you . . . one day. One day, when the moment is right. But you mustn't leave us. You must stay, here at the castle. It—it won't be for long, I promise you."

And Bridie hugged her close—what else could she do?— and whispered that of course she'd stay, and cried a little, and the two of them remained so, huddled together on the bed in the dim, watery light from the rain-lashed windows. Until abruptly, with the coming of a sharp tap upon the door, the mood was harshly broken and they parted.

Bridie got up and moved away a pace, to stand by a dying, yellow-leafed aspidistra on a red lacquer table in the window embrasure, while her great-aunt hurriedly straightened the bedclothes, as if to eliminate all traces of their affectionate intimacy.

"Come in," she called.

Old Peggy entered, stopped just inside the door, and folded her arms impressively across her considerable bosom. "There's a something for you outside, Madame," she announced enigmatically.

Lady Otranta clicked her tongue. "Not now, Peggy. I can't be bothered with all that. Just tell me who or what it is, and be done with it."

"A *something*, Madame," Peggy insisted, not budging an inch. "Surely Madame can discover it for herself?"

Bridie stared at her, totally bewildered. Had the woman

gone quite out of her mind? Her great-aunt, however, sighed resignedly and turned to Bridie. " I'm supposed to read the poor old thing's mind," she explained. " Mind-reading was my speciality back in the old days. A pretty enough illusion. But—"

" Come along now, Madame." Peggy wagged a minatory finger. " You know how you enjoys showing off your powers. And we mustn't keep the young lady waiting."

Lady Otranta leaned towards her great-niece. " Shall I humour her?" she murmured.

Bridie nodded. She was genuinely intrigued. And besides, she suspected her great-aunt's reluctance to be pretended. In fact, she wasn't at all sure which old lady was really humouring which.

" Come along now," Peggy repeated, severely straightening the round steel rims of her spectacles. " We mustn't keep—"

" Don't nag me, dear," Lady Otranta rebuked her mildly. " It's all a question of getting into the mood. . . ." She closed her eyes and began to smooth her forehead with the tips of her bony fingers. Then she frowned slightly. " You must try to concentrate, dear. The pictures are all confused."

Peggy sidled over to where Bridie was standing and nudged her delightedly. " She's off now, and no mistake," she whispered.

" *Concentrate*. You really must concentrate. . . ." Suddenly Lady Otranta's hands were still, her fingertips pressing hard against her temples. " I see a man. There's a man waiting in the next room."

" That's better." Old Peggy was positively hugging herself. " And what's this man's name?"

In the pause that followed Bridie listed in her mind the most probable male callers: Duncan Symonds, the butler Meredith, Sir Andrew or Robert. A four-to-one chance, she thought sceptically. Unless of course—oh, unworthy notion— one of these four men was in fact already expected.

Lady Otranta's frown deepened. " It's my son. . . . It's my son Andrew."

" Better and better." Peggy jogged up and down excitedly.

"Now then, tell us what he's got with him. What's he holding in his hand?"

"It's a . . . a piece of paper." Still Lady Otranta's eyes remained tight shut.

"Right first time," Peggy told her. "Next thing is, what's on this piece of paper?"

"I . . . I can't quite see." The old lady turned her head anxiously from side to side. Then she relaxed again, and smiled. "It's a list. That's what it is—a list."

But still Peggy wasn't satisfied. "Now comes the hard bit, Madame. See if you can tell us what's on this list. Maybe you can tell us the first word even."

"I . . . it's all so blurred . . . I. . . ." Effort was evident in every muscle of her body. Bridie came near to intervening. Surely this couldn't be good for her great-aunt?

"Just the first word, Madame," old Peggy insisted. "Just the very first word at the top of the page."

Lady Otranta's breath was coming in short gasps and there appeared to be sweat upon her brow. Then, all at once, she fell back against the pillows and opened her eyes. "What a lot of trouble for really so very little," she said, suddenly quite herself again. "The piece of paper is a list of guests for our coming festivities. And the name at the top of the page is Spiller. That'll be the Spillers from over near Alloa."

Fat old Peggy ran forward and hugged her. "I knew you could do it, Madame. I just *knew* you could do it."

"Of course I could do it." Though clearly much pleased with her success, Lady Otranta made a great show of shrugging Peggy off. "But you don't let me into your thoughts the way dear Henri did. The professor and I, we were like brother and sister." She turned to Bridie. "Wherever we went, child, everyone remarked upon the striking affinity of our minds. Beside him, poor Peggy here is scarcely more than a stranger."

Even so, Bridie had to admit that what she had just seen was most impressive—always assuming, of course, that what her great-aunt had predicted turned out to be correct. And she had little doubt but that it would. It was all the more impressive, she realised, from an old woman who had evidently got through a great deal of whisky in the few hours since waking.

All the same, she decided to check with her cousin Andrew later—solely in the interests of scientific accuracy—and discover if in truth he had been expected that morning. And, if so, whether he had been asked to bring with him a list of party guests at the head of which would be the name Spiller. For she had, it must be said, little faith in the genuinely supernatural powers of theatrical performers, even those as successful as her great-aunt, the Incredible Madame Otranta.

*   *   *

We got on at once, Sir James and I. He was gallant, and obviously very much a gentleman. So my dresser let him in, and cleared him a chair, and I asked him to be seated.

Did he often come to the theatre? I enquired.

He said he did not. But he had been on business in the city that day, and a storm had blown up during the afternoon to prevent him going home. He lived across the Firth, he explained, and didn't care to risk a rough steamship crossing. His wretched recent illness—not even the best doctors in Edinburgh seemed able to cure it.

Left therefore with the evening to fill before he could reasonably retire to his club, he had spotted one of Professor Salvador's play-bills and taken a chance on it. A chance that had paid off handsomely, he said.

We didn't talk long that first evening. But he visited me again a few days later. And again the following week. To be honest, he fascinated me. He was gentle, and a little shy —not a bit like the usual run of stage-door Johnnies. He didn't shower me with gifts. He seemed genuinely interested in listening to my conversation. I had my father's love of books, and we spoke of those a great deal. And politics.

He was modest. He didn't tell me in any of our first three or four meetings that he was steward to the Queen's Stirlingshire estates. Neither, less admirably, did he tell me that he was married. But, when he did finally make that admission, I have to say that I was past caring. I was in love.

He was older than I by fifteen years. He was a baronet. And he was married. He had a small daughter. But none of that mattered. It didn't matter, either, that his marriage was unhappy. Divorce, anyway, was out of the question—his position alone saw to that. We would be discreet, I told him, and snatch what happiness we could before my season at the Empire ended and I went back to London.

I meant it, too. In those early innocent days I was content with very little. We both were.

But shadows were gathering. Nothing ever stays still—especially in human relationships. If I quickly pass over those first few happy weeks it is because of the horrors that were already lurking, waiting to pounce. At this distance in time it is as if they had always been with us, right from the beginning. And indeed, in one respect at least, they had.

My Jamie's illness, the deathly pallor of his face, the way his clothes hung loose upon his emaciated body, and, most of all, his refusal to take it seriously, was horror enough. And the suspicion growing in my mind that there was a pattern to his attacks. A pattern that started me thinking the unthinkable. . . .

If I were to break off these memoirs, now would be the moment. A few pages more and there'll be no turning back. God knows, I'm tempted. How much simpler my life would be—and the life of the one who I'm afraid would rather see me dead than see this work completed—if I gave up here and now. Yet to stop would be cowardice. And, whatever else I've been, I don't think I've ever been a coward.

*   *   *

As things turned out, there was no need for Bridie to ask Andrew if either he himself or his list had been expected. One short minute's conversation between him and his mother convinced Bridie that they were not.

Respectfully, almost timidly, he came limping into the old lady's bedroom, the expected closely-written sheet of paper held unobtrusively down by his side. She glanced at him briefly, then attacked.

93

"I'd have expected you to know better," she slurred, "than to come pestering me about the shepherds' party. It's no concern of yours. None whatsoever."

He flushed. "I sometimes wonder," he said sharply, "if anything about the estate is any concern of mine. Or ever will be." He bit his lip then and lowered his eyes, clearly ashamed of his outburst.

His mother ignored it. "I shall discuss the party in detail with Duncan Symonds when the time is right," she murmured. "Naturally, if you have any personal friends you wish invited you will be given the opportunity to say so."

His head jerked up. "Duncan Symonds?" Again he could not restrain himself. "Since when had Duncan had anything to do with the guest list? Always it was Papa who—"

"Your father is dead." The words fell coldly, bitterly, killing all possibility of further discussion.

Andrew hesitated, seemed about to protest yet again, then shrugged his shoulders and turned wretchedly away. Bridie felt personally hurt by his humiliation and longed to go after him. But she dared not.

When the door had closed behind him her great-aunt turned to her. "I suppose you think I was unfair," she remarked harshly.

Bridie swallowed nervously. Old Peggy stepped forward to spare her answering, but she spoke up all the same. "Yes, Great-aunt, I'm afraid I do."

"I thought as much." Lady Otranta nodded. "At least you're honest with me, child." Suddenly her face crumpled. "Oh, he's so like his father—so like his father when I first knew him. Sometimes—I know it's terrible to say this—but sometimes I can hardly bear to have him in the same room with me."

Bridie struggled as best she could with her shock at this painful admission. "Have you ever tried to explain that to him?" she asked softly.

"Explain what I dare not understand myself?"

Bridie stared into her great-aunt's eyes, red-rimmed in her pale, painted-doll face. She tried to tell herself that all this was no more than the whisky talking. And yet, only a moment before, the old lady had seemed so normal.

"Would you like me to talk to him?" she suggested.

"Yes. . . . No. . . ." Lady Otranta flapped her hands in distress. "Oh, go to him—tell him what you will." Then, suddenly, she pulled herself upright, became utterly calm and sensible. "The old can be very foolish, my dear. Wild and hysterical. . . . Go to him by all means. But it would not be suitable, I think, for you to pass on the more ill-considered of my words. They would only plunge him into a still greater state of confusion."

Long strands of hair had fallen forward over her face. She pushed them carefully back, one by one. "Tell him simply that I'm sorry. And that if he were to bring his list of guests to me again when I'm . . ." she tensed her jaw against what might have been a sudden twinge of pain ". . . when I'm more myself, then perhaps we could discuss it together sensibly."

She looked sideways at Peggy, then back at Bridie, tilting her head, all at once positively skittish. "Hurry along now, child. We don't want him throwing himself from the topmost battlement, now do we?"

Gratefully taking her at her word, Bridie hurried along. Leaving her great-aunt's quarters she half-ran along the twisting passages. In the entrance hall she caught sight of Meredith, just going away through the green baize door. She called after him, asked him if he had seen Sir Andrew recently.

The old man turned back, pointed to an arched doorway. "The Laird went into the study a few minutes since," he told her softly.

She tapped on the door. After a long pause she heard a faint murmur from within, so she lifted the heavy iron latch and entered. Andrew was alone, standing by the window in a large, oak-panelled room sturdily furnished as an office, with large-scale maps pinned up on the walls and a swivel chair in front of a massive roll-topped desk. The unfortunate guest list was a crumpled ball in his hand.

"Bridie, my dear—forgive me . . ." Surprised to see her,

he came quickly forwards across the bare, satin-smooth boards. " I had expected . . . oh, that wretched man Duncan, I suppose. Come in, my dear. Sit you down."

He dropped the list on the table and swept untidy stacks of papers from a chair. " Sit you down, then. And what can I do for you?"

Bridie seated herself, looked up at him. " Your mother," she began—

" Shall we not talk of my mother?" He stiffened and turned away, his hands clenched tightly behind his back. " It is inevitable, no doubt, that we should have our disagreements, she and I. My only regret is that you should have been forced to witness one of them."

Bridie leaned forward. " She misses your father very much."

" Do not we all?" He swung round on her. " I tell you, it's more than two years now since Papa died, yet still I sometimes cannot believe it. This room now—" he spread his arms "—it was *his* room. Now it is mine. Yet still I feel a trespasser in it."

Bridie wondered if it was not rather his mother who made him feel the trespasser. " Sir James would not have left you the estate," she suggested, " if he had not wished you to take charge of it."

Distractedly Andrew ran his fingers through his silver-blond hair. " Do you think I have not said that to—?" He controlled himself. " It is not seemly for me to criticise Mama. But—"

" You're very like your father," Bridie cut in, looking up at him. " Physically, I mean. It must be hard for your mother to . . . to . . ." She hesitated, on the brink of saying what her great-aunt had forbade her to. Instead she shrugged her shoulders and left the sentence unfinished, hoping nevertheless that Andrew might be able to fill in her meaning for himself.

For a long moment he stared silently down at her, searching her face. Then, very slowly, understanding came and he relaxed.

" Isn't it sad," he murmured, " the way people like me can blind themselves to the obvious. Poor dear Mama— If only I'd realised before what pain I must be giving her."

He limped away, and sat down wearily at the open desk.

96

Then, all at once, he looked up, met her gaze, and smiled wryly, giving her a brief glimpse of his brother Robert. " You sit there so quietly, like a . . . like a small brown dormouse. And yet . . . You're as wise as you're bonny, little Bridie. And I'm truly grateful to you."

She blushed deeply. The wisdom was indeed not hers, for had not Lady Otranta personally spelled out the truth of the matter? And as for being bonny . . .

" I—I was only passing on your mother's message," she stammered. " Lady Otranta asked me to tell you she was sorry she'd been so abrupt. And to ask you to bring the guest list to her again when she was more herself."

He sighed. " And when will that be, I wonder?"

It was a question, as they both well knew, without an answer. Silence fell between them. Bridie's thoughts wandered. Suddenly she remembered that she'd intended to ask him about his morning. Just as a formality. Certainly not because she really thought he'd been anywhere near the runaway motor car.

" Is it a long way up to the sawmill?" she asked, ashamed at once of her deviousness. " You've been up there with Mr. Symonds all morning, haven't you?"

For a moment she could see that he was going to agree. Then, to her horror, a shifty, evasive look came over his face. It was as if he had planned to lie to her, but had realised she could of course easily check his reply with Duncan Symonds.

" As a matter of fact . . . as a matter of fact, I was too busy to go. Important matters came up that . . . that had to be attended to." He was lying still. She was sure of it. He went on, " So I decided to go this afternoon instead."

" I see." She felt profoundly cheated, that he of all people should be less than honest with her. Slowly she got up and moved away towards the door.

He called after her. " I tell you what, Bridie—why don't you come with me? It's a steep walk, but not over-long. And it promises to be a fine afternoon. What d'you say?"

She paused, her hand on the door latch. Well, what *did* she say? He was trying, she thought, to make things right with her. Anything else—any ugliness, any suspicion—was quite out of the question. If an act of faith were needed, she'd make it gladly.

She turned back into the room. " Thank you very much," she said. " I've never seen a sawmill before. I'd like that very much."

5

S ir James took to staying in Edinburgh for several days at a time. His wife didn't seem to mind this—by then they were hardly on speaking terms anyway. As for his work on the Queen's estates, he was far too ill to do it properly. And besides, Her Majesty always went south for the summer, to Osborne on the Isle of Wight, so his absences didn't really matter.

We'd meet in the late morning—at night, after the performance, I was always tired out and only fit for my bed. So I'd meet James about eleven and we'd walk a little, and then take lunch in some small eating house up in the Old Town, where he wasn't likely to be recognised. I didn't mind the secrecy. It was the price we both had to pay. After all, he was risking his reputation, his position in the Queen's service, every single time we met.

So we'd take lunch, and talk for an hour or so. Or rather, it was more often I who took lunch while he simply toyed with a glass of milk—and even that frequently disagreed with him. I had noticed, as I have already said, that there was a pattern to his illness. He'd arrive from Castle Tantallon a pitiful wraith of a man, unable to keep down even the blandest of food. His condition would then improve steadily, so that towards the end of a two or three day visit there'd be colour in his cheeks and he'd be eating almost normally.

Then he would return to his home, and by the next time we met he'd be back where he'd started again.

I was extremely worried. I took to having nightmares. No matter how strong his constitution was, he couldn't go on like that for ever. And besides, the implication—to me at least—was as clear as day. And so, one afternoon, as

99

casually as I could, I mentioned how strange it was that his health seemed to get better the longer he stayed away from his home.

His response was typical. First of all, he didn't take me seriously. Then, when I insisted, he offered his improvement as proof that I was good for him. My company was better than any amount of doctor's physic. Our meetings were all the world to him.

It was a pretty explanation, and I loved him all the more for it. Sadly, though, I myself wasn't so romantic. The truth as I saw it was rather less charming. But I didn't argue with him—he detested talking about his health at the best of times. And the explanation I had in mind wasn't one to be presented lightly. Proof was essential.

And proof, for my lover's sake, was what I was determined to find.

Deceit begets deceit. I know that now, and I knew it then. Yet, for all the long course of lies and subterfuges that I then put in motion, I'd like it remembered that the very first deceit, and the worst, wasn't mine at all. It was *hers*.

It makes me ashamed, really, to see how even after all these years I still can't bring myself to write her name. . . .

*   *   *

After accepting Andrew's invitation to go up to the sawmill with him that afternoon, Bridie went upstairs to her room to wash and tidy herself for lunch. Arriving in the dining room slightly early, she found only Robert there. He must have recognised her footsteps, for when she entered she saw him already deep in a pantomimed conversation, silent but highly dramatic, with the dismally moth-eaten stuffed bear which stood beside the fireplace.

He waved to her casually, then turned back to his ludicrous performance, pretending to become more and more exasperated with the creature's unresponsiveness until finally, in an access of wordless rage, he lashed out with his fist and punched the poor animal right on the end of its black leather nose. The shaggy form lurched, and fell stiffly back against the wall.

" And thus," her cousin proclaimed triumphantly, " perish all the foes of the proud *Seigneur Robert de Tantallon*!" Whereupon he hurried solicitously forward and restored the bear to its former upright position, apparently none the worse for the indignities heaped upon it.

Bridie was slightly bewildered, such youthful high spirits being rather outside her experience. All the same, *some* reaction seemed expected of her, so she applauded loudly. Robert bowed low. Then, suddenly, he lifted his head, the play-acting abandoned, his expression serious.

" Well?" he demanded, almost fiercely. " What did she say?"

Bridie stepped back a pace. " What did *who* say?"

" Come along, coz." He frowned impatiently. " You've been to see Mama, haven't you? So what did she say? Is she keeping on at her memoirs or isn't she?"

Bridie took a deep breath, only now catching up with the abrupt change in his manner. " Your mother . . . insists that she must go on with the work. But she won't let me help her." She hesitated, aware that Robert—for all his quixotic behaviour—would expect her to be honest with him. " And without my help I really can't see her making very much progress."

" I see." Her cousin walked away to the table, thoughtfully moved a chair a few inches to the right, then back again. " How far d'you think she's got?" he asked.

Clearly the matter was even more important to him than she'd thought. " If you want my opinion," she said carefully, " I'd say your mother hasn't even started. Certainly she's sent nothing down to Mr. Pugh-Hennessy in London. And to be honest, seeing how—seeing the way she is, I don't think she ever will."

" No. . . ." Robert was silent a moment. Then his mood lightened as suddenly as it had darkened. " That doesn't mean our city cousin will be haring off back to London, I hope?"

Bridie shook her head. " Your mother seems to want me to

stay, so I'll stay—as long as Mr. Pugh-Hennessy lets me, of course."

"Of course Mama wants you." He came to her then and put a friendly arm round her shoulders. "We all want you. You're our little ray of sunshine. And you can tell Mr. Pugh-Hennessy, if he objects, to put his head in a bucket of water and forget to take it out."

Laughing companionably together, they moved off to one of the high stone-mullioned windows, beyond which the rain still fell in a steady, though lessening downpour. Staring out at the rain, so Robert told her, was one of the principal leisure activities of people living at the castle.

"Just look at it," he exclaimed. "I bet poor Andy's glad he had that dust-up with Duncan. Otherwise he'd be trekking down from the sawmill at this very minute, and getting soaked to the skin for his pains."

Bridie pricked up her ears. "What dust-up was that?" she enquired.

"Poor chap—I'm sure he'd rather I didn't tell you. It was all quite horribly humiliating. All the same—" he lowered his voice. "The thing is, you've probably realised how touchy that man Duncan is. Well, I don't really understand these thing, but it seems there's been some break-down up at the mill, and my brother said he'd go up with Duncan this morning to look at it. At which friend Duncan ups and says Sir James always trusted him to do what was best—and there's no need for my brother to concern himself in the matter." Robert sighed. "Which is fair enough, in its way. But it's frustrating for Andy—to be continually kept out of things."

"So Mr. Symonds went up to the sawmill alone?" Bridie queried.

"Don't ask me." Robert shrugged and turned back into the room. "Duncan's a law unto himself these days."

At which point the far door opened and Melissa came briskly in, her twisted ankle clearly much improved, and the question of Andrew's "dust-up" with the estate manager was tactfully abandoned. But Bridie was profoundly glad that it had been mentioned, for it explained completely his earlier evasiveness : he would hardly have wished to share still another humiliation with her.

After lunch, therefore, she was able to set off with him, her mind perfectly easy. They went together up the steep track through the woods that she had seen from her bedroom window, walking mostly in silence. Occasionally, though, he would pause and stiffly draw her attention to scurrying rabbits, or squirrels busy with the pine cones, or, once, to a pair of buzzards that circled, mewing faintly, high overhead. As he had predicted the sky was clearing, and shafts of sunlight struck down here and there between the tall columns of the trees. The air was still moist, however, and by no means warm, and the pace he set, in spite of his limp, was brisk enough to have her soon breathless.

At last he stopped, waiting for her on a brief stretch of level track, and turned to look down on the castle spread out below them and beyond it the white-flecked waters of the Firth.

He wiped his forehead on a generous red bandanna. " I've hurried you," he said.

" Not at all. I—"

" It's this wretched foot of mine," he went on quickly, as if the explanation were an unpleasant task he'd set himself. " It seems I always have to be proving it doesn't make me any . . . any less than the next man."

She felt a sudden flood of sympathy for him. " Anyone who thought that," she said stoutly, " would be a fool."

He nodded absently, seeming hardly to have heard her. " I got it in a shooting accident, you know. Back in '98. In the gun-room at the castle." He gestured down at the turrets and battlements below. The sight distracted him. " What a ridiculously pompous place it is, to be sure."

Bridie frowned. " I don't think so," she said. And meant it, for from up there the sprawling, mock-medieval hulk of the castle generated a strange aura of power. It crouched in a hollow among the trees, almost like a great rocky outcrop of the hill itself.

Her cousin laughed softly. " Neither do I, really," he said.

103

"I love it. And I want to bring life back to it—the sort of life it knew in the days when my father was busy and happy, back in the old Queen's time. . . ." He broke off, stood for a moment staring silently down. "It killed Papa, you know, when King Edward sold off all her Stirlingshire estates. What a position he'd had in the old days, he and Mama! Always something going on, toing and froing, Her Majesty's visits to Stirling to be prepared for. I was twenty when the old Queen died, so I remember it well."

He paused. "And then, almost overnight it seemed, it was all taken away, and Papa was just an old man put out to grass. He lasted scarcely eighteen months. Died out here in the woods—of a heart attack, so the doctors said. That is as good a way as any of describing a broken heart, I suppose."

His voice had been growing steadily softer and more husky. Now, abruptly, he cleared his throat. "But all that's now two years ago and more," he said briskly. "And it's high time we put some life back into the place. That is why this party we're planning is so important. It's to mark a new beginning, you see."

He turned then, and started away again, up the track. Bridie followed him, not saying a word. It was as if he had principally been talking to himself, and she felt privileged to have been allowed to share his thoughts.

After he had gone a few paces he stopped again. "By the way," he threw back over his shoulder, "you may well hear unkind gossip about what happened in the gun-room when my foot was injured. 'Lissa was there, you see. . . ." He lowered his head. "But that's all nonsense, of course. It was an accident. I was actually holding the gun when it happened. She had nothing whatever to do with it. It was all a stupid accident."

He swung round on her, fixed her with his piercing gaze. "Do you believe me, Bridie?"

She stared back at him. "Of course I believe you."

"Good. Good. . . ." He relaxed. "It's the sort of story that can do so much damage. And I wouldn't want you to feel uneasy with poor 'Lissa. She's the dearest, kindest person."

He smiled down at Bridie, then held out his hand. " Shall we be on our way, then? I'm afraid the track gets steeper now."

She took the hand he offered. It was broad and strong, and its touch warmed her through and through. They began to climb again. And they chatted together now, easily, openly, his earlier remoteness quite forgotten. It was as if the accident in the gun-room had been preying on his mind, and he had not been able to talk with her freely until it had been dealt with and got safely out of the way.

He told her about his mother, about the difficulties she must have experienced in getting herself accepted into Victorian society, and the magnificent way in which her dignity and strength of character had gradually overcome all prejudice. From this it was the simplest transition to the present, discussed readily, without any great drama, without either despair or foolish optimism.

" Your mother has asked me to stay," Bridie told him.

" Excellent. I would have asked you myself otherwise." He paused, helped her round a deep rut in the track. " And what of the memoirs?"

She told him what she had told his brother. He asked her then about her employer down in London, how long she thought he'd let her stay. It was a question that Bridie, walking there on the sunlit hillside, didn't care to think about.

" Oh, for a good while yet," she told him, pretending a greater confidence than she felt. " He's not expecting my work up here to be easy."

" Oh, splendid. Excellent. . . !" He swung her hand. Then added hastily. " I know 'Lissa will be delighted to hear it. She'll want you to accompany her when she sings her piece at the party. The last time Robert did it he played faster and faster till she lost her temper and hit him with her music stand and stormed away up to her room." He checked himself. " I shouldn't laugh. It was heartless of him—inexcusable, really."

Bridie thought of poor awkward Melissa, publicly shamed, weeping alone in her bedroom, and agreed with him. And yet . . . and yet, had she *really* hit her half-brother with her music stand? The thought was irresistibly comic. So that, try as she might, she could not but laugh aloud as she climbed hand-in-hand with her cousin Andrew, and he laughed with her.

Her cousin Andrew . . . her second cousin really, who only the day before had seemed such a distant and threatening figure. She remembered the stiffness of his courtesy the previous night, handing her a candle when bedtime finally came after their painful discussion about Lady Otranta in the vast, shadowy dining room. And how his reserve had suddenly melted—*You're one of us*, he'd told her—and how his words had sent her cheered and light-hearted to bed. The previous night—was it truly only the previous night? Already she felt as if she had known him all her life.

The sky was blue now, and almost cloudless, the sun warm on their backs, the air soft with the scent of pine needles. They came to a rushing mountain stream, tumbling over polished stones between mossy boulders, and crossed it by a broad, thickly-timbered bridge. The stream came from the tiny loch up among the hills that fed their mill-wheel, so he told her. And the bridge had been built for the wagons heavily laden with planks that came down when the mill was working.

They climbed again, the track swinging across the hillside, then doubling back till at last, quite without warning, it ended on a wide ledge cut out of the forest, a ledge carpeted with golden sawdust, soft and moist and aromatic.

To the rear of the ledge stood the mill-house, a long stone building with a water-wheel towering beside it. Three massive timber wagons were drawn up nearby, their shafts empty, the sawdust around them deeply scuffed with horses' hooves. The mill-wheel was stopped now, and the only sound was the tumultuous murmuring of water, close at hand yet unseen and mysterious.

Her companion paused at the very edge of the surrounding trees. " When the mill-leet is closed," he explained, indicating a built-up stone channel on a level with the top of the wheel, " the water from the loch is drawn off through an underground passage. It surfaces a hundred feet or so further down the hill."

Bridie looked where he now pointed, saw a flash of sparkling white water among the trees below. "Did your father build all this?" she asked.

He smiled. "Not he. The buildings and earthworks must be two centuries old at least. Papa renovated them, however, and installed all the very latest machinery."

The sound of voices now came from the mill, followed by loud clanging hammer-blows that echoed unpleasantly against the rocky cliffs at the back of the clearing.

"They're fitting the new saw-blade," Andrew told her. He took an uncertain pace forward, then stopped. "I only hope they're getting it properly aligned this time," he said. "No doubt Duncan knows his business well enough, but . . ."

He tailed off, shrugging his shoulders. Bridie realised that he felt a trespasser here too, as he had in his father's study. Was Duncan Symonds then really so formidable? Certainly he had not seemed so during her long conversation with him on the train.

She stepped out onto the soft carpet of sawdust and her cousin followed her. Clear of the trees now, she could see the full gleaming width of the Firth, and the far shore gently blurred with summer mist. A steamer, tiny and toy-like, was coming down on the tide, trailing a long plume of white smoke behind it in the still air.

Andrew stood beside her, looking out. "That'll be one of Galloway's excursions," he murmured. "They sail up as far as Stirling. It's a beautiful journey, up past Blackness Castle and Dunimarle—you should take it some time. Papa, of course, couldn't bear the sight of those steamers. But then, that's hardly surprising."

Bridie was puzzled. "Why was that?" she asked.

"Did they not tell you?" Her cousin frowned. "It was from just such a ship as that that Papa's first wife, Melissa's mother, met her death. She fell from the platform above one of the paddle casings."

"How dreadful." Bridie shuddered at the thought. "What a terrible way to die. How did it happen? Was there no handrail?"

"Certainly there was a handrail. It's a bit of a mystery really." Behind them the sound of hammering broke out again, louder than ever. Andrew raised his voice. "An eye-witness said that the wind seemed to catch at her hat, and she lurched out to reach it."

"What did your father do?"

"He was not with her. Everybody is agreed that she went onto the platform alone."

The words were spoken firmly, a sharp denial of whatever Bridie might have been tempted to suspect. And yet, why should she be expected to think such a thing? She caught her breath. "I didn't mean to suggest—"

He swung round on her. "The rest of the world did, though. . . ." He controlled himself, smiled, reached out and took both her hands in his. The hammering from the sawmill had stopped, but somewhere nearby a dog was barking. "Forgive me, dear Bridie. It's a sore subject." Briefly she saw pain return to his eyes. "It all happened before I was born, of course. But the gossip was still going round when I was growing up. They weren't happy, you see, Papa and the first Lady Tantallon. And there was talk he'd been seen with Mama in the weeks before his wife's death—had been seen with a vulgar music-hall performer. The talk may even have been true, for all I know. Papa's marriage was miserable, and he and Mama certainly adored one another. But that does not mean. . . ."

He broke off, looked down at her, shaking his head sadly. "How cruel people are. Even your grandfather, Papa's own brother. . . . And it was all so unfair! Papa was nowhere near the platform—a dozen witnesses said so."

In his anguish he was crushing her hands in his. Then, gradually, he relaxed his grip, managing a wan smile. "But it's all ancient history now. Over and done with. I should never have mentioned it. I'm sorry."

Bridie did not remember her grandfather: he had died when she was a baby. But she was pleased that her father, when explaining the family quarrel to her, had chosen to suppress this least charitable aspect of it.

"Of course you should have mentioned it," she said earnestly. "If it concerns you, then it concerns me also."

The words, sincere, impetuous, unconsidered, were out before she could stop them. And she was glad.

For a moment her cousin was disconcerted. Then he lifted her hands to his lips and gently kissed them, first one and then the other. "Bless you, Bridie," he said. "I should have known you'd feel like that." He released her then, and stepped back a pace. "After all, you're one of the family," he went on briskly. "You're a Tantallon through and through."

Did he really not know, she wondered wistfully, that that was not what she had meant at all?

At that moment, however, she heard a shout behind her and a black and white collie dog came bounding down the path. She turned to see Duncan Symonds standing in the big open double doors at the end of the mill building.

"Noble, come here," he called. "Come here, sir, you devil!"

Then, seeing Andrew and Bridie, he moved forward. "Is it you then, Sir Andrew?" He snapped his fingers and the dog came to heel, to sit quietly at his master's feet.

Bridie clicked her tongue. "Who else does the silly man think it might be?" she hissed at her cousin, unreasonably irritated at the interruption.

"Hush now." Andrew patted her arm. "It's the Scotsman's way—it simply means *hullo*." He raised his voice. "It's a fine afternoon, Duncan," he said guardedly.

"It is, sir." The estate manager smiled, his gaze shifting to Bridie. "You've been admiring the view, then?" he suggested.

Bridie agreed that she had.

Her cousin shaded his eyes. "The repairs are progressing?" he asked.

"Fine. . . . Aye." Symonds stroked his beard thoughtfully, then advanced a few careful paces out into the sunlight. "Though now that you're here, sir, I'm thinking that you might be able to gi'e us a wee bit advice. Angus and me, we canna get the main pulley to run true."

Bridie stared at him, amazed. It was not that she would have judged Duncan Symonds to be a man to stand foolishly upon his pride. If he genuinely needed another's help, then he would surely say so. Nevertheless, his behaviour to her cousin now was in surprising contrast to what it must have been earlier in the day.

Andrew himself, however, made no comment. He excused himself politely from her side, joined Mr. Symonds, and together the two men disappeared into the shadowed interior of the sawmill. The dog Noble, having sniffed Bridie's skirt in mild curiosity, trotted off.

For a time, Bridie wandered about the clearing, peered up the broad logging paths that led away from it deep into the surrounding forest, stared timidly at the heavy steam crane, mercifully cold and silent now on its wide metal track, examined the stack of tree trunks, straight as telegraph poles, that lay waiting to be sawn into planks. Then, inquisitive, she approached the open doors of the mill itself and looked inside.

The sight that met her eyes was impressive indeed. In the centre of the floor, mounted upon well-greased iron rails, she saw a huge metal-topped table. A slot ran the length of the table, and through it projected a great, jagged-toothed saw-blade, rays of sun from the skylights overhead glinting wickedly on its blue-steel sides. While beneath the table yawned a deep pit, its concrete sides thick with yellow dust. Other machines, equally menacing, were positioned to one side of the table, massive structures set with gleaming blades and wheels and levers, all connected via great swooping lengths of loops and pulleys to a series of ponderous overhead shafts. In the midst of which, spanning the entire interior of the building, was a heavy girder bridge, also running on rails, and hung with grapnels like the claws of some gigantic iron bird, clearly powerful enough to lift even the biggest tree trunk as if it were a matchstick.

The men, Andrew, Mr. Symonds and another, dwarfed by the sheer size of their surroundings, were up on the gantry, deep in hushed conversation. Tentatively, Bridie moved further into the building. The men overhead seemed not to notice her: they were discussing something high above them, up among the roof beams, their voices lost to her in the awesome silence of the place.

She was about to call out to them when the man Mr. Symonds had called Angus suddenly turned, reached down, and pulled a lever. For a moment nothing happened. Then slowly, mysteriously, with an evil, silken rustling, the wheels about her all began to move, gathering speed with incredible rapidity until, in a matter of twenty seconds, no more, the entire building was filled with a nightmare chaos of sound and movement. Axles pounded, pulley wheels whirled their belts faster than sight itself, and Bridie cried out shrilly, cowering back against the wall as the giant saw-blade, now seemingly only a few inches away from her face and blurred to a leaping shimmering disk, began to keen an hypnotic lament as its thousand jagged teeth spun faster and faster, tearing mindlessly at the empty air.

Bridie felt herself drawn towards it as if mesmerised, terrified of its hideous power yet unable to turn away. Already she seemed to feel the wind of its passing cool upon her cheek. . . . So that she was hardly aware of the change when, her cries heard by the men above, the machinery began to slow. Footsteps clattered towards her down the iron ladder at the side of the gantry.

"Bridie! Bridie! For God's sake . . . are you all right? Are you hurt?"

At last she managed to drag her eyes away from the still whirling saw-blade. Andrew was close beside her, his face pale beneath its weather-beaten tan. She leaned back against the wall, shaking her head weakly. "No, not hurt. Only—"

"Thank God for that." He supported her, his arm about her waist. "You must never—you must *never* come in here again without letting the foreman know you are here. Can't you see how dangerous it is?" He shook her, half angrily. "With these long skirts of yours, you might easily have been. . . ."

He didn't need to finish. She found she was trembling.

"I'm truly sorry, Andrew. Could . . . could I sit down a minute, please?"

"Of course. Of course." He led her away, through a door and into an office with neatly whitewashed walls. There he sat her down and poured her a glass of water from a carafe on the desk.

She drank it gratefully. "It was silly of me to get upset," she stammered. "I was really in no danger—no danger at all."

"That's as maybe." He stood over her. "Supposing the band-saw had been operating too, and you'd backed away into that?"

She closed her eyes. It was right for him to say such things, to show her just how foolish she'd been.

"Well, well. . . ." He relented. "It's over now, and no harm done. We were testing the overhead pulleys, you see, and they seem to be running fine."

She opened her eyes and smiled up at him. On the wall behind him, almost as if it were looking over his shoulder, hung a portrait of the old Queen, severe and in her habitual mourning, above a large green-painted safe. There were wooden filing cabinets also, and samples of planking, all carefully varnished and labelled, in small portable frames.

"Did you fix them?" she asked him. "The pulleys, I mean?"

Andrew appeared doubtful. "I *checked* them . . . gave a grub-screw an extra turn here and there, you know." She didn't, but nodded knowingly. He straightened his back. "Anyway, if they weren't running true before, they certainly are now. So I must have done *some* good, I suppose."

All the same, Bridie wondered, collecting her thoughts and remembering the "dust-up" Robert had described between his brother and Mr. Symonds, it was strange that the estate manager should have asked for Andrew's help in what now appeared to have been such an unimportant matter. Unless of course the request had been intended as a peace offering. But it still didn't explain why the difficulty had occurred in the first place. It was almost, Bridie thought, as if there had been some reason why Duncan Symonds hadn't wanted her cousin up at the sawmill that morning—a reason that no longer applied.

*   *   *

The proof I needed was come by all too easily. Perhaps I had hoped my theory would turn out to be wrong. I don't know. If it had been wrong I'd have lost my Jamie, of course—to death if not to his wretched marriage—for he couldn't have lasted much longer the way he was. But I'd have gained in peace of mind, perhaps. And I wouldn't now be a tormented old woman, trying vainly to glue together the broken fragments of her life.

But my theory wasn't wrong.

First of all I found a chemist willing to do what I wanted and ask no questions. This wasn't difficult—Professor Salvador regularly bought spirits of mercury for a trick of his that involved turning water into something that looked like wine. So the man was used to the secrecy of us theatricals.

Next—and I make no apology for calling a spade a spade—I discreetly obtained samples of Sir James' vomit and took them to this chemist for analysis. He promised me the results the next afternoon. And when they came they confirmed my worst suspicions.

He found poison. To be exact, he found antimone—and in such quantities, so he said, as to suggest that, since the patient was still alive, the poor fellow had developed a partial immunity to it. He wasn't at all surprised that the patient was being sick. Antimone worked that way. Clearly, in his opinion, the patient was being systematically done to death.

I believed him. He had, I knew, no reason to lie. And I left his shop with a heavy heart.

Fearing the worst, I had broken my rule and already asked Jamie to meet me after the performance, at the stage door, with a carriage. How I got through that night's two performances I shall never know. Our coming meeting hung over me like a deathly cloud. To say what must be said would be the most difficult thing I had ever attempted.

The moment, when it came, was so agonising that even now, thirty years later, I remember our conversation virtually word for word.

A growler was waiting at the stage door. I had already planned where I would ask the driver to take us—some hour or more's journey out to Arthur's Seat, a prominent local landmark. Time enough, I thought, for all that had to be said between us.

The cabbie made no comment. Probably he assumed a romantic assignation. Dear God, if he had guessed the truth of the matter. . . .

Jamie was waiting for me inside the carriage. We kissed as it lurched away beneath the flickering gas-lamps.

I disengaged myself. He tried to take my hand. " What's the matter?" he asked.

I told him I had something very difficult and upsetting to say to him. Naturally enough he jumped to the wrong conclusion. " Your season at the theatre here is ending," he said wretchedly. " You have to go back to London."

I shook my head. " I'm to be here until the end of September. That's six weeks off."

" Then what is it? Are you trying to tell me we mustn't meet? Are you saying you don't care for me any more?"

I'd promised myself I'd stay calm and sensible. But I couldn't bear it. I burst into tears and blurted out, all higgledy-piggledy, what I had discovered.

When it was done he sat in silence for a long time, while the growler creaked and swayed through the steep dark streets. Then he sighed.

" Antimone, you say? But how could it be got hold of?"

So his first question had been *how* rather than *who*. I dried my tears, believing that our talk was going to be easier than I'd feared.

" First," I said, " I'm going to ask you a question. And you must answer it truthfully."

"I'm always truthful with you, Otranta."

I knew it. "Then tell me, James, are you a drunkard? When you're at home, are you a drunkard? So that someone who lived with you would be justified in trying to cure you of it?"

He began to reply, but I stopped him. "Don't answer quickly. Take your time, my dear. God knows, from what you've told me of your life I wouldn't blame you if you were."

He turned to me. I remember clearly how the fusty horsehair seat squeaked beneath him. "I swear to you, Otranta, never more than a glass or two of wine, and the malt at bed-time. But a drunkard—never!"

I'd known that also.

He touched my arm. "Why do you ask?"

"Because," I told him, "there is an easy way to obtain antimone. It is in the powders you can buy by post from a certain English doctor. It's put in small quantities into the wine of an excessive drinker. The intention is innocent— simply to associate in his mind the act of drinking with sickness, and thus cure him of his habit."

"I see." He seemed to draw away from me. "Clearly then, even if—as in my case—there were no need, no possible excuse for such powders, they could still be obtained." He paused. "And still be given. And not in *small* quantities either."

He had chosen his words carefully, spelling things out so that I should see he understood me. I didn't answer. There was no need.

For a time neither of us spoke. Then, with a weary groan, he stirred himself, lowered the cab window, and leaned out. "Cabbie," he called, "we've changed our minds. I'll still pay you the full fare, mind. But I'd be obliged if you'd take us back to the Caledonian Club in Prince's Street."

I didn't hear the driver's reply. But the carriage stopped and began to turn with a clashing of hooves. Sir James sank back into the seat beside me.

"You've given me a great deal to think about," he said. "I'm not sure that I thank you for it."

Suddenly, although we were still together in the same carriage, I felt there were a hundred miles between us.

"What'll you do?" I whispered. "Surely you won't return to the castle?"

"It's my home."

"But your wife is—"

He slapped his hand violently down on the buttoned leather between us. "I'd prefer you to keep Margaret out of this."

At which I rebelled. "But she's trying to kill you!" I cried.

"No!"

"Who else could it be? She doesn't love you. You've said yourself how—"

"No, I say!" His voice was anguished. "Anyone but she. I can't believe it—not of Margaret."

I was sorry I'd insisted. Obviously he believed it very well.

"You're quite right," I said gently. Hypocritically. "Nobody should be judged guilty on so little evidence."

"Very true." He drummed his fingers on the window ledge. "Of course not."

His tall hat and gloves were on the seat opposite. After a moment he leaned forward, picked up his gloves, fingered them aimlessly for a few seconds, then put them on. He could not meet my eye. I watched him sadly, realising that he had never, in all the time since we had first met, been as far from me as he was then. Shut away from me by what I knew. By what we both knew.

"This English doctor," he said at last. "Would he be a Doctor Smithson of Brighton, by any chance?"

I was wary, wondering how he knew so much. "That is the man's name, I believe."

"Aye. . . . Aye, I thought as much." He sighed, took his gloves off again, held them up, examining them as if they were the most interesting things in the world. "I—I saw the name on a packet at the back of Margaret's bureau. A matter of two or three weeks ago, this was. I asked her what the packet might be, and she said it was medicine for her migraine. I asked her then what was wrong with our local doctor's medicine, and she flew into a rage. . . ."

He spoke levelly, listlessly, as if by rote. " I believed her. I had no reason not to, you see. After all, it was just like her to go writing off to some fancy English quack with a row of invented letters after his name."

He stopped, leaned his head back against the lining of the carriage. Then, all at once, he began to sob uncontrollably, his whole body racked with misery. I moved towards him, hating to see him suffer so, and touched his hand. At last he came to me, and I comforted him as best I could.

It wasn't easy to have given a man the knowledge that his wife was a would-be murderess. What little comfort I could offer was a poor thing. The future still remained a time to be dreaded, dark and impenetrable. Solutions would be found, of course—they always were, for good or ill. Life went on. . . . Just then, all I could think was that I loved him, and he loved me. What had to be done would be done. The strength would be found : I swore it silently, and held him close to my breast. . . .

*　　　*　　　*

Mr. Symonds had joined Bridie and her cousin in the office, and had introduced her to the mill foreman. Angus Robertson was a shabby, raw-boned, unshaven giant of a man, but his greeting had all the dignity and soft-voiced courtesy of a born aristocrat.

The hand he offered her was pathetically mutilated, three fingers chopped off short, presumably in some terrible piece of milling machinery. She shook it bravely, hiding her revulsion, and was glad she had done so, for his grasp was warm and friendly.

" I'm gey glad to see ye've come to no great harm, Mistress.

The mill floor is no place for a young leddy, I'm thinking."

She nodded, fervently agreeing with him. Andrew cleared his throat. " The fault was mine, I fear. I should have warned my cousin."

" Aye. . . ." The engineer nodded gently, without rancour. " Weel, there's no great damage done, so ye shouldna reproach yoursen owermuch, sir." He turned back to Bridie. " We'll be seein' ye again when the mill is workin', I hope. It's a grand, powerful sight, y'ken."

" I'd like that very much." Bridie did her best to sound enthusiastic, though in truth she dreaded the very idea. She could not forget his hand, nor the baleful, vertiginous attraction the whirling saw-blade seemed to have for her.

Andrew leaned forward and lifted her to her feet. " We're keeping Mr. Robertson from his work," he said. " There's still a lot to be done if the mill is to be back in service by tomorrow."

Duncan Symonds stood back from the doorway to allow them passage. " They tell me the new Argyll nearly ran you down, you and Mistress Melissa," he said concernedly. " It's survived verra weel, I find—not even a scratch. But they're treacherous things, these motors." He paused. " I'd like you to know, Mistress Bridie, that the blocks were secure beneath its wheels when I left it. I wouldna have you thinking I do not know my responsibilities."

She hesitated. His eyes were guileless in his handsome, bearded face. How could she doubt him? " Of course not," she said. " The blocks must have slipped on the wet cobbles, that's all. It wasn't your fault. It wasn't anybody's fault." And now, as the event receded in her memory, she believed her words. Anything else was out of the question.

Later, on their way down from the mill, Andrew wanted to know what Duncan had been referring to. She realised that at lunch that day Robert and Melissa had chosen to talk of other things—possibly so as not to add to his many other worries. Making as little of it as possible, she described briefly what had happened.

He was horrified none the less. " What a terrible thing! In

future the Argyll shall always be left at the lower end of the courtyard, facing the wall." He took her arm. "You've had quite a day, my dear. I wouldn't want you to think life at the castle is always so perilous."

She laughed then, and they walked on in companionable silence down the track. When they reached the stream he stopped, and they leant together on the rail of the bridge, looking down into the rushing water. She sensed there was something he wanted to say to her. So she waited quietly, the soft breeze cool upon her face, and let him take his time.

At last he spoke. "My mother. . . ." Frowning, he cleared his throat. "What do you really think of her? Is Robert right? Does she really possess some terrible secret?"

Bridie paused. She did not want to be thought to be answering hastily. "Lady Otranta is a very unusual woman. . . . But she must always have been like that, I think."

"Unusual, certainly. But hardly so unusual as to—"

She knew his words would be harsh so she did not let him finish. "She has suffered a tragic bereavement. But that, I think, is not all that is troubling her. It is as if there were indeed some hidden torment, something she dare not speak of—scarcely dare even *think*. . . ."

He sighed. "You're saying that Robert is right?"

She nodded, remembering the hunched figure of her great-aunt, suddenly small and vulnerable in her arms. "Yet she seems to trust me. Now that I'm here to help her, perhaps she—"

"Help her? Can anybody help her?" Despairing, he turned away. "We know Macnab can't. For all his long words and his new ideas, he hasn't been able to do a thing!"

"But she's talked to me." Bridie went after him, timidly touched his sleeve. "It'll take time, I know. But I'm sure I can help her. I'm sure I can."

He didn't react. It was as if he had neither heard her nor felt her touch.

"You know," he said suddenly, "sometimes I think she must be utterly mad. Insane. Certifiable. The tricks she gets up to. That room she lives in. . . ." He beat angrily upon the rail of the bridge, then controlled himself. "Mind you," he admitted, "the room was always like that, even when Papa was alive—but in those days it was a joke between them. *Mama's museum*, he called it. Now she hardly ever leaves it —except to shame us all with her behaviour every night at dinner!"

Mad? It was a thought that had occurred to Bridie also. One too painful to be allowed. "But she's your *mother*, Andrew."

"D'you think I don't know that?" He swung round on her, lowering his voice to an agonised whisper. "D'you think I don't remind myself of that every day of my life?"

Silence fell between them, strained and unhappy, broken only by a wood pigeon murmuring gently to itself in a nearby tree. Bridie stared up into his haggard face, desperately seeking words with which to comfort him and finding none.

All at once he relaxed, held up one finger. "Just listen to that wood pigeon," he said, a faint, sad smile playing on his lips. "There was a story Mama used to tell us about that pigeon when we were children. She wasn't always so . . . so unhappy, you know. It was Papa's story really, but Mama told it better."

He tilted his head, remembering. "There was a Highland crofter, you see, a man called Davy, who was up before the magistrate for stealing two of his neghbour's cows. And he claimed he was innocent. He told the magistrate it wasn't his fault. There was a wood pigeon that always sat on the roof of his cottage—it was the pigeon's fault."

His smile broadened. Above him the branches shifted, dappling his pale hair with golden sunlight. "The magistrate asked him what he meant, of course. Davy leaned across the edge of the dock. 'But hae ye no hear't it yoursen', y'r Honour?' he replied. 'On and on, like the de'il hissen' . . . *Tak' two coos, Davy . . . Tak' two coos, Davy. . . .* I tell ye, y'r Honour, time came when 'twas morena flesh and blood could stand. So I just gi'ed in . . .'"

Andrew laughed aloud, then stood looking down at her. Puzzled, Bridie concentrated on the bird's gentle, rhythmic song. Suddenly she understood what the man in the story had meant. *Tak' two coos, Davy*—she heard it clearly, the exact words. *Tak' two coos, Davy, Tak' two coos, Davy. . . .*

She joined in his laughter. " Did the magistrate let the man off ?" she asked.

" Of course he did. The poetic imagination is much appreciated north of the Border."

He grasped her hand and led off cheerfully down the track. " Oh, I know it's not much of a joke, really. But we loved it, Robert and I. . . . Dearest Mama, what *fun* she used to be." His grip on her hand tightened. " And will be again, Bridie. And will be again—I swear it."

He quickened his pace, and she with him, running through the shadowy, pine-smelling woods. She knew it was a promise he was making—a promise to his mother, and to her also. A promise for the future, a time for happiness.

They came to the castle, circled its outer walls, crossed the drawbridge, entered through the towering doors. On the flag-stones of the entrance hall the sunlight lay in brilliant latticed oblongs, brightening even that dismal place. She left him then and climbed the staircase to her room with a light heart. Her hand on the door-latch, however, she changed her mind. She would go and cheer up her great-aunt, take to the old lady all the hope and determination that had come to her and Andrew up on the summer hillside, among the soaring trees.

The sitting room, with its bizarre furnishings, was empty. Bridie crossed it lightly, tapped upon the closed bedroom door, waited a moment, then burst impatiently in.

And froze. Appalled.

Old Peggy, arrested in the act of unbuttoning the collar of Lady Otranta's dress, glared bitterly across at her, accusing her wordlessly for her brash intrusion. The dresser was seated on the edge of the bed, her glasses knocked crooked on her nose, propping up Lady Otranta where she lay, sprawled across the heavy crimson covers. The old lady's legs stuck gracelessly out from beneath her rucked-up skirt, her head lolled, her eyes gaped sightlessly at the opposite wall. While from her grotesque, painted-doll mouth there issued a slow, moist, unmistakable snoring.

Bridie's horror lasted only a moment. Then she started forward, filled with compassion.

Only to be brought up short by Peggy's harsh words. " For Gawd's sake, ain't there *nothink* we can't keep to ourselves, me and Madame? Ain't there *no* bloody privacy left in this rotten world?"

She hugged the old, unappealing body to her. " We managed right enough before she come, didn't we my pet?" she crooned. " And we'll manage right enough after she's gone, too." Again she lifted her head and glared at Bridie. " Which can't 'appen too soon for my liking, neither!"

Silently Bridie backed from the room, closed the door, and stood, leaning her forehead helplessly upon the hard, cold wood of its ornately-painted panel. Her resolve had not weakened. She would never give up trying to help her great-aunt. But there were areas where she dared not trespass. For the old lady's sake there were sights that it was better for her not to have seen. Humiliations of which she should remain generously ignorant.

PART II

6

*O*bviously *I've reached the ugliest part of my story.* **One** to which the reader already knows the beginning (that Sir James was being systematically poisoned by his wife) and the end (that he and I were eventually joined in what some might call unholy matrimony) but not the middle. For thirty-odd years now I've done my best to forget what came in between. But now at last, if I'm ever to find peace of mind, it must be faced.

There are no excuses for what I did. Returning one wrong for another can never be honestly defended. There were reasons, of course, and persuasive ones too, but the strongest of them was blatant self-interest. And anyway, it's a crime to take the law into one's own hands, whatever the provocation.

I've already stated that there's one who I believe would do just about anything to stop me finishing these memoirs. It's a harsh thing to say, but I'm afraid it's true. How then, you may well ask, do I dare to go on? And the answer has to be, *by deceit.*

It's hardly the first deceit in my life, and certainly not the worst. And I'm hoping it may turn out to be the last. All the same, it has caused—and will go on causing—a lot of unhappiness to a lot of innocent people. I admit to it, therefore, with great reluctance.

Put baldly, *my deceit is to pretend drunkenness.* No more and no less. These days, you see, my entire household, save one whom I think I can trust, believes me a helpless alcoholic. It's not a pretty deception, nor an easy one. Day after day I'm forced to act the drunkard, seeing all the time the misery my squalid performance is causing to those I love.

But the sad fact is that I haven't been able to think of another that would work even half as well.

You must understand that mine isn't a large household. It was once, when the old Queen was alive, but it isn't any more. Most of the time we've a pretty good idea what each one of us is doing. While, to make matters worse, I'm not in good health and therefore in many ways have even less privacy than the others. So the only way I can think of to get some time to myself is to pretend to be badly the worse for drink. It's a repugnant business. But at least it allays the suspicions of the one above all whose suspicions *must* be allayed.

Do ends ever justify means? I hope so. Certainly common justice demands that my story be told. And not only the story of James and myself and his wife Margaret either. Solutions are found, and life goes on. Certainly mine did. For one thing, I became accepted into the intimate circle of the late Queen. And there are things about her also that need bringing out into the open before the myths surrounding Victoria become too firmly entrenched. It's not simply what I saw and heard during her visits to her Stirling estates —many others saw and heard the same and put upon it whatever interpretations suited them. But I have documentary proof also.

I'm not just promising scandal. That would be cheap and silly. I'm promising, rather, unique insights into a sensitive and much-misunderstood woman.

But I'm straying from the point, the situation facing Sir James and myself in that August of the year 1878. . . .

*   *   *

For Bridie life at Castle Tantallon had quickly settled into a predictable, but not at all burdensome, routine. The middle two hours of each day, when Lady Otranta had recovered from her excesses of the night before and was not yet too disordered by the new day's folly, were the best time for her to visit the old lady and try to talk to her. More often than not she was good company then, reminiscing about Sir James' proud years in the old Queen's service, and the part she had played in them : the difficulties her very different social position had caused at the start, and the manner in which she had overcome them.

"Quiet persistence, my child. Exemplary behaviour. A steady, but unobtrusive dedication to local good works. And a convenient blindness to the unmannerly behaviour of my social superiors."

She'd paused then, frowning slightly as she so often did, as if from some sudden twinge of pain. "Between you and me, child, such people are a thoroughly poor advertisement for their wealth and the length of their genealogies."

Often, in the course of these conversations, Bridie asked questions intended to lead round to the problem of the memoirs and the reason—for reason there must be—why she was finding them so difficult to complete. And always, in the gentlest, most patient way possible, her great-aunt evaded her. So that, as far as Bridie could see, the veil the old lady cast over her most private hopes and fears was utterly impenetrable.

She reported as much to the family. Robert she'd found— as he was often to be found—at the organ, a Bach fugue on the music stand, seemingly lost in the intricacies of fingering a particularly difficult passage. Music, Bridie had soon discovered, was Robert's passion. He had facility and talent, but not the genius he craved. And because he could not excel as he wished, he tended to make light of his ability, as he did of most things. For the rest, although he occasionally accompanied Andrew in his rounds of the estates, he seemed a young man with little to do but "buzz" about the neighbourhood in the Argyll.

He listened to her as she described her most recent conversation with Lady Otranta, nodding sympathetically. "Keep plugging," he told her. "Who knows, if this goes on long enough, she may give up the idea of the book altogether."

Melissa, arranging flowers in the garden room, refused to be drawn into the matter at all. "If you want to go on wasting your time, well, that's your business," she said, cocking her head at a bowl of chrysanthemums and bronzed autumn leaves. " Let's not talk about it, shall we? I was going to ask you to come down to the village with me, to visit poor old Mrs. McFadden." Then, with the surprising mixture of compassion and off-handedness so characteristic of her, Melissa added, " She's bedridden now, and I swear that daughter of hers'll be glad when she dies."

While Andrew, growing more haggard by the day, paced restlessly up and down his study, his hands clenched tightly behind his back. " I wish I could be sure that what we're doing is right, Bridie. Obviously Mama likes having you here —we all do." He smiled at her with sudden warmth. " But—" and the smile disappeared as quickly as it had come " —well, can you honestly say you've seen any improvement in her . . . condition?"

Much as she would have liked to, Bridie couldn't. And could only stare wretchedly at her cousin, wondering if he would ever have the chance of a life of his own, simple and uncomplicated, in which she herself might play a part. And all the time feeling—in such a household, at such a time— deeply ashamed of the unsuitability of such a thought.

Apart from the two hours or so spent each day with her great-aunt, Bridie's time was her own. Frequently, remembering her responsibility to her employer—for would not Mr. Pugh-Hennessy, in return for her wages, be expecting rather more strenuous efforts?—she was racked with guilt at her idleness, which she assuaged in long letters to him, hinting as clearly as she dared at the difficulties facing her, making no promises, and offering repeatedly to return to London at once if he was dissatisfied with her. His letters in reply she opened fearfully, terrified that he might take her at her word. But he was always patient and encouraging, begging her to persist, repeating the faith he had in her eventual success. If only he knew, she thought, what little faith she had in that herself.

For the rest, she was busy enough, walking in the woods with Andrew, going on bicycle rides with Melissa, playing the organ, or the piano in the long, oak-galleried music room, practising accompaniments for the songs Melissa would sing at the coming party, or jaunting with Robert in the motor car down to Kincardine village and along the shore of the Firth to Culross, from where the stupendous Forth Bridge could be viewed. She took riding lessons also, in the care of the sympathetic Mr. Symonds, but these were a source of much pain and little satisfaction to her. She was far too much a city girl, she decided, ever to be anything but a thoroughly indifferent horsewoman. If she had to ride anything, she'd much rather stick to one of the castle's stable of bicycles. At least they stopped more or less when you wanted them to.

Inevitably there were interruptions, not always looked for, in her routine. One of these came on the Monday of her second week at the castle, when the yellow Argyll, driven by Duncan Symonds and bearing a portly stranger in a wide-awake beaver, clattered past her and Melissa as they were returning on their bicycles from a morning visit to the head gamekeeper's wife, just three days delivered of a fine little baby girl.

Melissa wobbled dangerously and put her foot down, beating irritably at the clouds of dust and smoke that billowed in the car's wake.

" That horrible Macnab—looking as pleased with himself as ever, I see. Duncan will have been down to meet him from the ferry. Such a performance ! As if the local Alloa doctor wasn't good enough for Mama."

Tentatively Bridie suggested that perhaps an Edinburgh doctor was better versed in cases such as Lady Otranta's.

Melissa snorted. " He'd have you think that, of course. . . . But I mustn't be uncharitable. Anything that might help my poor step-mother is worth trying." She edged her bicycle a little closer to Bridie's and lowered her voice. " But I do wish he wasn't just back from Vienna, and so full of peculiar stories. There's some German doctor there, he says, who claims that we women are all in love with our fathers. An odd idea, wouldn't you say? If not positively disgusting?"

Bridie considered. She wasn't quite sure what being ' in love ' meant. But she remembered with painful clarity the depth of her affection for her own dear father. " I don't know," she ventured, then glanced sideways. " Your father now, old Sir James, weren't you perhaps just a little in love with him?"

" In love with Papa?" Suddenly all the spirit seemed to go out of her companion. She hunched her shoulders. " Yes, perhaps I was . . . at least, when I was little."

She stared at the ground, pushing stones about with her foot. It was as if she had forgotten Bridie's presence. " But not . . . not afterwards. I blamed him. It wasn't fair, I knew, but somehow I decided it was all his fault. All of it. Everything. Even my mother's. . . ."

She broke off. Bridie wondered if such things were not better brought out into the open. " You blamed him for your mother's death?" They were friends enough to be frank with each other, she thought.

Her cousin looked up sharply. " Good Lord no," she said. " My mother's death was an accident. Everybody knows that." She hoisted herself back onto the bicycle saddle. " Anyway, I wasn't a bit in love with Papa. He wasn't that sort of man. But I *was* frightened of him, I think—which probably amounts to almost the same thing."

So saying she clapped her hat firmly down upon her head and pedalled off up the road in the direction of the castle, leaving Bridie thinking that that was probably the most extraordinary definition of being ' in love ' she had ever heard of. But at least it gave her an explanation for why her cousin was still unmarried. Of all the young men Bridie had so far met on her jaunts round the district, not one of them could possibly have been thought frightening by someone as robust as Melissa.

After a moment she came to her senses. " Wait for me," she cried breathlessly, bending over her pedals in pursuit of her rapidly disappearing cousin.

Up at the castle the family was gathered in the small sitting room, waiting anxiously for the result of Dr. Macnab's examination of the old lady. It was a long time coming.

" What on earth can the stupid man be doing?" Robert burst out at last. " Taking her tonsils out on the spot?"

"He talks to her, I think," Andrew said quietly. "Tries to get her to confide in him."

"If little Bridie here hasn't yet managed it, I don't see what chance he thinks he has."

Andrew rested his head in his hands. "Dr. Macnab has to do what he thinks best. Mama trusts him. Besides, what else is there?"

Melissa drummed her fingers. "If only he didn't always seem so *pleased* with himself," she said.

"Perhaps he's simply trying to cheer you all up," Bridie suggested.

"Not him. In fact, he's as good as said the whole thing's our fault. Though how he works that out I can't imagine."

Bridie was silent, observing how obsessed Melissa was that morning with *fault*. She remembered how her father had always said that blaming people was a fruitless exercise. And besides—

But at that moment the door opened and Dr. Macnab came in. And she had to admit that he did appear irritatingly self-satisfied. Considering, that is, what they all knew about the condition of his patient.

Andrew leapt to his feet. "Well, doctor?"

Macnab spread his legs, clasping the lapels of his jacket with fat pink hands. "As well as can be expected, Sir Andrew."

Robert swore beneath his breath. "And what does that mean?" he demanded.

"It means that your mother's arthritis is a progressive disease. We cannot cure it. The most we can hope to do is slow its progress. Which we appear to be doing quite satisfactorily."

"We're not children, doctor." Melissa moved to stand close in front of Dr. Macnab. He was not a tall man, and indeed had to look up slightly to meet her gaze. "It's silly of you to pretend to us that you come all this way just to see to Mama's 'arthritis'."

He smiled imperturbably. "Has it never occurred to you, Miss Tantallon, that the patient's unfortunate drinking habits might be connected with her arthritis? That they might indeed simply be an escape from pain?"

Robert got up angrily and strode away to the window. "My God—is that really the best you can come up with? And after all these months?"

"I have to say that in my experience the most obvious explanations are often the best ones."

"But Mama doesn't even *have* arthritis." Robert swung round. "Does she?"

Dr. Macnab stepped carefully past Melissa and went to the empty fireplace where he turned and positioned himself as if warming the backs of his legs at the non-existent flames. He was nearly bald, with the sort of ruddy, well-polished complexion that betokened many years of good living. "You must have seen for yourself that the patient suffers almost continual discomfort," he said. "I've prescribed laudanum, of course, but I've had to warn her of its addictive properties. If she prefers to resort to alcohol I for one cannot wholly blame her."

Andrew sank down wretchedly into a chair. "I don't understand it," he said. "Last time you were here you seemed to have some completely different theory. You talked about the memoirs Mama was writing, and—"

"Ah yes, those memoirs. . . ." Dr. Macnab rose on his toes and flexed his knees slightly. "In view of what I have learned today I suspect that they may have been something of a red herring."

"I'm glad to hear it." Andrew looked up. "But what exactly has made you change your mind so completely?"

"Naturally my conversations with the patient are confidential. But I think I may safely say that the memoirs are not at all a significant factor. The patient, in fact, has given up all idea of ever writing them."

Bridie stared at him incredulously. Nothing Lady Otranta had said to her had suggested anything of the sort. "Are you sure of that?" she queried.

Dr. Macnab appeared to see her for the first time. He bowed. "We haven't been introduced, I believe. You must be Miss

Bridie, the patient's great-niece recently arrived from London. How d'you do."

Bridie nodded shyly. She wished he wouldn't keep referring to her great-aunt as 'the patient'. It made Lady Otranta seem somehow less than human.

"The patient has spoken of you most highly," the doctor continued. "She hopes that you may be persuaded to extend your visit. To be honest, I hope so too."

Bridie blushed. "I . . . I'll stay as long as I'm needed," she said. Though how she could square that with Mr. Pugh-Hennessy if her great-aunt had really decided not to write her memoirs she couldn't imagine. She'd stay on anyway, she decided—even if he chose to dispense with her services.

"I'm delighted to hear it." Dr Macnab beamed. "The patient has need of all the support she can get. And now, if you don't mind, I'd best be on my way." He produced an enormous gold watch from his waistcoat pocket. "The next ferry leaves in forty minutes, I believe."

Andrew rang for Meredith and asked the old man to tell Duncan to bring the car to the main entrance. Then he turned back to the doctor. "You're telling us we can expect no rapid improvement," he said resignedly.

Dr. Macnab pursed his lips. "In the patient's general condition, no. She is not as young as she was, you understand, and—"

"You make her sound as if she's an old woman," Melissa put in. "Good Lord—she's only fifty-seven!"

Bridie was shocked. If she'd been asked she'd have said that her great-aunt must be at least ten years older than that. It didn't make sense, of course, when one remembered how young her children were. Yet to be only fifty-seven and to look so thin and old and pale and drawn. . . .

Piously Dr. Macnab clasped his hands. "I'm afraid the ageing effects of alcohol are well established," he murmured.

They talked for a few moments longer. Then the clatter of the approaching Argyll was heard through the open windows. Dr. Macnab moved quickly to the door.

"Now, don't any of you disturb yourselves. Naturally you

will have things to discuss. If Miss Bridie would kindly escort me . . .?"

She looked across at Andrew, who gestured wearily for her to go. So she followed the doctor out into the hall. She didn't mind him treating her like a sort of poor relation. After all, that was what she was, more or less.

They intercepted old Meredith, coming at his snail's pace to announce that the car was waiting, and took from him the doctor's coat and hat. On the steps outside the towering, black-studded doors Dr. Macnab paused.

"You must forgive me for that little ruse, Miss Bridie. But I wanted a word with you alone."

She looked at him warily. Below them on the cobbles of the courtyard the yellow Argyll throbbed and emitted puffs of thick black smoke. "A word with me alone, Dr. Macnab?"

"Yes indeed. . . ." He lowered his voice. "You see, I have to admit that there are things about your great-aunt's condition that I do not altogether understand. And since she seems to be particularly fond of you, I was wondering if—"

"What sort of things don't you understand, doctor?"

He frowned. "It would be better, I think, if I did not lead you. Rather let me say that if there's ever anything that does not seem to you to . . . as it were, to make *sense*, then I'd be most grateful if. . . ." He tailed off, rummaging in one of his smaller waistcoat pockets. Beyond him she saw Duncan Symonds, at the wheel of the Argyll, make an impatient gesture.

"A lot of the things my great-aunt does don't seem to make much sense," she said sharply. Did he want her to be a spy? Was that it?

"Ah yes, but they do, you know. Mostly, that is. If you think about them." Suddenly his gaze was direct and his tone utterly serious. "That is why this . . . this other matter is so puzzling to me."

He found the card he had been seeking, and presented it to her. "Believe me, I have Lady Otranta's interests deeply at heart. And I certainly would not ask you to betray any confidences. But if you *did* happen upon anything that you thought might be helpful. . . ." He prodded at the card. " You know now where to find me. I'm available at that address between ten and mid-day." He took her hand and squeezed it. " I'd be grateful. Really most grateful."

She didn't know what to say. He went away then, down the steps. On the cobbles he stopped and turned back. " She trusts you, you know. And now that I've met you I think I can understand why. You care for her. You've a wise head on your shoulders, and you're outside all . . ." he gestured widely with his hat ". . . outside all this."

She watched him climb into the motor car. A moment later it was gone, driving out under the wide stone archway, leaving behind it a fine haze of smoke that cleared slowly in the still summer air.

She looked down at the card in her hand: *Reginald Macnab MD. 12, St. George's Square, Edinburgh.* Perhaps he wasn't quite the fool he'd seemed. All the same, she wasn't at all sure what it was he expected of her. A wise head on her shoulders? She very much doubted it. Yet he'd been right when he said she cared what happened to her great-aunt. And she *was* outside the various under-currents of life at the castle.

Her cousins accepted her return to the sitting room without comment. The atmosphere following the doctor's visit was understandably subdued, both then and later, over a particularly dreary lunch in the forbidding dining hall. Lady Otranta was sleeping—Dr. Macnab had given her some drops, so old Peggy reported. Afterwards, therefore, they all went their separate ways, united only in depression that he should have given them so little to hope for.

But Bridie was to be forcibly reminded of just those under-currents he had referred to only the very next day when, on her way to visit her great-aunt as usual in the early afternoon, she was brought up short just outside the open door to the old lady's sitting room by the sound of raised voices. She turned, intending to go away and come back later. Private family quarrels were surely no concern of hers.

Then, suddenly, to her utter astonishment, she realised that it was Robert, the seemingly always so easy-going Robert, who was haranguing Lady Otranta. And in terms so violent as seriously to suggest that the old lady might need Bridie's protection. So she returned to the open doorway and looked in, across the incredible clutter of conjuring cabinets and other theatrical gim-crackery, to where Robert was standing, leaning over his mother in her high-backed chair, shouting into her face, almost beside himself with inexplicable rage.

*   *   *

The weather was fine that August. It mocked our misery, Jamie's and mine. He'd returned to the castle the day after our midnight cab-ride, just as he'd said he would. We settled nothing, then or the next time we met. Somehow he got through the days spent under the same roof as his wife. What he ate there I don't know. He didn't want to talk about that time, and I didn't press him. But he'd already told me he wasn't going to challenge his wife with what we'd discovered. Not at once. Not until he'd decided what he was going to do about it.

For myself, I'd have gone straight to the police. I hated the woman. I'd never met her, never even seen her. I knew nothing of her, or of her reasons. But I hated her.

Not that her reasons mattered. Nothing in the world could have excused what she was doing. She deserved arrest, imprisonment, every hardship and humiliation society could heap on her. For James, though, things were less simple.

He got away from the castle again as soon as he could. He was so desperate that morning that he called for me at my rooms, a risk we'd always avoided. We sat and talked in a quiet corner of Prince's Street Gardens.

The police, he told me, must be a last resort. Apart from anything else, he blamed *himself* for his wife's monstrous behaviour, certainly too much just to turn her over to the constabulary. If he'd been anything of a husband to her, he said, she would never have been driven to such desperate straits. It wasn't true, of course—from what I knew of him her actions could never be his fault, no matter what: murder, and by poison too, of all things the coldest, most calculating and vile of weapons. . . . It broke my heart to watch him humbly search his own soul, when the true reason had to be in the twisted workings of that woman's mind. But I let him talk.

He'd been neglectful, he said. The building of Castle Tantallon had taken so much of his time and attention. That and his work on the Queen's estates. Then again, there was his daughter. He'd wanted a son, and his wife knew it. Perhaps she'd resented that, and felt he didn't care enough for the little girl. She wasn't yet two years old —had he really seemed unloving towards her?

To me that was so incredible that I faced him with it. Had he really not loved his own child, I said, simply because she was of the wrong sex? He stared at me wildly. Of course not, he answered.

Round and round he went, trying to achieve the impossible. Trying to find an excuse for murder. He would, I knew, have liked to blame our association, his and mine. But he'd been ill, thank God, months before that had started.

Obviously in some strange way he still felt a perverse loyalty towards the wretched woman, while I, seeing what she was doing to him, hated her all the more, and made my plans. She was vicious and cruel. Quite merciless. And as for the child—she cared nothing for her, otherwise she'd never be scheming to kill the child's father. She deserved death herself. She was a monster.

Strong words. But I believed them, and I believe them still. She can't be harmed by them now, of course, being dead. . . .

*　　　*　　　*

As Bridie watched, Robert stooped and shook his mother's shoulders.

" A millstone round your neck," he shouted. " Round all of our necks. And for what? Out of loyalty? To 'Lissa?"

He released the old lady, just as Bridie was about to intervene. Her great-aunt remained astonishingly calm. " Be quiet, Robert," she said coldly. " You just have to live with the fact that your father loved her. Jealousy is hardly—"

"Jealousy? *Jealousy*?" Robert swung away. "My dear Mama, what a ridiculous—" He caught sight of Bridie standing in the doorway and stopped abruptly. She saw his expression change, the habitual mask of mocking indifference return to his angular Tantallon features.

She swallowed, and went bravely forward into the room. "I'm sorry," she said. "I didn't mean to eavesdrop. But the door was open, and I. . . ."

"It really doesn't matter." Her cousin folded his arms. "You'd have to find out sooner or later. For a place this size the castle keeps its secrets really very badly. The thing is, you see, poor 'Lissa's been up here again, ranting on at poor Mama about those rotten memoirs. And Mama lets her, I—"

"That's enough, Robert." Lady Otranta struggled to her feet. "I'm sure Bridie will form her own opinion as to who was ranting and who was not."

Robert shrugged elaborately. Then he strolled past Bridie to the door. "Very well, Mama. And I'm sorry I lost my temper. But we all know what a horror dear 'Lissa has of those memoirs. She may try to keep it to herself, but it's there all the same. And I honestly can't imagine why." He turned to Bridie, tilting his head. "Can you, fair coz?"

She met his gaze. "No, I can't. And to be frank, I don't believe it." She glanced in her great-aunt's direction, expecting support. But the old lady appeared totally absorbed in straightening the collar of her long black dress, which Robert's rough handling had disordered. Was it true then after all, what he had said?

"Oh, Bridie, Bridie. . . ." He smiled at her sadly. "How little you know about us. We're a nasty twisted lot beneath our smiling exteriors, we Tantallons. And anyway, if you don't believe me, why not ask her? You saved her life, so she owes you the truth, which is more than I've ever been able to get out of her."

He moved closer, and lowered his voice. "Be nice to poor Mama. I know I've behaved disgustingly. But . . . well, I hate to see Mama taken advantage of. It brings out the worst in me." He sighed. " You're thinking it's 'Lissa I should have bullied. And you're quite right. But she takes these things to heart so. And she's so . . . vulnerable."

A millstone round our necks . . . was that really the way the family thought of the child of Sir James' first marriage? If so, then it was no wonder Melissa took things to heart, was so vulnerable. Robert went away then, and Bridie stared after him, wretchedly disheartened that such jealousy and unhappiness could exist in any family.

" People seem to think that because I'm old I'm deaf." Her great-aunt's brisk voice roused her. " But I'm not, you know. Not in the least. And you mustn't take Robert too seriously. He's a great coward, I'm afraid. And he has all of his father's temper, with none of his father's iron self-control."

Bridie turned back into the room. Lady Otranta had moved across in front of the ornate fireplace—in which, in spite of the warm weather, a gigantic log fire was burning—and had positioned herself beside the dummy chess player, one hand resting on its Turkish silk shoulder.

" Come in, child, and sit down. It's high time Az Rah and I told you all about some of the tricks we got up to, we and his master. The great Professor Salvador."

Bridie did as she was told. And, in spite of the painful scene she had just witnessed, tried her best to concentrate on what her great-aunt was telling her.

" There was a time, child—in Boulogne, I seem to remember—when the French police actually forbade poor Az Rah's performances. They had some ridiculous theory about a wretched young man hidden inside his body, and accused the Professor of being cruel and inhuman. It was quite nonsensical, of course. In point of fact the lad was under-sized for his age, and anyway didn't mind at all—as *he* saw it he was simply being paid to play chess, which was his favourite game! But it's no use trying to reason with the police. Never was and never will be."

The old lady poured herself a drink from a bottle on the mantelpiece, then came round in front of the cabinet on which Az Rah's chess board was laid out, and began opening the various doors. "Watch closely, my dear, and I'll show you how the trick was accomplished."

Bridie watched, and nodded her head in obedient amazement. But her thoughts were still preoccupied with what Robert had said about Melissa. She was treated to several other demonstrations that day—a cabinet in which the disappearances were all done by mirrors, a trunk with a sliding panel so closely fitted as to be totally invisible, table-rapping that was engineered by means of a simple electro-magnet. Seldom had her great-aunt been so forthcoming. It was almost as if she was trying to take Bridie's mind off Robert's inexcusable behaviour. This only made the girl, a Tantallon to the core, all the more determined to get to the truth of the matter.

By three o'clock Lady Otranta's frequent visits to the bottle on the mantelpiece were obviously taking effect, so Bridie was able to tuck her drowsily up in her chair, stoke the fire still higher, and make her escape.

She went at once in search of Melissa, finding her cousin finally in the oak-panelled music room, seated by the piano at the far end, picking out the tune of a mournful Scottish folk song with one finger. She looked up from the keyboard as Bridie came in.

"I can't seem to get the stupid thing right," she called. "Do come and play it for me."

Now that Bridie had found Melissa she didn't quite know how to begin. Slowly she walked the length of the room. There should have been some tactful way of leading up to the question she had to ask, but for the life of her she couldn't think of one. Her cousin stood up, offered her the piano stool. She took it, poised her hands nervously above the keys.

She lowered them again, and folded them in her lap. "These memoirs," she said baldly, "I didn't think you minded very much whether Lady Otranta finished them or not."

Her cousin's eyes widened. Then she turned angrily away. "It's Robert, of course—what's the little swine been saying?"

"Only that you didn't want the memoirs finished." Already Bridie felt ashamed. "I . . . I have to know, you see. After all,

I'm supposed to be helping her with them. But I wouldn't want you to—"

"Why can't Robert mind his own business?"

Bridie tried to explain. "It . . . it was just something I overheard. I'm sure he didn't *want* to tell me. But—"

"A fat lot you know about it. He'd just love to tell you. If he could, of course. But he doesn't really know anything—not a bloody thing!"

Her cousin's bad language shocked Bridie. But it convinced her more than anything else that there was indeed something to know. . . . She got up from the piano. "I'm sorry, 'Lissa . . . I'm sorry I poked my nose in. Please forgive me. It's really nothing to do with me."

"No, it's not." Melissa swung round on her. Then, suddenly, all her anger melted away. "Oh Bridie, Bridie—how rotten life is. We shouldn't be quarrelling, not you and I."

There were tears in her eyes. Bridie moved forward impulsively and put her arms about her cousin. "It doesn't matter, 'Lissa. Whatever it is, it's not important."

"But it is, it *is*. . . ." Melissa's shoulders were shaking uncontrollably. "Oh God, if only I could tell you! If only I could tell just *somebody*. . . ."

"Hush now. Hush. . . ." Bridie hugged her closer. The deserted music room seemed vast about them, and somehow threatening, its carved oak gallery darkly shadowed, full of unseen eyes. "Here—I'll play that tune for you now. *Ye banks and braes*, wasn't it?"

Her cousin straightened her back. "Oh, to hell with it," she said, giving her short, sharp, familiar laugh. "Robert's quite right, of course. He doesn't know why, though. But Mama knows—my step-mother knows very well. Still, it won't be the end of the world, I suppose, if she puts it all down in this rotten book of hers, I mean."

Bridie returned to the piano. It seemed that she had—at least in part—misjudged Robert. These memoirs—what trouble they were causing. First Andrew and Robert, and now Melissa. She understood the men's objection—their mother's wretched condition seemed unmistakably connected with Mr.

Pugh-Hennessy's ill-advised commission. But Melissa, what reason could she possibly have for such evident fears?

"I honestly don't think you have to worry, 'Lissa," she said quietly, "you heard what Dr. Macnab said about the memoirs. And I'm sure he knows what he's talking about."

"Are you?" Melissa mopped briskly at her eyes. "That's more than I am. He's a fool, that man. A pompous nincompoop."

Bridie would have agreed with her, had it not been for the curious private conversation she'd had with the portly doctor. But she didn't argue. "I still don't think you have to worry," she said. "I've been here nearly two weeks now, and I'm sure there's not a single word been written."

She began to play. After a few bars her cousin cleared her throat and joined in. Her voice, though still husky, was sweet and true.

Ye banks and braes of bonny Doon, how can ye bloom sae fresh and fair . . .?

Suddenly she broke off. "You really are a trump, you know. And I'll tell you all about it, one day. But not now. . . . Try to understand, will you?"

Bridie nodded. Suddenly she thought she knew what was worrying Melissa. The accident in the gun-room that had maimed her half-brother, Andrew : perhaps her part in it had not after all been entirely blameless. She'd know she could rely on Andrew's discretion—Bridie remembered how guarded he had been on the subject. But if Lady Otranta knew the truth also. . . .

Not for the first time Bridie wished devoutly that she'd never even heard of the confounded memoirs. She smiled at Melissa as reassuringly as she was able, then bent again over the piano keys.

How can ye chaunt, ye little birds, and I sae weary, full o' care. . .?

It was at dinner that very evening, however, that Bridie was brought to think she understood at last the full extent of her cousin's misery. And it was the gentle Andrew, of all people, who precipitated the crisis.

Lady Otranta seemed unusually subdued that night, and less interested than was her custom in the wine from the castle's fine cellars. Andrew therefore took the opportunity to raise again the question of the coming party, and of the guests who still had to be chosen. With the day now scarcely two weeks off, he said, the invitations must be sent out as soon as possible. Tactfully making no mention of Duncan Symonds, he wondered if his mother had any strong feelings in the matter.

Listlessly Lady Otranta toyed with the stem of her wine glass. "I suppose we have to have this party?" she said at last. "I feel so tired these days. I almost wish. . . ." Her words tailed off into silence.

Suddenly the old lady revived. "You understand what I mean, of course," she said harshly. "I have no wish to disgrace you, you see."

"Disgrace us?" Andrew hesitated. It was impossible to pretend he didn't know what she meant. "I'm sure there's no fear of that, Mama. You don't even have to attend if you don't want to."

"So I'm to be banished upstairs, is that it? The skeleton in the Tantallon cupboard?"

Andrew pushed back his chair, an angry flush on his haggard cheeks. "I do wish you wouldn't insist on misunderstanding me, Mama."

Unpredictable as always, his mother smiled. "Well said, boy. I'm a boring old woman, and it's high time you told me so."

Inevitably he began to apologise, but she talked him down. "This party, then. *This party*, I say. . . . We'd better begin by finding out whom all of you would like to see invited. Melissa, dear—you first. You're the oldest."

Bridie turned, saw her cousin fuss awkwardly with her starched white cuffs. "I'd rather you left me out of it, Mama."

Andrew leaned forward. "But 'Lissa, what about the Craigs?" he said gently. "I know Gordon would like to—"

Melissa got convulsively to her feet. "Leave me out of it, I said." She began to back away.

"Sit down this instant, Melissa!" Lady Otranta's words fell like hammer blows. Then she relaxed. "You really must not try to run away, child, every time we discuss anything remotely concerning you."

Slowly Melissa returned to her seat. Bridie felt desperately sorry for her. Was this a scene that had often been played out? she wondered.

"Gordon Craig is a thoroughly nice young man," the old lady continued. "And I know he thinks highly of you. Yet you avoid him like the plague. Do you really dislike him so much?"

"Honestly, Mama!" It was Robert now, surprisingly, who intervened. "If 'Lissa doesn't want to see the doughty Gordon, then that's *her* business. Surely she doesn't have to explain herself to the entire family?"

Boldly he met his mother's gaze until she turned away and reached uncertainly for her wine glass. But Melissa was sitting very straight now, and quite in control of herself. "Thank you, Robert, but no—Mama's quite right. It's time for a little plain speaking." She glanced sideways at Bridie. "I'm sorry if this embarrasses you, old thing. But that's family life for you . . . Tantallon family life, at any rate."

She placed her elbows firmly upon the table. "Gordon's not at all a bad fellow," she began. "He likes me and I like him. *Like*, I said—nothing more as yet. Though I'm not saying things mightn't develop, given the chance. But he's old-fashioned—or at least, his parents are. They'd expect a financial consideration before they gave their beloved oldest son away. And—"

Andrew cut her short. "But of course there'd be a dowry, my dear. You know as well as I do that the estate can well afford it. And even if it couldn't, we'd never—"

Lady Otranta drained her glass dramatically. "Certainly there'll be a dowry," she declaimed. "A *magnificent* dowry!"

There was a pause. Melissa's reply, when it came, was barely audible. "I . . . I knew you'd say that. And I'm very grateful. But . . . well, the thing is, I couldn't possibly accept it." She stared down at the tablecloth, blushing furiously.

" Please . . . please don't let's have an argument. I just couldn't accept it. You've given me so much—a home, a fine education, a—"

" But for God's sake, Melissa, it's your *right*." Andrew's voice was harsh with emotion. " You're as much a Tantallon as any of us."

Melissa lifted her head. " Please—I've said I can't accept a dowry, and I mean it." She smiled wryly. "After all, this is the twentieth century. If a man wants to marry me, then he must take me for what I am. Not for the money I bring."

It was a brave enough explanation. But Bridie, for one, didn't believe a word of it. Robert's words still rang in her ears: *A millstone round all our necks.* If that was really how he felt, then Melissa was sensitive enough to have guessed as much. And guessed also, perhaps unjustly, how his mother also might feel towards the child of her husband's first, unhappy marriage. . . . Poor Melissa. For all her sensible, modern talk, it was no wonder that she didn't want to accept any more of the Tantallon money than she had to. It was no wonder, either, that she spent so much of her time in good works about the district. She had a debt to repay, a debt that was none of her making.

7

To be frank, Jamie's indecision infuriated me. He was going to have to go to the police sooner or later, so why not get it over and done with? Yet it would have been tactless of me to say so straight out—it was something he had to come to in his own time.

I had a matinée to do that day, so I was forced to leave him shortly after one. There was no alternative. But I promised to meet him again that same night, after the evening show. I was deeply worried for him—he looked so utterly wretched, sitting there in the sun on that bench in Prince's Street Gardens.

There were three performances to be got through that day, and they left me little time for thinking. Possibly, if I'd been wise, I'd have gone to the police myself. James might well have welcomed being spared the responsibility. Certainly both our future lives would have been immeasurably simpler if I had. But I was afraid. Afraid to have to admit my own involvement with the Tantallon family. And afraid of Jamie's incomprehensible loyalty towards the woman who was trying to kill him. Somehow that had to be dealt with, got out of the way, before there could be any real future for him and me together.

Even then, you see, I was already thinking of the future, his and mine. And I was determined, with the ruthless determination that only a woman in love is capable of, that it should, *come what may*, be ours together.

A calculating creature, you say? Rather, I hope, a young woman faced with a hideous situation and trying desperately to wrest from it some hope of happiness for herself, and for the man she loved.

He met me at the stage door. We walked. If there was danger in Edinburgh's darkened streets at that time of night, we didn't think of it. We had other concerns, other problems. He told me he'd decided not to go to the police. At that I staked everything, asked him if in spite of everything he still loved his wife. He said he didn't know.

Besides, he went on, that wasn't the point. There was his daughter to think of—how could he have her growing up knowing her mother was a murderess? And as for himself, the scandal would certainly ruin him.

His reasoning didn't convince me. I asked him again—I *had* to—did he still love his wife? He stopped beneath a street lamp and turned to me. I remember his face to this very day. And his words also.

" I loved her once. Perhaps I always will. But I hate her too, and all the more because of that love. . . . Do you think you can understand that, Otranta? That a man can love a woman and hate her at the same time?"

I couldn't. But it didn't matter. If he said that was how he felt, then I had to believe him. " Jamie . . . Jamie, what are we to do now?" I said.

He didn't answer. We walked on again, into the shadows. Suddenly he was taken with a horrible spasm of pain. He leaned against some railings outside a high, dark house, retching dryly. I held him tight. Several days had passed since I'd seen him as bad as this. Dear God, how the poison lingered.

When the worst of the agony was passed he lifted his head. " I wish she was dead," he whispered. " God forgive me, Otranta—I wish she was *dead*."

I helped him back through the streets to the door of his club. Little else was said between us. But the seed was sown. And at last he and I were in total agreement. . . .

*   *   *

The castle had a garden, a place of bright lawns—one set out for croquet—and roses and lavender, with wide paved paths thick with fragrant alyssum, and a fountain playing in the middle of a dark, cool lily pond. On all sides it was sheltered from the wind by high stone walls, against which grew wistaria and honeysuckle, and espaliered fruit trees facing the south. Only to the west were the walls low enough to be seen over, and there an arcaded terrace had been built, with seats and great stone tubs of hardy escallonia.

It was to this sunny corner, looking out over a broad expanse of soft, thickly-wooded hillsides, that Bridie often came in the late afternoon. It was her ' thinking place ', where she could sit quietly and review the events of the day, indeed, of her entire short life. Often she remembered her father, and wished that he were still alive, and there with her. She would have told him about so many things, and asked his advice upon so many matters.

And it was here, one afternoon a few days later, that she found Andrew, leaning absently upon the stone parapet, staring out at the view with tired, unseeing eyes.

He had not heard her approach, and she was in two minds as to whether she should creep away again. But she had spoken to him on her own so seldom in these last few days, and he seemed so utterly dejected now that her heart went out to him.

She sought a pebble with her toe, and kicked it across the grey paving stones. At the sound he stiffened, and turned warily. Seeing her, he relaxed.

"Bridie my dear, forgive me—I'm afraid I'm intruding on your private corner."

She moved forward. " It's hardly *my* private corner," she said. " It was here a long time before me and I'm sure it'll be here a long time after."

Andrew looked away. " But you've made it yours," he murmured. " Certainly I shall always think of it as yours."

She didn't know how to answer. Suddenly there was an electric tension in the air between them. By what means did he know how often she came there? He had seemed so absorbed in the affairs of the estate recently, almost as if he was avoiding her.

"I . . . I like it here," she stammered. "It's so . . . so peaceful."

"And the rest of the castle is not? Well, I can hardly blame you for thinking that." He made room for her to stand beside him at the wall. She leaned on the sun-warmed stones, feeling the golden moment slip away. And there was nothing she could do to stop it.

Andrew shifted his feet. "At least I've got that guest-list sorted out," he said. "I went over it with Mama yesterday evening before dinner. She was . . . well, surprisingly coherent."

Bridie hesitated. If he wanted to talk about his mother, then they would talk about his mother. "I think she's getting better," she said.

"Do you? Do you really?" He turned to her eagerly. Then the hope in his eyes faded. "But she won't listen to sense about the Craigs, I'm afraid. Once she gets an idea into her head, nothing will change it."

"Poor Melissa." Bridie shivered slightly, as if a cool breeze had suddenly come up from the valley. "Still, there'll be a lot of other guests at the party, I expect."

All at once Andrew straightened, and limped distractedly away down the terrace. He stopped by a pillar. "You know, none of this is what I wanted to say at all." His back was still turned to her. "I wanted to tell you . . . oh, so many things. But. . . ."

He paused, swung slowly round. "Bridie, dear, you must try to understand. I'm not my own man. You'll think me weak, perhaps, not to stand up to her. But I—"

"Not weak, Andrew." Never weak. It took great strength —and love—to bear all that he did so patiently. "Your mother's ill. Naturally your first thought must be for her."

Despairingly he ran his fingers through his hair. "One day, maybe, when all this is over . . . yet who can say when that will be?" He beat his fist against the pillar's side. "I have so little to offer, Bridie. A nightmare. Nothing more."

Her eyes blurred. She longed to run to him, but dared not. "It won't go on for ever," she whispered.

"But what about you? What about *your* feelings? I haven't even asked—I'm sorry—I'm doing this so badly." Returning to her, he took her arm and drew her down beside him onto one of the long wooden seats. "Look—I'd better begin again properly, from the beginning. I . . . I care for you very much, Bridie. You're good and beautiful and true. You're—"

She put up her hand to cover his mouth. "Please Andrew —don't."

He grasped her hand and kissed it. "How long have you been here—three weeks? It might as well have been a lifetime. I *know* you, Bridie. I've watched you and I've listened to you, and I *know* you."

Her heart was pounding. "And I know you too, Andrew."

He wrenched away. "But what do you know? A limping wreck of a man, with a troubled household, an uncertain future, and . . . a mother who—"

Bridie interrupted him. "I know *you*, dear Andrew."

He stared into her eyes. She saw doubt pass across his face, then wonder, then joy. Then despair again.

"But it's impossible. How can I talk like this when there's so much in the way, so many problems?"

She found herself cradling his face in both hands. "I don't mind waiting," she said.

"Oh, Bridie. . . ." He kissed her then, lightly at first, his lips soft and gentle on hers. At their touch her whole being seemed to dissolve. And as his passion grew, so hers grew to match it. Until suddenly, breathless and more than a little afraid at the powerful, unfamiliar urgings of her body, she thrust him away.

"No Andrew," she gasped. "No. . . ."

He stared anxiously into her face. His hair had fallen forward unheeded over his brow. "I love you, Bridie. D'you know that?"

She nodded. She wanted to tell him she loved him also, but she was all at once too shy. She blushed, and lowered her gaze.

"Should I not have . . . have kissed you, my dearest?"

Her eyes darted up. "Oh, *yes*."

He smiled. Then he laughed aloud. He laughed so that she

was almost afraid, the sound echoing back at her from the high rear wall of the terrace.

He pressed her closely to him, her head against his breast. " I was afraid I'd been too bold. And clumsy perhaps."

" Clumsy? Oh no, not clumsy. . . ." She relaxed into his arms, feeling their strength, and the reassuring breadth of his shoulders. He smelt deliciously of tweed and sweet camomile soap. The sensations that crowded in upon her were beyond expressing.

" I have a confession to make," he told her, laughter still in his voice. " I was waiting for you here. I was hoping, praying that you'd come."

She'd suspected as much, yet hadn't dared to admit it even to herself. " I'm glad you did, Andrew. I . . . I'd thought you were avoiding me."

Suddenly serious again, he eased her reluctantly away. " And so I was. It seemed the only honourable way. I'd made up my mind never to tell you how I felt, you see. I had so little to offer—it wouldn't be fair, I thought. And no matter how wretched life here may be, I can never leave. It's my *home*. So I did what I thought was right, and avoided you." He lifted her chin with the tips of his fingers and stared down into her eyes. " But then, this afternoon, my love got the better of me. I simply couldn't let another day pass without. . . ." He leaned forward and kissed her lips with infinite tenderness.

" Things won't always be like this," she said earnestly. " Your mother *will* get better."

" Do you honestly believe that?"

Thoughts fluttered in her mind like imprisoned moths. No, she did not believe it. " *Something* will happen," she cried. " I know it will !"

He held her close again. " Good and wise and true. . . . I knew you wouldn't lie to me."

An idea came to her in her despair. " Perhaps Lady Otranta would be happier, perhaps she'd see things differently if we were to—" She broke off then, horrified at what she'd nearly said, biting her lip.

But he'd guessed her meaning. " If we were to be married?" he suggested. Suddenly his face was radiant. "You mean, you'd agree? You care for me enough for that?"

She thought her heart would burst. Of course she'd agree. Of course she cared enough. But she hesitated, seeking the right words with which to answer his question, the most important question she would ever be asked. And as she hesitated, his elation died and he released her, letting his hands fall limply, miserably down by his sides.

"But it wouldn't work, Bridie. Believe me, that's the only reason I haven't suggested it myself ages ago—well, at least a week ago." He managed a wan smile, then sighed. "My dear, you've seen how Mama treats me. I'm denied even the smallest authority. She thinks of me as a child. I tell you, I couldn't endure her scorn, the cruel things she'd say to us both. And the purgatory she'd make our lives afterwards."

"That's not true!" Bridie was near to tears. "You sound as if you think she's wicked."

"Not wicked. Only ill—and desperately unhappy. And so impossibly touchy where I'm concerned. . . . You told me yourself how much I reminded her of Papa, and how she hated it. What d'you think she'd feel if—" He stopped abruptly and tensed, looking over her shoulder, back along the terrace. She turned, fearing she knew not what, and followed the direction of his gaze. And there, standing on the path not twenty feet away, was Peggy, her bright button eyes behind the thick lenses of her spectacles screwed up against the late afternoon sun, her whole attitude one of sly outrage.

Andrew moved away from her and got to his feet. "Well, Peggy?" he demanded brusquely.

"Well what?" the fat old dresser returned, quick as a flash. "A person can walk in the garden, can't she? It's a free country, innit?"

It was on the tip of Bridie's tongue to observe that creeping up on other people and spying on them was unacceptable, no matter how free the country might be. Then she remembered how easy she herself had found it unwittingly to approach the terrace without Andrew hearing her.

Andrew folded his arms. "Well, you can get on with your

walk now, Peggy," he said firmly. " There's nothing keeping you here."

" That's as may be. Knowing what I knows, I might well say as a word of kindly warning's called for."

" *Kindly?*" Bridie dared query the word. She refused to be cowed by the old woman. Besides, fighting back was the only language Peggy understood.

" Kindly I said, miss, and kindly I meant." But her expression remained as sly as before. " You see, miss, there's no future in it. None at all. Not for neither of you."

Andrew frowned, and went purposefully towards her. " We really don't need your advice, Peggy, thank you."

But the old dresser stood her ground, hands on hips. " No future, I say. When Madame's bloody memoirs is done it'll mean ruin for the lot of yer." She smacked her fat lips. " Ruin, I say. Out and out ruin."

Andrew turned back to Bridie. " Come along, my dear. It's time we were getting back into the castle."

But she restrained him, putting her hand on his arm. " Peggy," she said carefully, " what exactly do you know about Lady Otranta's memoirs?"

" What I knows?" Peggy thrust her head pugnaciously forward. " I'm not stupid. I can put two and two together as well as many. Better than most. Then again—it's *which* two you puts together with *which* two . . . and I was close to Madame back in them days, closer than any other living soul. And I'm telling you, if Madame writes the truth in them memoirs, the whole truth about what she done like what she's threatening, then it's ruin for the lot of yer." She rocked ponderously back on her heels. " And I wouldn't put it past her, at that."

" But Lady Otranta isn't even writing her memoirs," Bridie said quickly. " You know that as well as I do."

Briefly old Peggy was outfaced, and fiddled uncertainly with the ribbons and other oddments attached to the front of her dress. Then she recovered.

" Yers . . . well, I'll tell you what that one is—cunning as a cartload of monkeys, that's what Madame is. I wouldn't put that past her neither—having us all on—while she pegged away on her own, it'd be just like her."

" But that's ridiculous."

" Yers." Peggy shrugged. " Maybe it is. But she ain't one to give up. She'll come back to them memoirs one of these days. And then it'll be ruin for the lot of yer." She paused. " For me, too, I shouldn't wonder," she added, folding her arms in strange, masochistic glee.

Andrew laughed. " How melodramatic you are, Peggy," he said lightly.

But Bridie could see he was worried all the same. She glanced calmly at her little gold fob watch, not wanting to give old Peggy the satisfaction of seeing her distress. " Dinner in a quarter of an hour," she said, copying his casual tone. " You'll excuse us, Peggy, I'm sure."

Andrew took her arm then and they walked together up the path between the long beds of dusty pink roses.

Old Peggy watched them go. " I tell you, there's no future in it," she called after them. " Dead or alive, that one'll be the ruin of us all. You mark my words."

Andrew stooped sideways, still mocking. " Hark to the gypsy's warning," he murmured in Bridie's ear.

But when they had entered through the low arched doorway to the garden room and were about to part on the gallery above the sombre entrance hall, he hesitated and looked down at her, anxiety now showing in his eyes. " D'you think that old witch really knows anything?" he said.

" Of course she doesn't." He looked so distressed that Bridie reached up on tip-toe and quickly kissed his cheek. " Besides, Lady Otranta's your mother. You don't honestly think she has some terrible guilty secret?"

Her question had hardly been serious. He took it as such all the same. " I don't know," he murmured, looking round almost furtively, as if he were afraid of being overheard. " The thing is, Bridie, *I just don't know.* She's such an extraordinary woman—she might have done anything, anything at all. With the best of intentions, of course. Dear Mama has always had the best of intentions."

He essayed a smile, but it faded quickly. Shrugging his shoulders, he stooped briefly to brush her lips with his, then dejectedly limped away down the corridor.

*   *   *

It was necessary that Jamie's wife should die. That much, if nothing else, was certain. The manner of the deed, where and when—and how he and I were ever to bring ourselves openly to discuss it—all that was still in the future. Only the fact, the necessity, existed.

I thought then, and I still think now, that she deserved to die. After all, does not the Church itself demand that we take the wish for the deed? In which case the woman was already many times a murderess, both in her own heart and in the name of all that was just, having sought, day after day, grain by grain, the death of another. No matter *how* indifferent a husband he might have been (which possibility was anyway utter nonsense) such actions could never be justified. And as for the laws of this country, I have always felt that the difference they make between murder and attempted murder is totally misguided.

That Jamie's wife should die, therefore, was not only necessary but just. That, and the exact method, never worried me. As far as James and I were concerned, the only problem that remained was how to say the words.

I knew there was no point in beating about the bush. His position at home was intolerable. And if it was up to me to play Lady Macbeth's part, then so be it. I spent the rest of that sleepless night formulating a plan. And I broached it to him the very next morning.

We were in the gardens again, sitting upon the same discreet bench. He refused my plan pointblank, of course. He had to. Apart from anything else, there was danger to myself in it. We argued for a long time, going over the alternatives. He was, I know, absolutely genuine in his reluctance to agree to my scheme. But finally I persuaded him there was no other way. He wept then, a grown man sitting there in the sun, the tears streaming unheeded down his cheeks.

I did not weep. I knew I had to be strong enough for the two of us. And there was much to be arranged.

I hope I will be forgiven now if I cheat a little. For to divulge the details of my plan at this stage would be to rob my story of half its momentum. And I wasn't Professor Salvador's assistant for nothing. I still know the value of keeping a trick or two up my sleeve.

*   *   *

Unlike her cousin Andrew, Bridie had every confidence in Lady Otranta. Thinking about it that night in the candle-lit privacy of her little chintz room, she had to concede that she hadn't known the old lady quite as long as he had. But then, she'd only known him for exactly the same length of time, yet she was willing to stake her life on his never having done anything to be even remotely ashamed of. No, Peggy was simply a sour old creature with an evil imagination, who couldn't bear to see others happy. Her warning was just so much hot air. There was nothing unworthy in Lady Otranta's past. There couldn't be. Even allowing for the strangeness of her recent behaviour—dinner that evening had been particularly difficult—she was far too . . . too *sensible* for that.

And besides, Bridie needed to trust the old lady for she was in love, and wanted nothing more than to talk about her beloved. Who else would receive her confidences more kindly than her beloved's mother?

Andrew had spoken of the old lady's scorn, of the cruel things she would say. Frankly Bridie didn't believe a word of that either. She understood the confusions in Lady Otranta's heart, but could not credit that she would allow them so profoundly to warp her judgement. No, in spite of her many awkwardnesses, she loved her son. And Bridie had reason to think that she loved her also. What, then, could make her more content than that these two people whom she loved should find happiness together?

That much decided to her complete satisfaction, Bridie leaned from her bed, snuffed out her candle, and composed herself for sleep. Almost immediately, with a start, she sat up again. A thought had occurred to her, one not altogether comfortable. If she married Andrew, she'd become Lady Tantallon. And she wasn't sure she could live up to it.

Then she smiled to herself in the dark and lay back again. It didn't matter. Andrew was quite strong and wise enough to live up to it for both of them. And anyway, she wasn't really such a ninny. As she drifted comfortably off to sleep her father's voice came to her, as fond and gently bewildered as it had always been: "You aren't really a ninny, my pet. It's just that in company you will persist in behaving like one."

Next morning she should have had a riding lesson with Mr. Symonds, but she excused herself. She'd hoped to spend the time with Andrew, but she found he'd gone out early with the head shepherd, up onto the hill pastures to check the arrangements for the sheep-juicing, now less than a week away.

So she sought out Robert instead. She'd seen little of him since their stormy meeting in her great-aunt's room, and she was afraid she'd misjudged him. Certainly he'd done his best to help poor Melissa concerning Gordon Craig's invitation to the party.

Advised by old Meredith, she discovered him at last on his back under the motor car, tinkering with its insides. But he wriggled out readily enough when she spoke to him, and hurried away to wash his hands and face at the sink in one of the stables. He emerged a moment later, drying himself vigorously on a coarse striped towel.

" I say, coz—how about a game of croquet? Usually the lawn's like a bog, but I wouldn't be surprised if this spell of fine weather's dried it out."

Gracefully he swung an imaginary mallet. "Oh, do come on. I'm a positive wizard at it, and I haven't had a chance to show off for absolutely ages."

She laughed. " I'm afraid I'll give you a rotten game," she protested. " I haven't played since my school days."

" Doesn't matter in the least. Just close your eyes and tonk me to Kingdom Come. Do say you will."

She nodded.

" Champion. Champion. . . ."

As he rushed off through the castle, it was hard to believe that this and that other figure, brow-beating his mother, were one and the same. If he'd got his quick temper from Sir James, then he'd got his sense of fun from Lady Otranta.

The croquet equipment was in a small wooden summer-house. He hauled it all out, and set up the game. They started to play, two balls each. He played as well as he'd boasted he would, with flair and the sort of good luck that only true gamesmen attract to themselves, but he fooled around so much that Bridie, by plugging earnestly along, was able to keep up really quite well.

" Roquet!" he cried, swiping wildly and managing to hit his foot instead of the ball.

As time went on they played less, and chatted more. He was full of the coming party. One of the shepherds was a master fiddler, and there'd be Highland dancing. He crossed two croquet mallets on the grass and demonstrated the sword dance for her, hopping in and out as neatly as a cat. Bridie was reminded that Melissa had promised to teach her the reels, but that somehow nothing had come of it.

" Pooh on that," he said. " I tell you, all they do is prance round and round in ever decreasing circles."

He grabbed her hands and dragged her off, revolving faster and faster until he caught his foot in a croquet hoop and fell sprawling. He sat on the grass looking up at her, his head on one side. Suddenly he was serious. " You know," he said, " that brother of mine's a jolly lucky fellow."

She blushed, not quite sure if he meant what she thought he did.

" Oh, come now," he said, getting slowly to his feet. " You'd not expect that abominable old Peggy creature to keep a titbit like that to herself, now would you?"

She blushed still deeper. " Then it's . . . it's all round the castle?"

158

Dramatically he held up one finger. "If you listen very carefully you can hear the mice telling it to their children at this very moment."

He was so comical she had to laugh. But she was suddenly anxious all the same. "What about your mother?" she faltered.

"Dissolved in a flash of blue light and a thunder clap, I shouldn't wonder." He checked himself, seeing her expression. "Seriously though, as far as Mama is concerned, I've no idea. She might jump any way, or no way at all. Still, Andy's old enough to know his own mind, I'd say. And that's all that matters."

Bridie fell silent. His brother was indeed old enough to know his own mind. But she didn't care to tell him just how unhopeful that mind might be.

Robert picked up the mallets, and they got on with the game. He was as cheerful as ever, and even let her win. But somehow, with the reminder of all Andrew's painful misgivings, the fun had gone out of the game for her. When it was over she excused herself and went to her room. There she stood for a long time, staring thoughtfully down at the dry, sun-soaked trees. Then, to settle her mind, she took the cover off her fine green-and-gold Barlock and typed a short letter to Mr. Pugh-Hennessy, telling him she honestly believed now that he was wasting his money on her services. Lady Otranta would never write her memoirs—even her doctor said so.

Bridie went on to say that she was willing to return to London to report to him in person if he so wished, but that otherwise she would be staying on at Castle Tantallon for—her fingers hesitated, then rapidly tapped out the rest of the sentence—for a few weeks longer as a guest. She apologised briefly for her failure and suggested that he cancel Lady Otranta's contract. If he cared to write to her great-aunt himself she was sure that the old lady would be reasonable about the advance she had received.

Bridie read her letter through, ripped it from the machine, signed it, put it in an envelope which she addressed, and took it down to the box for out-going post in the entrance hall. She tucked it through the slot with a sigh of relief. That was one at least of her worries dealt with. Now it was past mid-day, and time to go and see Lady Otranta. In deference to Andrew's fears she would proceed cautiously with the old lady.

Her great-aunt was waiting for her, sitting in her black-upholstered chair, the inevitable bottle and glass on a table at her elbow, a book open upon her knee.

"Come in child, come in. I was beginning to think you had abandoned me."

"Not at all, Great-aunt." Bridie crossed the room and sat down in her usual place, very close to the old lady, who was so short-sighted as to be almost blind without her dark-rimmed lorgnettes. "It was just that I had a letter to——"

"It's no matter. You're here now. And I have come to a most important decision."

"Oh yes?" Bridie faltered, quailing inwardly. In spite of what Robert had told her, she'd still hoped she might be able to break the news of herself and Andrew to her great-aunt in her own way and in her own time. Clearly, however, old Peggy had forestalled her after all—and goodness only knew with what sort of garbled version.

"Yes, my dear." Lady Otranta closed the book on her knee with a snap, so that Bridie almost jumped. "I have decided to let you into the secrets of mind-reading. . . . Not that they're exactly secrets—this book explains everything for those who care to read it. But it's not a book in general circulation—and anyway, I understand that people these days use some completely different system. But this was the one Professor Salvador and I employed, and you've seen it in action for yourself. It was not unimpressive, I think."

Bridie couldn't believe her ears. Mind-reading? What on earth was her great-aunt thinking of? Had Peggy then said nothing to her of what she had seen down in the garden?

"I've felt a bit guilty," Lady Otranta went on, "ever since that little demonstration. You're very dear to me, and it didn't seem fair to leave you possibly believing in mystical powers that I certainly don't possess. Mystical powers, no. An excellent memory and a head for figures, yes."

Bridie had to stop the old lady. She was so full of herself and Andrew that she could not, positively *could* not, sit through some long and complicated explanation. " Forgive me, Great-aunt, but just before you tell me about the mind-reading, I wonder if I could—"

But she might just as well not have spoken. Lady Otranta, once launched, was virtually unstoppable. " Later, dear, later. . . ." she murmured, then returned to the attack with renewed vigour. " There are *trigger phrases*, you see. Twenty-six of them. One for each letter of the alphabet. And for twenty-six groups of words also. And in each group twenty-six words—colours, shapes, materials, and the sort of items that might reasonably be in the pockets of a member of the audience. That's six hundred and seventy-six words to be memorised, and in their correct order too."

She turned triumphantly to her great-niece, then peered closer. " You appear muddled, child," she accused. " And it's really very simple. Take any trigger phrase you like. *Come along now* : well, that's an easy one. It's the first one on the list, so it stands for the first letter of the alphabet. Which, as even you must be aware, Bridie, is A. Old Peggy used it, you may remember, when she asked me who was waiting outside. *Come along now*, she said so I knew at once that it must be someone whose name began with A. Therefore, Andrew."

In spite of herself, Bridie was intrigued. " What if there'd been two people it might have been whose names began with A?"

Lady Otranta clicked her tongue impatiently. " Then Peggy'd have gone on to give me the next letter in his name, of course. And the next after that, if necessary. *Hurry up,* she'd have said. Now that's the fourteenth trigger phrase. And the fourteenth letter of the alphabet is N. For D she'd have given me *Try harder*—that's the fourth trigger phrase. And so on. . . ."

Bridie thought she understood. " And there really are twenty-six of these phrases?"

"Certainly there are." The old lady closed her eyes and began to rattle them off. *"Come along now; Do your best; Now then; Try harder; I want to know; Concentrate; We want to know; We'd like to know. . . ."*

The words ran together insanely in Bridie's ears. "But surely," she interrupted, "you can't spell out everything? It would take too long. And someone might notice."

"Aha!" Lady Otranta opened her eyes, "That's where the lists come in. Phrase number one, for example, *Come along now*—that refers to list number one also. And list number one is colours and shapes, twenty-six of them. Yellow, green, blue, red, brown, pink, purple, black. . . . I needn't go on. First you're given your list number, then the number of the word upon that list. You understand?"

"I . . . I think so."

"Of course you do. For example, that piece of paper Peggy wanted me to guess. Now, 'paper' is word number twelve on list number three. So she gave me the two trigger phrases: first of all *Now then*, for the list, and then *Tell us* for the word. You can string the phrases together, you see. And nobody ever notices."

"It sounds like an awful lot to remember."

"And so it is, child. Twenty-six trigger phrases, and six hundred and seventy-six words. But I've never forgotten them. And neither has that disreputable old Peggy. She helped me to learn them, you see, when I was just beginning. Anyway, they're all here in Robert Houdin's book."

She held it up. "He should never have written it of course. I'm only glad dear Henri never lived to see it published. He'd have had a fit. But then, as I've said, it's all old stuff now. Goodness only knows what the young ones get up to these days. . . . I've never been to see them, you know. I don't think I could bear to."

She handed the book to Bridie who riffled through it, seeing page after page of bewildering lists and numbers. "I think you're wonderful to be able to remember so much," she said.

"The Incredible Madame Otranta?" Her great-aunt

smiled. "It's not really so wonderful. An actor learns many more words in the course of his training. Now, child, we'd better put that book away safely. You're privileged, my dear. I've never before let anyone—not even the boys—into my little secret."

She turned then to the little table close by her, poured whisky into her glass, and drank from it. "Take the book, Bridie, and put it in the drawer over there." She pointed to a little shallow glass specimen cabinet with solid sides, standing on four spindly legs. Bridie stared at it—the cabinet had a glass top and bottom and front and back, so that she could see right through to its transparent back. There was no sign of a drawer, nor room for one. But she carried the book over to it all the same—she'd learned enough in earlier visits to know that little in that room was what it seemed to be.

And indeed the cabinet, on very close inspection, proved to be yet another cunning deception. Inside, at the bottom of its glass front, a mirror sloped up diagonally to the back top corner, beautifully fitted against the solid sides and perfectly reflecting the triangular inside of the cabinet above it so that the space appeared both rectangular and perfectly transparent. While behind and beneath the mirror, as Bridie saw when she went round to the back of the cabinet, there was room for a tapering drawer quite big enough to accommodate the book her great-aunt had given her. Bridie stooped and put the book in and closed the drawer with a click.

"Well done, child. We'll make a magician of you yet." Lady Otranta nodded approvingly. "But now, my dear, if you don't mind, I'm just a little bit tired. Perhaps you would be good enough to call Peggy for me."

Bridie straightened her back, realising unhappily that she was being sent away. She'd said to her great-aunt none of the things that she'd intended to, and now she was being sent away. "But please," she protested, "please let me stay just a little bit longer. There's something very important I have to tell—"

The old lady interrupted her, beating furiously with her bony fists upon the arms of her chair. "Really, child, if you refuse pointblank to do as I say, I shall simply have to call the old fool myself!"

"Oh but please, Great-aunt," Bridie blurted out, "I . . .I love Andrew—I love him so much. And he loves me. And we—"

"Indeed?" Lady Otranta stared at her coldly. "I was afraid you were going to tell me some such nonsense. No tact, you young people. Can't take a hint. Can't take a hint at all." She groped for her stick and began pounding the floor with it. "Peggy? *Peggy*? Where are you, you great, fat, idle creature?"

Bridie felt wretched, understanding now, now that it was too late, what all that talk of mind-reading had really been about. Of course the old lady knew all about herself and Andrew. And she'd made it as plain as she could that, for some incomprehensible reason, she didn't want to discuss the matter.

Abruptly Lady Otranta paused in her pounding, and fixed Bridie with a blurred, uncertain eye. "You'll be hurt, m'dear. Give up the whole ridiculous notion—now, while there's still time. Take the advice of an old woman and look for a husband elsewhere."

"But—"

"And it's no use asking for explanations, because you won't get 'em. Not from me. Not now. . . . Stay here long enough, of course, and I expect you'll find out for yourself. And you won't like it. No—be wise, m'dear, and go back to London and try to forget that you ever even met the accursed Tantallons."

Her speech was slurred now as she began to pound again and call for Peggy. Bridie watched her dumbly, in utter bewilderment, until at last the fat old dresser, in her own good time, opened the door and sailed imperturbably in.

"Now, what's all this, Madame? Did I hear a little birdie singing?"

"God Almighty, woman, you did *not*." Lady Otranta flailed the air unsteadily with her stick. "You heard your wretched employer shouting herself hoarse for the want of a little simple attention."

Peggy caught the stick and removed it peaceably from the old lady's grasp. "Well, old Peggy's here now, so we won't be needing that, now will we?" She leaned it beside the fireplace. "And there's no call to get all aeriated. You're upsetting poor little Az Rah. Not to mention Miss Bridie there."

Surprisingly, this childish nonsense seemed to placate Lady Otranta. She reached again for the whisky and slopped some into her glass. "I'm fit for neither man nor beast," she muttered thickly. "If I stay here long enough perhaps someone'll be good enough to come along and wheel me away."

Suddenly she was near to tears. Peggy looked across at Bridie, caught her eye, and nodded in the direction of the door. "Now, Madame, we mustn't talk like that, must we? We know what Dr. Macnab said about feeling sorry for ourselves. Just you come along of me. Just you come along of old Peggy."

As Bridie backed from the room and closed the door her great-aunt was being hoisted gently to her feet. She didn't seem even to notice Bridie's going.

Outside in the small octagonal room with the lancet windows Bridie paused. If she hadn't actually seen Lady Otranta's rapid deterioration with her own eyes she would never have believed it possible. How much had the old lady drunk—half a tumblerful? Hardly more. Bridie knew little about such things, but could it really have been enough to have such a drastic effect? She gazed in puzzlement at the closed door. It struck her that her great-aunt might almost have been putting on that pitiful performance as a way of getting rid of her.

Acting on impulse, she returned to the door, quietly opened it a crack, and peered through. Lady Otranta, leaning heavily upon old Peggy and muttering incoherently, was being led away into her bedroom. Bridie closed the door guiltily. If her great-aunt was in truth putting on an act, it was clearly one that her devoted servant wasn't a party to.

And anyway, why? Why should Lady Otranta do such a thing? If she wanted Bridie to go away there were surely easier methods? Unless of course the performance was in fact aimed at Peggy, and not at her at all. Bridie thought back, seeming to remember other occasions very similar. The horrible scene with Andrew, for example, when only a few moments before her great-aunt had seemed so sane and sensible.

Even so, the question why was still unanswered. And anyway, yet another picture remained in her mind, that of old Peggy struggling with Lady Otranta's graceless, comatose body. That at least couldn't have been an act on the old lady's part, no matter what. No—the whole idea was quite ridiculous.

Slowly Bridie turned and made her way back to her room. For once its chintzy cosiness didn't comfort her. She sat on the bed, staring unhappily at her neat button boots. She didn't know which was better—to believe her great-aunt's drunkenness an act, or to believe it genuine. Either possibility was dismal in the extreme.

She lifted her eyes, took in her typewriter on the table by the window, just as she had left it. Her gaze moved idly away, then returned. The typewriter, she saw, was *not* just as she had left it. There was a piece of paper now wound crookedly onto the roller.

With a curious sense of foreboding she rose and went to the table. An uneven line of words was spelled out on the paper. She wound the paper out of the machine and stared at it. The message was clear, and unpleasant.

a word from a freind. go back to london. youll be sorry if youdont. i mean it.

Impulsively she crumpled the paper into a tight, angry ball. A friend, indeed! How dare he! Or she, perhaps . . .? She looked down at the paper in her hand, then smoothed it out and read the words again. They told her nothing, except that the writer was vicious and cowardly. She was trembling all over, both from fury and from a profound sense of shock. Still, after all these weeks, there was someone at the castle who disliked her enough to play this sort of cheap, cruel trick on her. Someone who offered courtesy to her face, possibly even affection. Who could it be?

Everybody knew she visited her great-aunt at mid-day. Everybody knew her room would be empty then, and un-

166

attended. Robert, Melissa, Duncan Symonds, Peggy, even dear old Meredith. It could be any one of them. Slowly she tore the paper into small pieces and threw them into her waste-paper basket.

It could have been any one of them, just as it could have been any one of them, she realised, who had staged the episode of the runaway car at the very beginning. They'd disliked her then, when they scarcely knew her, just as they disliked her now. She leaned against the table and closed her eyes. She couldn't honestly believe she was in any real danger. No— they simply wanted to frighten her. Well, they'd failed. If she felt anything, it was disgust. All the same, from now on she must be careful. She must watch and listen, and trust nobody.

Could she live like that? She had to. Certainly she wasn't going to give in and go running back to London. Lady Otranta needed her. And so, she believed, did Andrew. And, dear God, how much she needed Andrew.

Distantly she heard the sound of the gong for lunch. She went to the wash-stand, splashed water in her face, and dried it. Someone, no doubt, would be watching her to see signs of how well their evil trick had succeeded. She stooped in front of the mirror and tidied her hair, thrusting pins into it with savage determination. Come what may, she wouldn't give them the satisfaction. She'd show them she wasn't a Tantallon for nothing.

8

On Thursday the twenty-eighth of August the ferry from Kincardine across the Firth of Forth to Leith docks at three-thirty in the afternoon, the *Lord Morton*, was a little late in leaving. The delay was caused by the arrival on the jetty at the very last minute, just as the gangplank was being withdrawn, of the carriage and pair belonging to Sir James Tantallon.

It is doubtful, in fact, if the *Lord Morton* would have waited at all, had not the equipage been so well known in the district. Sir James was steward to Her Majesty's Stirlingshire estates, and for such a man mere ferry steamers—and even, upon occasion, the trains of the Great Northern Railway—were proud to suffer some slight delay.

So the man at the gangplank lowered it again, and waited respectfully. He saw Sir James and Lady Margaret descend from the carriage. He was to concede later that he had been surprised at this for, like most locals, he was well aware that Lady Margaret had not been seen abroad in the company of her husband for several months. He was not to know, of course, that the entire enterprise was the result of a long and painful confrontation between Sir James and his wife the previous evening.

Neither was he to know, as he saw Lady Margaret come towards him up the gangplank on the arm of her husband, that her lowered face and the copious veiling about it were also the outcome of that same long and painful confrontation. Lady Margaret had been first profoundly outraged and later profoundly ashamed and distressed by what Sir James had had to say to her. She was distressed still, and in fact near to weeping.

Evidence would be given later that she and her husband

had almost certainly had a quarrel, even on the way to the ferry. Their original intention, it seemed, had been to travel by train to Stirling and then on down to Edinburgh, on account of Sir James' ill health and consequent dislike of the ferry crossing. Reaching the nearest station to Castle Tantallon, however, they had apparently changed their minds and made posthaste for the jetty at Kincardine instead. Upon being pressed in court to give a reason for this, Sir James had said the decision was entirely his: since the weather was so exceptionally fine and calm he had chosen to spare his wife the tedious train journey and go by boat after all.

This explanation for such a curiously last-minute reversal was generally accepted to be a thoroughly gentlemanly attempt to add nothing further to his wife's already considerable reputation for selfishness and ill-humour.

Be that as it may, once at the Kincardine jetty the couple went quickly aboard the *Lord Norton* and retired at once to her First Class main saloon, lavishly appointed with Greek carved pilasters and alcoves panelled in solid oak, while the gangplank was brought back on board and the ship began to reverse away from the jetty, her paddles thrashing energetically. She made a lot of smoke that afternoon, the delay having put the engine room chief artificer into a thoroughly bad humour.

The next person to report seeing Sir James Tantallon and his wife was the First Class saloon steward. He brought the couple tea at approximately four o'clock and was not able to say that he remembered anything strange about them. They were quiet, certainly, and did not seem to be talking to each other. But that was often the way with the gentry.

The *Lord Morton* passed Grangemouth and the ironworks at Bo'ness, sailed under the future site of the stupendous Forth Bridge, stopped briefly at South Queensferry as was her custom, then skirted the rocky islet of Inch Garvie and set out across the Firth for the harbour at Leith.

It was as the paddle steamer was navigating the narrows by Inch Garvie that several people, all of them fellow First Class passengers, reported seeing Sir James Tantallon and his wife walking together upon the upper promenade deck. They leaned on the starboard rail and, although they were not seen to communicate, they appeared to share an interest in the island and in the ruined castle which stood upon it. The water was calm, and they seem to have stayed there for most of the rest of the voyage, sheltered by the ship's superstructure from the coolish easterly breeze that was blowing that day.

At one moment, when the ship was nearing her destination, it is thought that Lady Margaret went briefly below decks. But she quickly returned, and the reason for her going was discreetly not enquired into. The ladies' rest room was just aft of the main companionway.

The next time the couple's whereabouts can reliably be established is not until the *Lord Morton* was backing up in the deep water outside Leith docks. By then they were separated, Sir James being on the promenade just forward of the funnel and wheelhouse, while his wife was out on the observation platform above the starboard paddle casing. This was an unusual position for her, since the *Lord Morton* had by then turned her port side to the Leith shore, and most passengers therefore tended to crowd to that side of the ship. So much so, in fact, that the Master stated it was not unusual for steamers to be in danger of capsizing, on account of the sudden redistribution of weight. This was why, he hastened to add, all ships of the Galloway Line were designed with great reserves of lateral stability.

No satisfactory explanation was ever found for Lady Margaret's going out onto the observation platform. A Miss Agatha Tweedie claimed it was on account of a furious argument she had witnessed between Sir James and his wife, but he denied this strenuously and, upon cross-examination, Miss Tweedie was disclosed to be not only rather short-sighted but also exceedingly deaf.

Suddenly a scream was heard, even above the pounding

of the *Lord Morton*'s engines. Many pairs of eyes were turned at once in its direction, in time to see Lady Margaret totter precariously over the rail, hesitate for one breathtaking moment, and then disappear from sight. A combined gasp of horror went up from all the onlookers. As one man they rushed across to the starboard side of the ship, while the Master in his wheelhouse frantically rang down to stop the engines.

The *Lord Morton* slowed to a halt, swinging gently on the tide. Afterwards at least a dozen witnesses were prepared to swear that nobody had been within a good thirty feet of Lady Margaret at the moment of her falling. Certainly Sir James had been nowhere near her—the ship's master himself was prepared to vouch for that, since the nobleman had been clearly in sight in front of his wheelhouse for around a quarter of an hour before the catastrophe.

As to the reason for Lady Margaret having fallen, the theory was put forward at the inquest on her death that the wind had caught her elaborate hat and veil, and that in reaching for them she had leant out too far and overbalanced. But since nobody could be found who had actually been watching her before the moment of her scream, this remained no more than a theory, plausible but unproven.

Within a few seconds of her screaming, however, at least a hundred people were leaning over the *Lord Morton*'s starboard rail, staring avidly down into the murky water. Some of them, no doubt, were expecting—nay, hoping—to see the bloody, mutilated corpse of the poor wretched woman, for the paddles of the ship had been backing up on maximum power at the time of the tragedy. In the event they saw nothing of the sort—simply her hat and cloak floating on the turbulent waters. Her body had disappeared completely, drawn down, no doubt, by the powerful currents prevailing in the Firth at that stage of the tide.

Rowing-boats put out from the harbour, and the search for a body was continued unsuccessfully for several hours. Thereafter a watch was kept along the shores of the Firth of Forth for many weeks, but the remains of Lady Margaret were never recovered. This was not, according to expert local opinion, an unusual circumstance. The tides were strong, and the currents unpredictable. Many poor souls had been lost that way, and their bodies denied a decent, Christian burial.

It was suggested at the subsequent inquest that the behaviour of Sir James Tantallon immediately following the accident had hardly been as grief-stricken as might have been thought suitable. But that is neither here nor there. Others, more charitable, privately considered that his dignity and self-control were no more than might be expected of a Scottish gentleman. Furthermore, since it was generally accepted that the marriage of Sir James and Lady Margaret had hardly been a happy one, surely it redounded to his credit that he did not hypocritically pretend a grief he did not feel?

He behaved, in fact, with complete propriety, going into full mourning for a twelvemonth and receiving the sympathetic understanding not only of his friends but of Queen Victoria herself. Admittedly, no more than another two months after the end of the mourning period, he remarried —and chose for the second Lady Tantallon a young person with the most disreputable theatrical connections. (Indeed, there were those who wondered how he could even have come to make her acquaintance, and him in mourning too.) But the gentry have always been allowed a certain latitude in these matters. And besides, since the Queen herself was thought to be on the point of accepting the second Lady Tantallon, what else could honest Scottish folk do but go along with her? In public, at least. . . .

*　　　*　　　*

'go back to london. youll be sorry if youdont. . . .' The threat was clear enough. In the days that immediately followed her finding the message on the roller of her typewriter, therefore, Bridie was wary. She remembered the runaway motor car and suspected that there might be another such attempt to frighten her off. At night she locked the door to her bedroom. And when she went about the castle she did her best always to keep one eye unobtrusively cocked over her shoulder.

As time went by, however, and nothing out of the ordinary occurred, she began to think her anxiety a little overdone—even ridiculous. All around her, life at the castle seemed to be going on just as it had before, growing slowly in momentum as it built up to the party being held on the Saturday night after the last of the Tantallon flocks had been dipped. Dancing lessons were started in earnest with Melissa, happy hours spent in the music room, learning the complex patterns of the reels. Menus were discussed, and plans made for cheering up the dismal castle rooms with festive decorations, flowers and branches of bright autumn leaves.

Meanwhile, answer had come from London to her letter to Mr. Pugh-Hennessy. He begged her to reconsider. He still had faith in her, he said. She mustn't give up. The Tantallon memoirs were important to him. He had, he confessed vaguely, giving no further explanation, a certain *personal interest* in them. She must persevere with her great-aunt. Rome, he said, wasn't built in a day.

She sighed, and put his letter to one side, and immediately, defensively, forgot all about it. She had, after all, other matters on her mind.

She'd told nobody of the threatening message—not even Andrew. It would only worry him to no avail, she thought. And anyway, as the days passed, she began to regard it less and less seriously. Certainly, watching the people she had first suspected, not one of them seemed capable of such a squalid, cruel trick. It was a vain threat, childish and without foundation. There were others at the castle, servants she had scarcely spoken to, who might have tapped it out on the spur of the moment, perhaps working off some minor secret grudge against the family. If its purpose had been to upset her, then temporarily it had succeeded. But not any more.

She *had* described to Andrew, however, his mother's reaction to the news of their love for one another. He'd been neither surprised nor particularly distressed. " It could have been a great deal worse," he told her. " If we bide our time and play things carefully, she's sure to come round before very long. And then—oh, Bridie, the life we'll have. So much to do, so much to show you. A mountain stream at sunrise . . . the hills purple with heather . . . Scotland's a wonderful country, my dear."

He kissed her then and she clung to him, forgetting everything in the excitement and magic of his love.

Even the weather remained kind to the lovers, an Indian Summer rare in those stormy northern regions, the first day of the sheep-juicing dawning bright and clear. Soon after breakfast Bridie walked up through the woods to watch, in the company of Robert and Melissa. The walk was long and steep, but finally they left the trees and came out on a huge curve of open hillside, softly grassed, divided into fields by snaking walls of massive black, wind-scoured stones. It was a high, wild place, as boundless as the infinite blue dome of the sky above, and today a busy, noisy, crowded place also.

Sheep, more than Bridie would have thought possible, seemingly thousand upon thousand of them, covered the hillside in a great shifting carpet, restless as treetops in a summer wind. Among them men and dogs moved ceaselessly, grouping them, funnelling them steadily down from field to field, then on through a narrowing pathway of hurdles to where the long wooden sheep trough waited, a gigantic cauldron bubbling over a fierce wood fire close by, sending out powerful fumes of boiling soap and tobacco.

Duncan Symonds stood at one side of the trough, Andrew at the other, their shirts open and their sleeves rolled up, heaving the sheep in one by one, dunking them unceremoniously then urging them on their way. They emerged, suddenly skinny-looking, on ridiculous little stick legs, and ran, protesting bitterly all the way, down to a lower paddock where they huddled together, pressed pathetically against their fellows in its furthermost corner. Already both men were sodden and mud-streaked, their voices hoarse as they shouted and prodded at the struggling animals. But there was laughter also, and a rough comradeship in which was included every single man on the busy hillside.

Bridie watched entranced, proud to see how Andrew—Sir Andrew, Laird of Tantallon—laboured willingly alongside his men, and was accepted by them. Often, in their conversations, he had told her of his father's training, how they had worked the estate together during the old man's final years, getting to know every shepherd, every woodsman, learning their skills. And here was the proof of it. She wished that his mother could see him now. And Duncan—what excuse was there here for his sly deferring to the old lady's jealous will?

Robert touched her arm. " Who'd be the artistic one now?" he said, pointing. " There's glory for you."

Bridie turned on him, suspecting mockery. But there'd been no bitterness in his voice, and there was none in his expression either—only unashamed admiration.

" Why not take off your jacket and go and join them?" she teased.

" What—and end up with a smudge on my nose and blisters? No thank you!" He laughed. " Mind you, that's what 'Lissa here would do, if she were a man. Wouldn't you, 'Lissa?"

His half-sister's eyes were bright with the day's excitement. " Maybe I would. . . . But it'd be a dull old world if we were all the same. And besides, you can't talk—you don't mind what sort of a state you get yourself into, tinkering with that rotten motor car."

He put an affectionate arm round her waist, smiled across at Bridie. " The thing is, fair coz, to know your limitations. I know mine. And the really rough work I leave to Andrew. He's so good at it, you see."

She turned back to the hectic scene round the sheep trough, Andrew joking now in Gaelic with the boy who stoked the fire beneath the cauldron, then stooping to lift a bedraggled ram bodily out onto the churned-up grass, the muscles of his shoulders straining mightily beneath his sodden, clinging shirt. Yes, she thought joyfully, he *was* good at it. Remembering his fear that she might think him weak she knew now, more than ever, how foolish that had been. He was *strong*—as strong as he was gentle.

At eleven the men broke for bread and cheese, and a great brew of scalding, milkless tea. Andrew came over to join them, Duncan's dog Noble at his heels. But he didn't linger.

"It's hot, wet work," he said, cheerfully wringing out his shirt tails, "and I'm not really fit for the fine company. Anyway, there's young MacNeil over there I must have a word with. He's tipped to win the Lowland sheep-dog trials, so they tell me. . . ." And he was off again, taking with him an undeniably powerful stench of drenched fleeces and tobacco water.

And so it went on every day that week, Andrew out on the high hillside from dawn to dusk, and Bridie trudging up, alone now, to watch for an hour or so, quietly, from the edge of the trees. She never tired of the ceaseless activity, the dark shapes of the sheep-dogs crouching and darting across the trampled grass, the men whistling their strange sharp signals, the shouts and splashes from the sheep-trough, the steam rising from man and beast alike in the still, cool air, and above it all the silent, soaring spaces of the pale autumn sky.

This, then, was the shape nature gave to the seasons at Castle Tantallon. This, and the spring shearing. She prayed that she'd be here to see that also. A shape to the seasons, and a shape to life itself—her life and Andrew's. Next year. And the year after that. And the year after that as well. A mountain stream at sunrise . . . the hills purple with heather. . . .

Then, on the morning of the day before the party, Melissa came knocking early at Bridie's bedroom door. She wanted, she said, to talk about what the two of them were to wear the following evening. They needed to be sure, she explained, that they neither clashed nor went in anything too similar.

Bridie could have hugged her, since she recognised the excuse for what it was—the dearest, most tactful way of offering assistance. She herself had been quite resigned to wearing her solitary evening dress—the one with the pie-frill collar and the little puff sleeves—yet again. But Melissa must have suspected from its regular appearances on every single night of her visit that it was the only one she possessed,

176

and have determined therefore, as discreetly as she was able, to do something about it.

Bridie admitted happily to her predicament. There was no shame, after all, in being poor—her years with her father had taught her that. And besides, as he had often pointed out, poverty gave other people the opportunity to be generous, and there was no experience in the world more delightful than to be able to exercise one's natural generosity.

Melissa, certainly, was delighted. She whisked Bridie off at once to her own room at the other end of the corridor, where the two of them spent a very pleasant hour or so sorting through the clothes of countless different styles and colours that tumbled from her cupboards.

" I know I'm taller than you," she commented excitedly, " and a bit more up and down. But once we've chosen something, old Peggy'll fix it. Whatever else she may be, she's a positive wizard when it comes to giving a little and taking a little."

She broke off, staring rather shame-facedly round at all the dresses spread out on the furniture. " Goodness knows what I ever thought I needed all this stuff for," she muttered. " Mama *would* get them for me—and I'm such a squirrel, you know—can never bear to part with anything. Why, some of these must date right back as far as—"

She stopped abruptly, growing suddenly tense. Then she shrugged. " Oh, eleven years at least," she finished, with an attempt at lightness.

For a moment Bridie was thoughtful. The evasion was too clear to be easily overlooked. She wondered at its reason. Eleven years ago her cousin would have been only eighteen. And it had been then, she suddenly realised, in 1896, that the accident to Andrew's foot had occurred in the castle gun-room. An unhappy memory? Nothing more than that? No, Bridie was convinced now that her earlier suspicions had been correct. That was indeed the secret in Melissa's life that made her so afraid of her step-mother's memoirs—she had in some tragic way been responsible for Andrew's injury, and the old lady knew it.

Bridie looked up, came near to speaking. But the moment slipped by, and Melissa was holding up another dress, this time in pale blue silk, and Bridie told herself that her cousin's past was anyway none of her business. When Melissa wanted to tell her about it she would. And to try to press her before she was ready would be both tasteless and cruel.

From all the dresses they chose finally a yellow spotted muslin over the palest green cotton, that would go well with Bridie's rich auburn hair and pale complexion, while her dark-haired cousin would wear a striped green and gold taffeta. They took Bridie's dress along to Peggy and cajoled the old woman into making the necessary alterations.

She stood Bridie up on a stool and slashed at the dress with tailor's chalk. "Needed termorrer, is it?" she snorted, her mouth full of pins. "Fat chance of that, I must say. I'm not ezzackly at the beck and call of you young ladies. It's Madame what needs me. You lot can go hang."

"Oh, Peggy dear, it only needs the tiniest bit doing," Melissa wheedled. "And Mama's always saying how clever you are with your needle. How you saved her life a hundred times, back in your theatrical days."

Peggy glared at her over her spectacles. "I'll have you know, Miss Melissa, as how flattery won't get you nowheres."

It did, however. In the end it got old Peggy to promise to have the dress ready for a fitting that same night. Bridie thanked her profusely, and thanked Melissa too.

"Oh, stuff," her cousin muttered. "The main thing is, you'll be the belle of the ball. You'll see—Andrew won't be able to take his eyes off you."

At this Bridie glanced anxiously in Peggy's direction. But the old dresser was busy matching cottons and either had not heard or was pretending for her own mysterious reasons not to have. And mercifully she appeared to bear Bridie no grudge either—even though she must have known by then that her dramatic warning had been ignored.

Hardly had Bridie finished changing back into her skirt and blouse before Duncan Symonds came through from Lady Tantallon's rooms, the accounts folder as usual under his arm.

She was horrified—a moment earlier and he'd have caught her in her chemise and petticoat. Not, she decided, that he was a man to make much of such an unexciting spectacle. He was far too wise and avuncular for that.

Suddenly she realised how very little she knew about Mr. Symonds' private circumstances. When he had passed civilly through and gone on about his business, she turned to Melissa. "Is Duncan married?" she asked. "I remember him telling me once he had his own quarters."

"Duncan married? Good Lord, no." Melissa gave one of her short, sharp laughs. "He's the born bachelor, I'd say. Lives over the stable block. Keeps his place like a captain's cabin. Clean as a pin. You should just see it."

Old Peggy looked sharply up from the mass of spotted muslin on her lap. "Mind you, there's them as would say he *was* married, though. In all but name, that is. To Madame Otranta."

There was a shocked silence. Melissa was the first to break it, smiling coldly. "What a disgraceful thing to say, Peggy. I suppose it's all that John Brown nonsense Mama's been filling you up with. Once and for all, Peggy, Mama is *not* Queen Victoria, and poor Duncan is *not* John Brown."

"Nonsense, is it?" The old woman tugged angrily at her needlework. "You've not seen what I have. Diaries. The actual diaries. Folks said as they was destroyed, and destroyed they should of been too. Let 'em both rest in peace, the poor souls—that's what I say."

Melissa frowned. "Diaries? What diaries are these? Mama's? Are you talking about her *memoirs*? Do explain yourself, for goodness' sake."

"Not me. I knows what I knows. And I reckon I've said too much, as it is." At which the fat old dresser bent over her work and began to whistle determinedly and tunelessly between her few remaining teeth, refusing utterly to say another word.

With an effort Melissa controlled her temper and turned to Bridie. "I do hope you know Mama well enough not to believe—"

"Of course I do." Bridie patted her cousin's arm. "Anyway, your mother'll be expecting me about now. Why don't we go in together?"

And before Melissa could protest she'd dragged her across to Lady Otranta's door and knocked upon it and gone in, leaving Peggy to her resentful, unmelodious whistling.

Lady Otranta was still in bed, sitting up among all the elaborate oriental furnishings, her pale face flushed, her eyes bright as if with some secret excitement. "*Two* visitors? Come in, come in. What a pleasant surprise."

Bridie listened for sarcasm in her voice, but heard none. "Melissa's lent me a dress for tomorrow," she explained. "We've just been getting Peggy to alter it a bit."

"That was thoughtful of you, Melissa, but then, you always were a thoughtful girl. And such a help when the boys were little." She patted the heavy crimson covers of the bed. "Come here where I can see you, and tell me about the dress you've chosen for your city cousin."

Melissa sat down and began to describe it. Bridie wandered away to the window. She was pleased to see Lady Otranta and her step-daughter getting on so well together. It happened all too seldom. Mostly the old lady lived a life completely isolated from her family. That this was by her own doing was neither here nor there.

"The yellow muslin? I remember it well. Wasn't that the dress you wore when your dear father was given the freedom of the city?"

Melissa laughed gently. "I don't honestly think so, Mama. That was twenty years ago at least. I can't have been more than eight."

". . . And the little boys wore sailor suits and looked *so* enchanting. . . . Then the muslin must be what you were presented to Her Majesty in—in '96. Or was it '97?"

Bridie leaned by the window, smiling quietly to herself. The aspidistra on the table close beside her caught her eyes. It was looking really quite extraordinarily sickly. Absent-mindedly she felt the soil in its pot—perhaps it wasn't getting enough water. No, the soil felt moist enough.

"You know, 'Lissa, between you and me, I was never quite sure if the muslin suited you. With your colouring, you see, I thought you could get away with bolder colours. But that wretched French dressmaker insisted. What was her name, now? Latouche? Labouche? Something like that. . . ."

Bridie took out her handkerchief and wiped her fingers. Then she stared at the grains of soil upon the linen. A faint but most curious smell was rising from them. She lifted her handkerchief to her nose and sniffed. Then she dug down into the pot with a sudden urgent movement, brought more soil out between finger and thumb, and sniffed again.

There could be no doubt about it. The soil in the pot positively reeked of whisky.

She stepped back a pace, bewildered. Behind her the voices of her cousin and great-aunt rose and fell peacefully. She peered at the plant—clearly it was no wonder that the poor thing was dying. But why *whisky*, of all things?

Until suddenly, astonishingly, the answer became clear. If a person wished to appear to be drinking far more than she actually was, there were only a limited number of places in which to dispose of the surplus spirits. The fire was one, of course—and a good one too. But what if, as in the mornings recently, the fire was not yet lighted? Where then could a person go to tip a glass or two, when she was sure no one was looking?

Always assuming, of course, that any person would be eccentric enough to wish to create such an impression of excessive drinking in the first place. . . .

*　　　*　　　*

I have cheated in my story, of course, just a little. With so many other deceits in my life, I feel sure that just one more will make no difference. By describing the events on board the *Lord Morton* that afternoon in August 1878 principally from the point of view of the world at large, however, I have managed to tell rather less than half the truth.

The story in fact begins two days earlier, on Tuesday

the twenty-sixth of August. On that day I took a First Class return journey across the Firth on the *Lord Morton*, alone. My plan, worked out in theory and from a casual observation of Galloway Line paddle steamers while they were in Leith harbour, needed testing. In particular I wanted to inspect the view from the observation platforms above the *Lord Morton*'s paddle casings, and accordingly I spent a long time upon each one of them, staring apprehensively down the ship's side at the frothing water below. Eventually I decided that my plan was feasible, if only just. And I reported as much to a haggard Sir James that same evening.

The Wednesday, being a matinee day, was uneventful. Uneventful for me, that is. For Jamie, poor man, it was the day on which he faced his wife with what he had discovered, and laid the alternatives for her future clearly before her. Either she fell in with his wishes or he went straight to the police. Needless to say, after a predictable amount of bluster and an equally predictable amount of weeping, she agreed to the former. I never questioned him about the confrontation—it was enough to me that it should have taken place, and with a satisfactory outcome.

Early on Thursday morning, wearing a long, light grey travelling cloak and a straw boater, I took a second return ticket on the *Lord Morton*, booking a First Class cabin at the same time. I went ashore at South Queensferry, walked to the railway station there, boarding the eleven thirty-seven train bound for Stirling, which I left at Alloa. A short walk around that town to purchase a newspaper was enough to convince me that it was a place to which I would never wish to return.

Two o'clock found me again at the station, buying a Second Class ticket to Aberdeen. I then repaired to the Ladies' Waiting Room, removed my cloak and hat, and placed both, together with the ticket to Aberdeen, on a bench just inside the door. Thereafter I sat down behind my newspaper in the farthest corner and did not emerge again for nearly half an hour.

Obviously the entire success of my plan depended upon Alloa railway station being more or less deserted on a Thursday afternoon between two and two-thirty. No trains were due during that time, so it was a reasonable enough possibility. And, as things turned out, the station *was* deserted. Quite deserted. And there is nothing, I believe, quite so deserted as a deserted railway station.

I didn't look up when the waiting room door banged open. Neither did I make an effort to peer round my newspaper while certain small rustlings took place. I had no wish to see Sir James' wife and I imagine she felt the same about me.

Only when the door had banged shut again behind her did I lay my newspaper carefully down beside me, get slowly to my feet, and move to the bench on which I had left my cloak and hat and ticket. In their place lay a cloak of far richer material, blue, and a broad, stolid hat with a great deal of veiling. These I picked up and, stifling my disgust, put on. They smelt of *her*. It was, I swear, the hardest part of the whole enterprise, though it took but a second.

Tying the veil firmly about my face, I left the waiting room. James was ready for me a short distance off, while away down at the far end of the platform stood a passable imitation of myself, in light grey cloak and straw boater, her back resolutely turned upon us both.

The rest is obvious. James and I hurried back to the coach. I climbed in, my head averted, while James shouted instructions to the coachman. He naturally asked no questions but set off immediately at a good pace, there being scarcely more than an hour in which to cover the ten miles or so back to Kincardine.

It was I, therefore, who accompanied Sir James onto the *Lord Morton*, and not his wife. She, the wretched woman, was by then well on her way to Aberdeen, to a new identity and a new life, whatever she cared to make of it. It was I also who took tea with Sir James in the First Class saloon. It was I who stood with him by the starboard rail. And it was I who climbed up onto the observation platform as the ship approached Leith harbour.

Observers who claimed later that we spoke little during the voyage were right. There was little to be said. We were launched irretrievably upon a desperate enterprise. And whatever words might be necessary between us had already been said.

A small technical digression is now necessary. The observation platforms on the *Lord Morton* overhung the paddle casings by perhaps three feet. Beneath them the sides of the hull swelled to a broad strip called, I believe, a rubbing strake. Above this strake, and some five feet below the platform, were the port-holes to the First Class cabins. By now, if I have made myself clear, the most desperate part of the entire desperate affair will be apparent.

I had previously, in the person of myself, secured the cabin immediately below the platform. And I had also, during the crossing with Sir James, slipped below briefly to make sure that its port-hole was firmly open. It was a fitting nearly two feet in diameter—a squeeze, certainly, but for a slim young woman with Professor Salvador's training behind her, no very serious problem.

The rest, as they say, is history. There was a nasty moment, admittedly, when the heavy stuff of my borrowed cloak encumbered my legs so that I almost missed my footing. But I overcame that, cowered briefly on the rubbing strake beneath the platform, just long enough to shed both cloak and hat into the water below, and then dived precipitately, head first through the open port-hole and onto the bunk within.

I lay there, panting. Images passed before my eyes, images of knife-edged paddle blades that flashed by only inches from my feet. Images of what would have happened had I slipped. But I had not slipped.

Briskly I got to the floor, smoothed my rumpled dress and tidied my hair in the mahogany-framed mirror above the washbasin. Then I left the cabin, ran up the main companionway, and unobtrusively joined the people hurrying to see what had become of the poor woman who—so appeared to be the general uncharitable consensus—had just committed suicide off the starboard observation platform.

It must be said, of course, that had the question ever been asked whether or not I, in the person of myself, had ever actually boarded the *Lord Morton* in Kincardine or anywhere else, nobody would have been able to give a definite answer. But the question was never asked. Indeed, why should it have been? The reasonable assumption has to be that if a person is seen to leave a ship, then she must necessarily have come aboard it first. And it is certainly possible that I was seen to leave the *Lord Morton*. Although frankly, in view of the crowds and the general commotion, I very much doubt it.

And as for the light grey travelling cloak and straw boater in which I had set out that morning—and which by then were well on their way to Aberdeen—who in the world was likely to ask after them? Except dear Peggy. And she, the pet, would believe just about anything I told her. . . .

*   *   *

Shoes. Green shoes. A pair of green shoes. If Bridie's evening ensemble were to be complete, this was the one thing she did not have. The one thing, that is, that could neither be supplied from the built-in resources of the castle nor from the single, turpentine-smelling general shop down in Kincardine. Her cousin Melissa might have a pair—after all, she'd have needed some to go with the dress, back whenever it was—but Melissa's feet were luckily at least three sizes too big.

No—if one wanted an excuse to go to Edinburgh, and nowhere else would do, then green shoes were a positive brainwave.

The thought of going to Edinburgh had not come to Bridie at once. She had stood in her great-aunt's bedroom, quite paralysed, seemingly for hours, listening to the inconsequential chatter of her cousin and the old lady, staring blankly at the grains of whisky-sodden earth still clinging to her thumb and forefinger. She had no idea what to do, who to turn to, where to go. Certainly she had toyed before with the idea that her great-aunt's drunkenness might be a pretence. But to have proof of this suddenly forced upon her. . . . She was appalled. Even slightly disgusted.

Somehow, when it was expected of her, she joined in the chatter. And somehow she watched without comment while Lady Otranta went through the now familiar ritual of filling her glass, drinking from it (quite moderately, in fact), and becoming progressively more incoherent. And somehow, finally, she made her escape from the room, she and Melissa together.

She went to her bedroom. Once there, she was able to think more clearly. And she thought, almost at once, of Dr. Macnab. He'd asked her to go to him. *If there's ever anything that does not seem to you to . . . as it were, to make sense,* he'd said. And this latest discovery made no sense at all.

She felt a sudden spasm of guilt, wondering why it was the doctor she was planning to turn to, rather than Andrew. Should he not be the first to learn that his mother was after all not the drunkard everyone thought her? Would he not be delighted? Bridie thought not. It explained nothing. Rather, it raised a whole host of new and uncomfortable questions.

No, she must confide first in Dr. Macnab. She trusted him. Only after that, armed with his expert opinion, would she go to Andrew.

The doctor's card was in a drawer. She got it out and stared at it. And at once the problem was forced in upon her of how to find an excuse for going alone to Edinburgh that everyone would accept. She must go at once. To delay would be unbearable. She could make the journey the following morning, and still be back in time for the party. But why? What reason could she possibly give?

It was then, with the gong sounding below her for lunch, that the inspiration came to her. The party . . . her dress . . . the shoes she'd need to go with it. Shoes from one of the smart Edinburgh shops. Green shoes.

186

Bracing herself, she raised the question of her shoes at lunch.

"*Shoes?*" Robert demanded. "Hoity-toity—whatever's wrong with the ones you're wearing? Very sensible for dancing in, I'd say."

He knew the answer to his question very well, of course, but it took the full force of Melissa's indignation to get him admit it. So the journey was fixed, by the eight-thirty ferry in the morning and then back from Leith at two. Then, to Bridie's consternation, Melissa decided to go with her—to make sure Bridie wasn't swindled, she said.

It was Andrew who came unwittingly to Bridie's rescue. "I'm sorry to be a bore, 'Lissa, but we really can't spare you. Not with all the arrangements for the party to be seen to. I'm sure Bridie'll be able to manage." He turned to her. "You don't mind, do you, my dear?"

Guiltily Bridie shook her head. Deceiving him, deceiving all of them, seemed suddenly so cheap and shoddy.

But Melissa gave one of her short sharp laughs. "You're quite right, of course, Andy. We all know what cook's like with sherry trifle. If I let her loose we'll have the shepherds' wives keeling over like ninepins before the evening's half done."

So the question was settled and Bridie was driven down to the ferry the following morning by Duncan Symonds.

He stopped on the road by the jetty and pointed across at the dark clouds massing above the distant shore line. "Yon marks the end o' the fine weather, I'm thinking. It's a mercy the last o' the sheep'll be juiced before the morning's out." He reached behind the motor car's front seat and produced a large umbrella. "You'd best be taking this, Mistress Bridie. When the wet comes down it'll be no wee bit drizzle."

Bridie thanked him and took the umbrella. The dog, Noble, sitting on the floor between them, whined and placed his head upon Bridie's knee. Absentmindedly she patted his head. The steamer was waiting at the jetty, the *Stirling Castle*, a ship very similar, she thought, to the one from which Lady Margaret Tantallon had fallen to her death some thirty years before.

"I'll be here to meet the two o'clock from Leith," Mr. Symonds told her. "So you mind you're on board her."

She thanked him again, got out of the motor car, and walked away down the jetty. A sharp breeze was coming in from the sea, blowing her skirts against her knees and lifting the water of the Firth into steep little waves. She went aboard just as the *Stirling Castle* blew her five minute whistle. Observing that she appeared to be the only person boarding at Kincardine, she wondered if this meant that other, wiser people were staying at home on account of the weather. She hoped not. But it couldn't be helped, even if they were. She had to go to Edinburgh that day. She had to.

Throughout the crossing the sky darkened and the wind grew stronger. But the waves were still short, and the *Stirling Castle* rode them easily. As the ship passed under the Forth Bridge Bridie stared wonderingly up at its soaring girders. On her way out a month before, in the company of Duncan Symonds, its sheer size had so frightened her that she'd scarcely dared to look. Now she saw three men perched high above her, painting the intricate web of metal. They seemed tiny and dangerously wind-swept, their task apparently without end. Sooner them than her, she thought.

At the Leith West Pier she took a horse cab direct to Dr. Macnab's address. The fare would be more than she cared to afford, but the time saved would be worth it. She had a lot to get through if she was to see the doctor and also buy the shoes that were her excuse for going. And at least the horse cabs were cheaper than the motor taxis.

The cab jolted along cobbled streets. In side alleyways she could see little barefoot boys scrambling in the gutters, tossing marbles, their cries reaching her ears even above the bustle and clatter of the streets. *Keps! Nae Keps! Nae high nickle!* She supposed it was English they were speaking, but it might just as well have been a foreign language. And there were ragged girls playing hop-scotch, their shrill chanting equally incomprehensible. Her stay at Castle Tantallon had made her forget what a strange and alien place Scotland really was.

They came to Edinburgh, to the staid black terraces and crescents she remembered from her previous journey. On a corner by Methven Simpson's Pianola Circulating Library they turned sharply left, up a steep incline to St. George's Square, the horse's hooves slipping on the polished stones. They were overtaken by a jerky little motor taxi, and its driver hooted derisively. She'd always known she hated the horrid, smelly, noisy things.

Then the cab stopped and they had arrived. She glanced at her watch: the time was eleven-fifteen. She heaved a sigh of relief. Between ten and mid-day, Dr. Macnab had said.

As the first large drops of rain were spotting the pavement, Bridie paid off the cab, knocked at the door of number twelve, and was admitted. She gave her name to the uniformed maid, and her umbrella, and was shown into a vast and dingy waiting room, quite empty, its heavy mahogany table set neatly with staggered yellowing rows of *Punch* and the *Illustrated London News*. She sat herself on the very edge of a hard, red leather dining chair. She waited.

When her name was called she jumped. Then she pulled herself together and followed the maid down a corridor and into Dr. Macnab's consulting room.

"Mistress Bridie Tantallon," the maid announced, then departed, closing the door behind her. Bridie stood where she'd been put, fidgeting nervously.

The doctor majestically laid down the paper he was reading, rose from his desk, and progressed towards her across the faded carpet. "Miss Tantallon—I'm truly delighted to see you."

He certainly appeared delighted—though whether at seeing her or at the glories of his own person Bridie was far from certain. She wished she hadn't come.

"Sit you down, Miss Tantallon. Sit you down." He held a chair for her. Then he returned to his desk. "Would you forgive me for just one minute? I was scanning the daily Hospital Bulletin." He picked up the paper again, the *Edinburgh Gazette*. "There's a patient of mine—number three seven two, I believe. I was interested to see how she was progressing. . . ."

"Number three seven two?" Bridie queried. "Don't you know her name?"

"Certainly I do." The doctor smiled at her, though a little barbedly. "But you'd hardly expect the *Gazette* to publish patients' progress under their own names, would you? For all the world to see?" Then he bent over the paper. "Good, good . . . she's not among the *Dangerously ill: friends requested to come out*. Nor is she *Seriously ill: no immediate danger*. Now, let me see. . . . Ah, here she is—number three seven two, *Not quite so well: no cause for anxiety*. Excellent. Excellent. . . ." He looked up. "Do they not have these reports in the London papers?"

"I—I believe so. I've never had any cause to notice."

"Lucky you, Miss Tantallon."

No, she thought, not lucky. Her father had not survived even as far as a hospital. He'd been dead by the time they got the cab horse clear of his body.

Dr. Macnab folded his newspaper and put it away. "And what can I do for you now, Miss Tantallon? Is it on account of yourself you've come?"

She collected her thoughts and shook her head. "You . . . you asked me to come if . . . if. . . ."

"Ah yes, Lady Otranta." He leaned back in his chair and blandly steepled his fingers. "She's an extraordinary woman, you know."

Bridie did know. And even if she hadn't, that—or words to that effect—was really all that anybody ever said about her great-aunt. The doctor was a fool. She should have trusted her first impression of him.

But she hadn't come all that way only to give up at the last minute. Clenching her hands in her lap, she told Dr. Macnab about her suspicions concerning her great-aunt's drunkenness, and about the proof of them that she had discovered the previous afternoon. "I'm not saying she isn't ever the worse for drink, doctor," she concluded. "Especially in the evenings. But I am saying that she consistently pretends to be worse than she is. And I find that worrying. It's almost worse than if her drunkenness were genuine."

Dr. Macnab sighed. " I'm afraid this doesn't really surprise me," he said.

"You mean you've suspected something of the sort all along?"

" Unfortunately not. The signs were there, I'm sure, but I was blind to them." Such a frank admission warmed her to him. He rose ponderously to his feet. " There was something, though, that I could not exactly put my finger upon. . . . I take it you've mentioned nothing of this to anybody at the castle?"

Bridie shook her head.

" Very wise. I said you were a wise young woman, and now there's proof of it." He turned and moved away to the window, tucking his hands thoughtfully up beneath the tail of his morning coat. " I'm going to tell you something, Miss Tantallon, that nobody else in the whole world knows. It's a breach of professional etiquette, and I might well be struck off the register for it. But you're a wise young woman, and I believe you will handle the knowledge wisely." He swung round. " This means you will tell it to nobody. And you will not allow it to affect your behaviour in the smallest particular. Do I make myself clear?"

She shrank down in her chair. " What use will this knowledge be to me, then?" she whispered.

The doctor softened. He came to her, stood behind her, put his hands softly on her shoulders. " *Understanding*, Miss Tantallon. To be truly wise you must first of all *understand*. Only then will your wisdom be soundly directed." His hands tightened. " This arthritis your great-aunt is suffering from. What do you think of it?"

" What should I think of it?" Bridie racked her brains. " That it is progressive, and—"

" The disease Lady Otranta is suffering from is undeniably progressive. But it is *not* arthritis."

She twisted round to face him. " Then why tell everybody—?"

191

"Your great-aunt is dying, child. Rapidly." He reached down for her hands and held them with a strange tenderness. "She is being consumed from within. Nothing I can do, nothing any man can do, can save her."

"How . . . how long?" Bridie shook her head from side to side. She had asked the question, but she didn't want to hear the answer.

Dr. Macnab released one of her hands. Discreetly, almost without seeming to do so, he gave her his own silk handkerchief. "A month?" he said. "A week? A day . . .? Every time I visit her I am astonished at her powers of survival."

Bridie stared at the handkerchief in her hand. He was expecting her to cry. But she had seldom felt less like crying. The doctor's news was far too terrible for that. "It's my great-aunt's wish that her family shouldn't know of this?"

"Her wish." He smiled gently. "She's a brave woman. The only thing she said she couldn't endure was to see them suffer with her. For her . . . And besides, there was something she needed to accomplish. I never discovered exactly what. But. . . ."

Bridie stared up at him. "Her memoirs?"

"It . . . could be. She said she needed to conserve all her energies for . . . whatever it was."

"But you told us—last time you came to the castle, you told us. . . ."

". . . That she'd given up all idea of completing them?" He smiled again. "That is correct. In the past she'd always seemed worried about the memoirs, so that I'd suspected some psychological cause. We all have things in our lives we're ashamed of, you understand. Even the most exemplary of us. . . . But the last time I spoke to her she seemed more than worried—she seemed afraid. She told me herself that she'd abandoned the memoirs."

"Did you believe her?"

"Not . . . entirely. But to set her mind at rest I promised to pass the information on to her family."

Bridie was thoughtful. "But what then of the pretended drunkenness?"

Dr. Macnab looked down at the mirror toes of his pointed shoes. " A ruse, would you not say? A way of convincing whoever might be interested that the all-important memoirs were not being worked upon?"

" While in fact they were? And still are?"

" Who can say?" The doctor hesitated, shrugged. " Certainly not I." Then he stooped over her. " But I doubt if it matters," he whispered. " If they're not finished soon, they never will be. . . . And you must be very brave now, Bridie. Your great-aunt will need your strength. And her family too . . . afterwards. They will need you very much."

Bridie caught her breath. No. No—Lady Otranta must not die. Then there would be no need, no need for an *afterwards*. Except that there always was. She believed the doctor. Her great-aunt would die. And the rest of them would go on. That was what life was all about. There always was an *afterwards*.

She bent her head then, in preparation for all that would be demanded of her, and the tears flowed.

9

Sir James and I did not meet for many weeks after his wife's 'death'. This separation was, of course, an essential part of our plan, so that no possible shade of suspicion should fall upon either of us. I myself even returned to London with Professor Salvador at the end of our season at the Empire without seeing him. But we wrote. Almost daily. And filled our letters with our longing. . . .

I'm tempted now to pause, and wonder if my readers were deceived by the foregoing literary trick. Did they read on avidly, expecting to be told how Sir James and I had committed murder? Were they really so untrusting as to believe us capable of that? I, a young woman of twenty-eight, so utterly degenerate? And Sir James also? And he a man so loyal to his wife that, in spite of all that she had done, he was willing to spare her the indignity of imprisonment?

Ah yes, they may say, but a police investigation would have ruined his career. Not to mention the squalid divorce that must follow it. To which I can only answer that all that may well be so. Nevertheless, he was a man so loyal to his wife, in spite of everything, that in all her future wanderings—and she wandered far, settling at last in a Continental watering place—an allowance from him followed her, generous to a fault, and as regularly as September follows August. An allowance that he paid, faithfully, in expiation of whatever wrongs he felt he might have done her, until the day of her death, from natural causes, some twenty-two years later.

It hardly needs be said that she kept her side of the bargain, changing her name, never contacting her daughter, never exposing the trick she had been a party to. Admittedly a word from her would have ruined us all, a fact that James and I lived with all our days together. But the ruin that word would have brought upon her must have been as bad, if not worse, than anything we could suffer. And anyway, possibly by then even she had come to feel just a little ashamed of what she had done.

Ruined us all, I say. And with good reason. James, and myself, and in due course our two sons. Our two bastards. For it must be obvious by now that the marriage ceremony James and I went through was illegal. He was a bigamist, and I his knowing accomplice. And our two children therefore illegitimate.

The true inheritor of the Tantallon estate is Melissa Tantallon, the daughter of Jamie's first, and only legal marriage.

There. It's done. At long last the record is put straight. James, right up to the moment of his sudden and unexpected death, had been insistent that for my sake the truth be concealed. Had death been slower in coming, and had he had time in which to reflect, who knows what he might have decided? But it was not to be. And the responsibility therefore passed to myself. The truth needed to be told—not simply in the bare, legalistic terms of a will but in all its full and subtle ramifications.

I do not seek to excuse, merely to explain. And even if these memoirs are never published, never finished perhaps, the facts are down in black and white, to be read by those who matter. All her life we made up to the girl as best we could. But no amount of generosity, of love, could compensate for the wrong we did her in robbing her of her rightful heritage.

It'll be hard on the boys, of course. But they're young and able. Life will deliver them harder knocks than this, surely, before it's finally done with them. I love them both dearly. And my belief is that, when they think upon it seriously, they will see how wrong, how inexcusable it would have been for them to continue to enjoy privileges rightfully belonging to their half-sister Melissa.

Others, also, will be hurt by the truth. As I have already

said, the truth is often hurtful. But it will out. And those, whoever they may be, who try to prevent it, must learn to accept the inevitable. We were happy, Jamie and I. But it was a stolen happiness. . . .

*   *   *

For Bridie the journey back across the Firth of Forth was a nightmare.

Wretchedly she huddled in the corner of the main saloon, clutching the small parcel with her shoes for the party inside it. How she had bought the shoes she could not properly remember. She had left Dr. Macnab in a daze. He had been deeply concerned for her, and would have called her a taxi himself to take her back to Leith. But even in her trance-like state she remembered the shoes—she dare not return to the castle without them.

Clutching her umbrella to her, she insisted upon walking the short distance down to the shops on Prince's Street. Reluctantly he let her go.

" Not a word of this, now," he called after her. " For your great-aunt's sake, not a hint in word or gesture !"

She walked away through the rain, now torrential from a sky that seemed to rest, dark and menacing, close upon the very chimney pots. Gusts of wind lashed the rain against her, soaking the lower part of her skirt. When she reached Prince's Street the castle, high above it, was lost in the clouds.

The pavements were deserted. Hoardings dripped dismally. Black Cat Cigarettes : $2\frac{1}{2}$d for ten. Stewart's Wax Works. A concert at the music hall on George Street, featuring the Electric Axeto Gramophone. . . . Somehow she found a shoe shop. Lord knows what the assistants must have thought of the sodden object she presented. They did have shoes, however, with waisted heels and pearl buttons, in all the colours of the rainbow.

Bridie cared less than nothing for heels or buttons. Indeed, the seeming frivolity of the entire operation shocked her profoundly. Lady Otranta was ill. Terribly ill, well-nigh unto

196

death. While she, Bridie, sat in a shop in Edinburgh, trying on shoes. . . .

She took the first green pair that fitted her, not even bothering to take the snipping from the hem of Melissa's dress out of her handbag by way of comparison. Green was green. No more could be expected of her than that.

Her odious task accomplished, she paid over an unconscionable amount of money—for the shop was chic to the point of criminal extravagance—and went out again into the street. And it was then, her spirits at their lowest ebb, that fate thrust yet another puzzle, yet another anxiety in her path.

As she stood in the arcade outside the shoe shop, staring out at the rain, a motor taxi splashed slowly by in the roadway. Suddenly it was hailed from a shop entrance not ten feet away from her, and slithered to a halt. A man hurried out across the pavement to it, an elderly man, tall, with sloping eyebrows beneath his high-crowned hat, and stood for a moment, the rain dripping from his hat-brim, while he gave the driver his instructions. Then the man got into the taxi, and it drove away.

The entire commonplace episode had taken perhaps thirty seconds. And Bridie had watched it in silence, so astonished as to be rendered quite speechless. For the elderly man in the high-crowned hat—and of this she was absolutely certain— had been her London employer, Mr. Pugh-Hennessy.

What in God's name was he doing in Edinburgh? She clearly remembered his most recent letter. He'd made no mention at all of coming north. He had faith in her, he said. If anyone could persuade Lady Tantallon to write her memoirs, then she could. Certainly he'd said nothing whatsoever about coming himself to Edinburgh. He might well have changed his mind later, of course. But if that was the case, then why hadn't he written, or sent a telegram, to tell her so?

Only one reasonable possibility remained : that such a communication would be waiting for her on her return to the castle. Yet instinct told her that would not be the case. He was here in the city without her knowledge because that was his intention. How long he had been here she did not know. How long he would stay—she knew not that either. And as to his reasons—these too were a total mystery to her. Except that they were obviously secretive, and therefore not to her liking.

The time was nearly one. Scarcely more than an hour remained before the ferry left Leith for Kincardine. And she knew the wretched shoes had so far depleted her purse that a taxi all the way was out of the question. In desperation she set forth beneath her umbrella, found a policeman in a shiny black cape standing under the trees opposite, and asked for his advice. His answer came in Scots so broad that he had to repeat it several times before she understood. North British Railway trains left from the Haymarket station for Portobello and Leith, calling at Blackford Hill and Craiglockhart. He pointed the way to the Haymarket station. It was, he said, a goodly walk for a young leddy.

She made it, or most of it, at a goodly run.

Miraculously, on such an ill-fated day, there was a train waiting that got her to Leith within ten minutes of the ferry's sailing. And at a price within her meagre resources. And so to the ferry, and to the unhappiest and most frightening journey of her life.

A full gale appeared to be blowing out on the Firth. The steamer lurched like a mad thing. Sometimes it seemed to stop dead in its tracks, and even to go backwards, the machinery screaming in protest as the paddles bit on air and raced, and checked suddenly with sickening violence. While, Bridie, in company with eight or ten other ill-advised passengers, cowered in the main saloon, its windows totally obscured with rain and breaking water, her thoughts as tumultuous as the elements about her, the soggy little package containing her new shoes pressed tightly to her bosom.

Her great-aunt had pretended drunkenness. Her great-aunt was dying. Her great-aunt had been working surreptitiously upon her memoirs. Mr. Pugh-Hennessy had come secretly to Edinburgh. Her great-aunt was dying. . . . Round and round the thoughts went. And round and round went her stomach also.

She scarcely noticed when the ship's motion eased, when bumping and hooting announced their arrival at South Queensferry. Soon they were off again for Kincardine, the sea a little calmer now as the surrounding hillsides began to shelter them from the full blast of the storm. Bridie sat up. In another three-quarters of an hour she'd be at the castle. She must put her mind in order. Not a word, Dr. Macnab had said. For her great-aunt's sake, not a hint in word or gesture. She only hoped that such a thing were possible.

Duncan Symonds was waiting in the car by the end of Kincardine jetty, just as he had promised. The dog, Noble, had wisely stayed at home.

Mr. Symonds swung the door open and she climbed in. "You got what you went for, then?" he said, pointing at her parcel.

She nodded. The first of many bitter lies. What she had really got she had certainly not gone for. The direst news.

"And you got a mite wet too, I'm thinking." He backed the yellow Argyll, and turned it. The mica side-screens were up, but leaking abominably.

"How is Lady Tantallon?" Bridie asked suddenly.

"Her Ladyship? Fine, fine. . . . And out about the castle too, here and there and everywhere, seeing to the preparations for the night."

The *party*—the only reason for the shoes, yet somehow she had completely forgotten it. Perhaps, she thought, the party would provide a merciful respite. People would be too taken up with it to notice how upset she was.

Then she remembered Mr. Pugh-Hennessy. "Mr. Symonds —has there been a letter for me today? Or a telegram?"

He glanced at her sideways, gripping the wheel as the car lurched through rain-filled pot-holes. "Not that I've hear't of, Mistress Bridie. Would it be something you were expecting?"

"Not really. Not at all, really. It doesn't matter." Another lie. It mattered very much. Even Mr. Pugh-Hennessy, now, couldn't be wholly trusted.

The castle was in turmoil. The huge table in the dining hall had been pushed back against the wall under the windows, covered with fine white cloths, and a buffet was being set out upon it. The rugs had been rolled up and taken away. The stuffed bear, too, had been banished to some nether region. In the music room chairs were being set out for the concert, while the entrance hall and the main drawing room which nobody ever used were being cleared for dancing. Already trails of mud led hither and thither, where servants had hurried in from outdoors with kegs of strong beer and bundles of branches for the decorations, and candles from the storerooms and endless armsful of logs for the fireplaces. While old Meredith chivvied a housemaid round behind them with mop and bucket.

The first person Bridie met was Lady Otranta, storming across the entrance hall, waving her stick. "Not the *crystal* punch glasses," she was shrieking, apparently to no one in particular. "It's not the Queen we're entertaining, I tell you!"

Seeing Bridie, she paused in mid-stride. Her face was pale, her eyes unhealthily bright. "Ah, there you are. The *King* I meant, of course. It's so easy to forget." Briefly she leaned on her stick. "You got back safely then. Didn't have to swim for it, I see."

"No, Great-aunt, I—"

But the old lady was already off again, "Not the *crystal* ones, you idiot," her hoarse cry fading rapidly beneath the general bustle of activity.

Bridie leaned for a moment against the carved stone newel post at the bottom of the stairs and closed her eyes. Knowing what she did, she could not bear to see Lady Otranta push herself so. Surely, if she was more careful, the disease that was wasting her might be arrested? But she'd asked Dr. Macnab that very same question and he'd shaken his head sadly. "A day more, a day less—the terrible thing will take her when it's ready."

And yet surely . . .? Bridie opened her eyes and pulled herself upright. Only five minutes in the castle, and already she was giving way to anxiety. Firmly she lifted her sodden skirts and made her way up the staircase to her bedroom, to change.

Word must quickly have got round that she was back, for

soon Melissa came hurrying to her room, and the new shoes had to be unpacked, and exclaimed over, and all the excited, breathless spirit of the coming party entered into. Bridie did her best and Melissa, chattering enough for the two of them, noticed nothing out of the ordinary. The shoes, as it happened, were a great success. The dress was back now from old Peggy, and they matched it to perfection.

The family—including Lady Otranta—had high tea in the small drawing room. For the first time Bridie noticed just how little her great-aunt actually ate. She really ought to try to eat more. Otherwise, how could she ever expect to—Bridie checked herself. She *must* stop brooding over the old lady. Her great-aunt had lived in her own way, and doubtless she would die in her own way also. *Not a hint in word or gesture,* Dr. Macnab had said.

On her way back up to her room to change for the party she was joined on the stairs by Andrew. She took his hand, trying to be gay. There was so much she wished she could say to him. Up until the previous evening they had shared so much. Everything. Even though he'd often been away from the castle, helping with the sheep, not half a day had gone by when they had not contrived a meeting, talked, kissed, made plans, exchanged those total intimacies only lovers can. Now, miserably, she felt the secrecy that Dr. Macnab had imposed upon her loom between them, an insurmountable barrier.

Mercifully, absorbed in thoughts of his own, he didn't notice her preoccupied air. At the door to her room he hesitated, as if steeling himself. " May I come in, Bridie? There's something I must ask you."

Instantly afraid, she looked anxiously up at him, all manner of thoughts whirling in her head. Was her secret already discovered?

He managed a smile. " Oh, I know it won't be quite proper, my dear. But I wouldn't ask if it wasn't—"

Proper? What did she care just then for what was *proper*? " Of course you must come in, Andrew."

She led him through the door and he closed it behind them.

Then he took her in his arms. "Oh, Bridie. . . ." He kissed her tenderly, passionately, so that she forgot everything, her great-aunt, Mr. Pugh-Hennessy, everything but the wonder of their love. "Bridie . . . my dearest, to go on like this is folly. We can't. We mustn't. . . ."

She lowered her gaze, her heart pounding till she thought it would burst. "But, Andrew, your mother—"

"Listen to me, my love. I want us to be married—you know that, don't you?"

She nodded, afraid to speak.

"And you want that too, Bridie?"

"You . . . you know I do."

"Very well then. May I announce our engagement tonight? At the party? May I tell them, may I tell the whole world that you've consented to become my wife?"

The cosy little room reeled about her. "But, Andrew— we've been through this so many times before. You—"

"You're thinking of Mama. But I'm my own man, Bridie. And she knows my mind. Even if she really wanted to, she knows there's nothing she could do to prevent our marriage."

Even if she really wanted to. . . . Bridie wrenched away. Who could guess what the old lady really wanted? Locked away behind the grisly charade of her drunkenness, battling with the certainty of her own rapidly approaching death, devoting only God knew how many of her few remaining days to the memoirs that had caused both her and her family such untold misery, who could possibly tell what she really wanted? Peace? Might it not, more than anything else, be peace?

She'd warned Bridie. "You'll be hurt," she'd said. "Give up the whole ridiculous notion now, while there's still time." But *why*? Why would she be hurt? Was there something that only Lady Otranta knew? Something unworthy? Something about her son Andrew, perhaps?

No. No, that could not be.

He took her shoulders and turned her back to face him. "I'm my own man, Bridie. And I love you. I cannot live my entire life under Mama's shadow. Marry me, my dear. Let me make the announcement tonight."

She stared at him. Her whole being cried out that she say yes. " But, Andrew—"

" Don't say a word." He walked her to the chintz-covered window seat and pressed her gently down. " There's something perhaps I should not say to you. But Mama is ill— we all know that. Possibly, though, we don't know just *how* ill. . . ."

She looked away. Outside her window the rain fell on the trees in a steady, unrelenting downpour. How near he was to the truth. Oh, if only she could tell him just how near.

" It may be," he went on, " that she does not have long to live. We must face that fact. I've watched her—she's thinner, weaker, every day." His voice broke, but he struggled to continue. "And I know she loves me. In her heart I know she wants me to be happy. She wants us both to be happy. . . . I want her to live to see that day. I want her to see our joy, yours and mine. I want her to understand, and be happy too. For us. And for the future generations of Tantallons who will come after."

His pleading was done. She turned back to him. There were tears in his eyes. She could resist no longer. " If you really want to marry me, Andrew—"

" I do."

" Then you may make the announcement."

She was in his arms again. The decision was made. And in all her life she knew she'd never regret that moment. She loved him with all her heart and mind and body. And his mother, seeing that, knowing that, would rejoice. She'd loved Sir James, had she not? Remembering that love she couldn't but rejoice.

* * *

Two months after his mourning period was up, James and I were married. It was a November ceremony, and as quiet as we could make it. He'd been down in London for a time before, and I travelled up with him at the end of

October to meet his relations, his little daughter and his younger brother's family.

Naturally both David and his wife opposed the match. I had expected that, if not the full violence of their opposition. David was a lawyer, a narrow man, of rigid Presbyterian principles, living on the outskirts of Glasgow with Mary and an earnest, bespectacled son called Arthur. The son was to lose his sight in later years, poor man, and to father in his turn the most delightful, intelligent, sweetest-natured daughter. . . . In his parents' natures, however, there was neither sweetness nor any very great intelligence. They did everything they could to prevent Jamie's marrying me. They'd never speak to him again. I was a gold-digger, a cheap little nobody who'd bewitched a man almost old enough to be my father. The Tantallon name would be disgraced for ever.

We, of course, who had already been through so much, were not to be put off. And when David and his sour-faced wife saw that they had failed, they stormed from the castle, never to return. They were as good as their word. From that moment on communication ceased between them and Jamie. It was, I fear, but one sadness among many. For our marriage, false both in the eyes of God and man, was hardly a moment for unbridled joy. The happiness we won came later, growing slowly as the months went by and the frenzied determination of our love blossomed into something profound and lasting.

Originally dear faithful Peggy had gone north with me simply to act as chaperon before my marriage. But when the nurse to Sir James' little daughter departed (in righteous indignation at the coming introduction into the household of anyone as lowly as myself—and *English*, too), Peggy insisted on staying to help me with the child. In the event, caught at first between a castle full of resentful servants and a bundle of local neighbours who studiously ignored me, I was very grateful, both for her and indeed for little Melissa herself. I was never one, you see, for that Biblical wish to visit the sins of the mothers upon the children. And the child was so enchanting, and so spontaneously open-hearted, that my inexperience in dealing with her kind was of no account whatsoever.

We soon became very close. In fact, we stayed that way for many years, right up to her eighteenth birthday. . . . Since the tragedy, I regret to say, things have never been the same between us. Guilt, perhaps? I don't know. Certainly I never blamed her for what happened. How could I, when I never even discovered exactly what it was? My son Andrew, who might have told me, remained impenetrably discreet. Not that I pressed him. The whole affair was far too wretched for that.

The fact remains that for many years, and especially in those early months, she was a great comfort to myself and her father. The whole district, you see, was as it were holding its breath, delaying a final decision on my social possibilities until they might learn of the Queen's reaction. And the Queen also delayed, having personal problems of her own. . . . And while she delayed, James and I were in a sort of limbo. Neither fish nor fowl nor good red herring. . . .

*   *   *

It was around eight when the guests started arriving. Andrew stood with his mother at the foot of the great staircase to welcome them, while Melissa and Robert hovered on one side, ready to descend on anyone who seemed uncertain and bear them off to the laden buffet table. The champion fiddler had come early—a tiny, bow-legged Scotsman in full tartan regalia—and was already scraping cheerfully away in the dining hall. And sufficient discordant wheezings filtered through the green baize door to the servants' quarters to suggest to Bridie that bagpipes were being warmed up somewhere in the background.

She knew very few of the guests, of course, and those she did know were principally the tradespeople up from Kincardine. The dominie was there, and several small farmers she had met through her cousin Melissa's bicycle visits to their aged grandparents and the like. Indeed, after half an hour or so of watching the arrivals, Bridie couldn't for the life of her imagine what all the fuss over the guest list had been about: it seemed to her that literally everybody, both the high and the lowly, living within a thirty mile radius of the castle had been invited.

She remarked on this to Robert when he drifted briefly into earshot, unaccompanied after leading one of the younger shepherds off to his friends around the punch-bowl.

Her cousin laughed. " At least we're not snobs," he said. " A laird and his people are one, you see. The Court in the old days was Frenchified and formal enough. But apart from that we've long been a fine democratic people, we Scots."

He spoke, she thought, with some pride and little of his usual mockery. Then he touched her arm and nodded in the direction of the big outer porch where a group of people, newly arrived from a carriage, were shaking rainwater off their cloaks and headgear.

" Watch out, coz. There are the Craigs now come. I must stand by to do my duty. Gordon's there, I see. And poor 'Lissa already hurrying away to the far end of the music room, unless I'm much mistaken."

He moved away. Bridie stared with interest at the young man about whom there'd been so much fuss. So *that* then was Gordon Craig, waiting respectfully a pace or two behind his parents, flanked by a very much younger brother and sister who nudged each other and giggled. He was a handsome man, she thought, with a distinguished, purposeful air about him. If he'd have her, Melissa should forget all the nonsense about a dowry and marry him. But he was hardly a patch on her Andrew. ,

She turned then, in time to see Andrew, one pair of guests safely despatched, lift his head in her direction. As he stood there in his kilt and white frilled shirt and dress sporran, she was reminded of the tall, commanding figure of his father in the portrait. He was his own man, he'd said. Old Sir James had been his own man also. Then, as their eyes met above the crowd, his expression softened. She blushed, pressing her clasped hands tightly against her breast, for all the world as if fearing that the beating of her heart might show. He was *hers*. And she was his.

She never did see Robert do his duty by the Craigs, for in the big drawing room couples were formed up for an eightsome reel, and at that moment a young farmer came shyly to claim her as his partner. She accepted gladly, safe in the knowledge of Andrew's love, afraid of nothing—not even the intricacies of the eightsome reel.

From that moment on, until the concert began at ten, she was never still. Mr. Pugh-Hennessy . . . the memoirs . . . all was forgotten. The yellow muslin whirled and the green shoes hopped and capered. And none too inexpertly either, thanks to Melissa's patient tuition. It was, she suddenly realised, the very first dance she had been to since the few stumbling children's events in the winter before her mother's death. The first real dance of her life. Yet even that excitement was eclipsed in the breathless expectation of what was to come.

Twice Andrew partnered her. In a lull he stooped and whispered in her ear. His face was flushed, his eyes shining. " Midnight, my love. At midnight I'll make the announcement."

Briefly, in spite of herself, she looked round, afraid that her great-aunt might have overheard his words. But the old lady was away on the far side of the room, sitting on a small dais that had been arranged, watching the dancing. Bridie turned back to Andrew. " I love you very much," she told him.

If Andrew dominated the proceedings that night by his handsome stature and boundless energy, his mother in her own way dominated them also—by the sheer magnetism of her presence. Her eyes burned like live coals in the pallor of her face and, although she moved slowly, leaning upon her stick, and sat often, she commanded respectful attention wherever she went. The space around her was never empty, and she had a kind, amusing word for all.

To Bridie however, who had eyes to see, it was clear that the old lady was burning up her reserves at a reckless rate. She drank, but only wine, and that sparingly. She listened well, and when she spoke her reply was worth hearing. She was Lady Otranta Tantallon. And if many of those present had heard rumours of her dissolute behaviour, they would go away believing these no more than malicious gossip. She was Sir James Tantallon's widow, and worthy of his proud name.

Watching her, Bridie came near to seeking out Andrew and telling him she'd changed her mind. There was cowardice in what he planned to do—the public announcement first, the *fait accompli* before which his mother would be forced to bow, her response one of pleasure, even if assumed. . . .

But something held Bridie back. The desperately-held belief that in the event Lady Otranta's pleasure would not need to be assumed. The realisation, too, that she herself, were she in Andrew's place, would be frightened of the old lady. Frightened of her wrath. Or, worse, of her scorn.

At ten the haggis was piped in with full Gaelic ceremony. Bridie had met haggis before—she thought of it as peppered porridge. But on such a night, and with the rest of the buffet such a triumph of salmon and cold game pie and mutton galantine and honey-glazed ham—not to mention Melissa's sherry trifle—she forgave the Scots even their haggis. Then, with forks and steaming plates in their hands, they all went into the music room and settled down for the concert.

Someone—the Kincardine postmaster, Bridie thought—led off in a fine tenor voice with *Trumpeter, what are you sounding now?* It made a fine martial introduction for Andrew who came next, reciting Sir Walter Scott as was his custom.

O, Brignall banks are wild and fair,
And Greta woods are green,
And you may gather garlands there,
Would grace a summer queen. . . .

He followed this with a patriotic verse that brought loud applause from the entire company:

Breathes there a man with soul so dead,
Who never to himself has said,
" This is my own, my native land !? . . . ."

After Andrew there came a tall, solemn gentleman with an incongruously tiny concertina, to the accompaniment of which he sang sea-shanties and music hall ballads. The proceedings were entirely informal, one performer bobbing up from the audience and coming unembarrassedly forward as soon as another was done. By the time Bridie's turn came with Melissa, she had quite forgotten to be nervous. They were all friends there, every one of them. Melissa sang very sweetly: two Scottish folk songs and a Schubert *Lied*.

Robert followed on the piano soon after, playing Chopin's Military Polonaise with great dash and bravura. There were patter songs from Gilbert and Sullivan. Even Lady Otranta herself performed, giving a reading from Charles Dickens, the death of Little Nell, that left hardly a dry eye in the room.

At last the concert ended, and dancing was resumed, now to the music of the piper. Robert came forward again, and danced between two swords crossed upon the floor, his hands held high, leaping and skipping. All evening he had been first with one partner and then the next, laughing, flattering, tossing his silvery hair, bewitching surely a dozen hearts with his outrageous charm. Never in all her life had Bridie been present at such a joyful gathering. How well it augured for her future! Under the influence of such universal good spirits what few misgivings she still had simply melted away.

As midnight approached she began to look round, a little nervously, for Andrew. She left the dancing and wandered from room to room. She spoke briefly with her great-aunt, who was sitting quietly now by one of the huge log fires, clearly tired out but refusing to give in and leave the party. In the dining hall she was happy to see Melissa, flushed and smiling, deep in conversation with the handsome Gordon Craig. Not even her cousin's gloomy doubts could survive the general gaiety.

She found Andrew at last, sitting on the edge of the stage in the almost deserted music room. A sudden fear gripped her, for the flush on his face had faded to a sickly greenish tinge and his shoulders were hunched as he leaned forward, staring morosely into his empty wine glass.

She touched his shoulder. " What is it, Andrew? Are you ill, my dear?"

He started, and looked blearily up at her. His eyes were scarcely focused. " Bridie?" He made a great effort. " How . . . how b-beautiful you are, little Bridie. . . ."

Her heart sank: obviously he had taken a great deal too much wine. " Come along now, my dear." She helped him to his feet. " It's so hot in here—perhaps a little fresh air would. . . ."

She tried to lead him away but he resisted, swaying as he pushed his face down at her. " Kiss me, Bridie. Kiss me—"

Dear God, was this mouthing lout her Andrew? Desperately she looked round for someone who might help—his brother Robert, Duncan Symonds, anybody. . . . But the room was empty save for a couple leaning on the piano with eyes for no one but each other.

" No, Andrew. No—not now. I—I think you should go upstairs. Lie down for a while. Until you're . . . better."

" Lie down. . . ." He seemed to think this a good idea and started away across the room, leaning heavily upon her arm. Suddenly he stopped and began to fumble feverishly for his watch. " I'm not late, am I? The announcement—I'm not late, am I?"

" Of course not," she lied. " There's plenty of time. Just you have a short rest first, and then. . . ." Once he was asleep, she thought, he'd stay that way till morning. Somehow he had to be prevented from disgracing himself in front of the assembled company.

But he'd got his watch out and was peering at it. " There's a . . . a minute to go, Bridie. Only a minute, I swear. . . . You must help me, my dear. I feel so strange, so unsteady. . . . I doubt if I can manage without your help."

" No, Andrew." She spoke sharply, almost hating him. " I shall not help you. You're in no fit state."

He broke away, suddenly angry. " Then I'll manage on my own, blast you."

He squared his shoulders and flung back his head. With faltering, pathetic dignity he made his crooked way to the music room door. She ran after him then, past him, pressing herself in front, trying at all costs to hold him back. But he thrust her aside with contemptuous ease.

"The announcement—you gave me your word. You shall not go back on it now. You gave me your word, Bridie."

There was dancing out in the entrance hall. She watched in despair as Andrew stalked blindly between the laughing couples, looking neither to right nor left. At the foot of the stairs he paused, and beckoned to one of the servants. The man went to him and they conferred together briefly.

Bridie saw the servant look anxiously round, then nod and move away. She caught sight of Robert and his mother, over beyond the staircase, standing in the door to the dining hall. She began to ease her way across to them. Perhaps it still wasn't too late. If she could only reach them in time, and make some sort of explanation, then Robert could—

But she was only halfway across the crowded floor when the sound of the great bronze dinner gong rose deafeningly above the piper's music. The bagpipes faltered, died with a discordant groan. The dancing stopped, the dancers looked round in bewilderment. After a short pause they began to chatter among themselves.

Andrew was three steps up the staircase, leaning upon the massive banister rail. "Again!" he shouted to the man-servant. "Again!"

And again the gong was beaten.

All heads turned now in its direction, and then to their host where he stood upon the broad sweep of the stairs. Silence descended. Andrew heaved himself away from the rail and lifted his arms. "Ladies and gentlemen. . . ." He swayed, then recovered himself. "My lords, ladies and gentlemen. . . ."

Bridie would have looked away, but could not. Instead she stared in helpless fascination at the lurching drunken stranger who was her Andrew.

"My lords, ladies and gentlemen, *friends* . . . I shall not take up much of your time. You are all of you my guests, and I welcome you."

He lowered his arms and stood for a moment in silence,

quite still. He seemed to have forgotten what he had planned to say next. Several of the dancers began to clap half-heartedly. The noise roused him. When he spoke again it was quietly, almost conversationally. "But I have an important announcement to make, you see. A very important announcement. . . ."

A commotion in the crowd dragged Bridie's gaze away. She saw Lady Otranta imperiously forcing her way forward. Up on the staircase her son had lifted his head and was looking out across the heads of the people. "An important announcement, I say. And a proud one, also—"

Abruptly he broke off, his eyes turning up in their sockets till only the whites showed. He lingered there a moment longer, then crumpled sideways, falling against the rail and tumbling slowly forwards down the stairs. He reached the bottom of the flight at the same time as his mother.

Someone laughed. It was a sound quickly stifled. With great presence of mind the piper began to play again. But the guests had no heart just then for dancing. They drifted away in small embarrassed groups, talking quietly among themselves.

When Bridie reached the foot of the stairs Robert was there also, his hand supporting his mother's arm. Andrew lay on the flagstones at their feet, unconscious, dead to the world.

Robert pulled Bridie closer. "See to Mama, will you?" he whispered urgently. "I'll deal with Andrew."

The old lady's skin, always pale, now had a translucency that showed the skull beneath with hideous clarity. She leaned on her stick, staring down at her son, breathing in fast, shallow gasps. Bridie put her arm about her waist. A moment later Melissa arrived, accompanied by Gordon Craig. Together the two men lifted Andrew and began to carry him away up the stairs.

"You go with him," Melissa said. "I'll look after Mama."

Bridie hesitated, then did as she was told, catching up with the pathetic trio on the gallery. Robert glanced at her, appalled. "Did you *see* Mama?" he said. "Dear God, did you *see* her?"

Bridie nodded wretchedly. They shuffled along to Andrew's

door, Gordon Craig discreetly silent, Robert cursing all the way under his breath. They opened the door, went in, laid the unconscious man on the bed. Bridie wetted a towel from the water jug and began to bathe his forehead.

Suddenly she became aware of Robert's hostile presence. "You're wasting your time," he said savagely. "He's done this before. He'll be out till morning."

She didn't believe him. "What d'you mean?" she demanded.

Robert turned from the bedside. "Nothing at all. I mean nothing at all."

The other man had moved away and was hovering awkwardly by the door. Robert leant down over her. "Forget I ever spoke, dear coz," he whispered. Then he reached out and loosened his brother's collar with rough affection. "And forget all this too, if you've any sense."

She laid the towel gently across Andrew's forehead and backed from the room. The last she saw of him was one of his hands trailing lifelessly from the bed as Robert and Gordon Craig lifted first one foot and then the other to remove his shoes.

Downstairs Lady Otranta had rallied miraculously and was circulating among the crowd, encouraging the dancing, offering dignified words of apology here and there for the behaviour of her son. But the guests began to leave soon after. Bridie for one didn't blame them—the evening was ruined, a dismal shadow cast over the entire proceedings.

But it wasn't until the very last of them had gone, and her great-aunt safe in old Peggy's care, that she could go to her room and find release for all the pent-up misery within her. Andrew—oh, *Andrew*. . . . She cried herself to sleep that night.

10

Obviously there are people who would prefer that these memoirs so far had not been written. People who fear for Sir James' reputation, or for his wife's reputation, or even (bless them) for my own reputation. Not to mention those who stand to lose materially by what I have revealed.

As to the rest of these memoirs, there will also be people anxious to prevent *their* publication. You see, the monarchy, as conceived by Queen Victoria, was a strange institution. By setting itself above common humanity it made itself vulnerable because it was itself, in spite of everything, still completely human. Touchingly so. And I speak from intimate personal knowledge. . . . And there are people still today who would seek to deny that fact, to deny that humanity.

The man, for example, who helps me every day with these memoirs, is a good man, an honest man. Yet I've had to make him swear never to read a single word of what I've written—for I know he'd move heaven and earth to stop me if he guessed the nature of what I am about to reveal. His overriding loyalty, you see, would be to what he thinks of as the late Queen's memory. By this he means the myth of her inhumanly faultless propriety. His affection for her is such that he even owns, to this very day, a collie dog called Noble, just as she once did.

I myself, on the other hand, have evidence written with her own pen, that she was blessedly neither more nor less human than the majority of her subjects. But I anticipate myself. There's first the episode of my miraculous acceptance into the Queen's circle to be described. It came on a day in early spring, when. . . .

For three days after the party Lady Otranta held her own. Dr. Macnab was sent for and departed smiling as blandly as when he had arrived. Bridie watched him from a distance. Knowing what she knew, she could not have borne to be a party to his soothing lies.

On the fourth day, however, the doctor was sent for again. And this time, when he came to the family where they waited in the small drawing room, his smile was gone.

" I have grave news," he said, looking earnestly round from face to face. " Lady Otranta's condition is very serious." He paused. " She may not last the night."

Bridie closed her eyes. She could have told him that. Most of her waking hours she'd spent with her great-aunt. And she'd seen the change for herself, the gathering in of the old lady's resources, the strange new quality of peace.

Robert leapt to his feet. " But that's impossible," he cried. " Either you've been lying to us all along, or. . . . You're wrong, I tell you. She's had these turns before—but she's always recovered. She's always recovered. . . ."

Dr Macnab's face was expressionless. " Your mother's heart is very weak. She's experienced much pain. Now she's . . . simply tired out. Sleep will be a mercy."

Melissa stifled a sob and turned away. Robert clenched his fists. " You're wrong, I say. You've been wrong right from the start. I was with Mama last night, I tell you. And she was better. She was *much better*."

" Please, Robert. . . ." Andrew had not risen. Now he leaned forward, his head in his hands. " Does Mama know she's—she's dying?" he asked the doctor.

Dr. Macnab cleared his throat. " Yes. She knows." He hesitated. " I think she's known for a long time," he said.

" Which is more than *you* have, you blundering idiot!" Robert came near to striking him then. Dr. Macnab didn't flinch. But neither did he justify himself.

Bridie gazed at him, wondering at his obstinate courage.

Surely it wouldn't matter if he owned up to the truth, not *now*?

Finally Robert swung away. "Dear God," he muttered, "she can't be dying. She can't be. . . ." He leaned his head upon the mantelpiece and wept.

Andrew seemed about to say something, then changed his mind. Helplessly Bridie watched his quiet anguish across the gulf which—since the night of the party—had separated them. He had come to her the very next morning, disdaining apology for his behaviour, simply in quiet, formal tones releasing her from their engagement. And she, distressed and uncertain, had accepted her release without argument.

Yet she did not really believe in it, seeing it simply as a way of gaining breathing space. She knew she still loved him. But his behaviour at the party had terrified her. She needed time. . . . Since then, however, his mother had become so ill. Events crowded in upon them both. And still the gulf between them remained unbridged.

Composed again, Melissa turned back into the room. "Is there anything we can do?" she asked. "Should we get a nurse over from Edinburgh?"

"There's no need." Dr. Macnab went to the window, pushed back the edge of the curtain and stared thoughtfully out at the rain that by then had been falling virtually continuously for four days. "Lady Otranta is comfortable. Nothing else remains to be done."

He sighed, then lowered the curtain. "And now, if you don't mind, I'd like to get back to my patient." At the door he paused. "Lady Otranta has accepted the truth. She's a very courageous woman. But she needs the support of every single one of you." Slowly, compassionately, he looked round the group. "The time for grieving will be later," he said.

Then he left the room.

Bridie hurried after him, catching him on the stairs. "Why did you not defend yourself?" she whispered. "Why did you not tell them that—"

"Hush, my dear." He put a finger to his lips. "Your great-aunt knows her own mind. And things are bad enough for her family without them also having to know, and be grateful for, the many months of misery she's spared them."

He went away then, up the stairs and along the vaulted gallery. Only when he was out of sight did Bridie turn and thoughtfully retrace her steps back across the sombre entrance hall to her three cousins.

As she entered the room Robert was facing the door, his back to the fireplace. "What's this, then?" he demanded loudly. "Secrets, is it? Secrets between our little Bridie and the good doctor?"

Bridie blushed, lowering her head in confusion. Before she could manage some sort of reply Andrew had risen and limped across to his brother. "Don't bully her, Robert. We've troubles enough without that."

"But—"

"Don't *bully* her, I said."

For a moment the two men glared at each other. Then Robert subsided. "Well," he said bitterly, "at least if Mama dies now it'll solve a lot of our problems."

He made to walk away but Andrew grabbed angrily at his arm. "What exactly do you mean by that?"

Defiantly Robert faced him. "You know very well what I mean."

"I do not."

"Then I'm not going to tell you."

It was Melissa who broke the impasse. "We've none of us very much to be proud of," she said coldly.

"Dear God, that's true enough!" Robert wrenched his arm from Andrew's grasp and strode away. "We're a pretty lot, we Tantallons."

Nobody contradicted him. Still in her position by the door, Bridie watched, horrified. She was seeing three strangers, stripped of the everyday selves she thought she knew so well. Was this always the way when the ultimate reality of death came to a family?

She backed from the room. None of them seemed to notice her going. She closed the door and ran. For her great-aunt to be dying was bad enough. But for the old lady's family to wrangle so was past all endurance.

She went to her room, and flung herself upon the bed, and wept. How long she lay there she didn't know or care. But she was roused at last by a gentle tapping at the door.

" Bridie, my dear. . . . Bridie, it's Andrew."

Instantly fearing bad news she leapt up and flung the door wide. " What's happened, Andrew? Is it your mother? Is she—"

" It's nothing, my dear. I just wanted a word with you."

She stepped back, weak with relief, and let him in. He went and knelt upon the window seat, his head averted.

" When . . . when all this is over," he began, " there'll be nothing to keep you here. You'll be going back to London, to your old life there. . . ."

He paused. She saw very well what he was trying to say. He knew what that old life had been. He knew also how much she loved him—dear God, had she not told him often enough? But the time was wrong. She couldn't concentrate on such matters, couldn't make decisions, not now.

He turned to look at her and she lowered her tear-smudged face, avoiding his gaze. " Is there . . . is there no news at all of your mother, Andrew?"

" A little. Dr. Macnab says it's all right to go to her. Robert and Melissa have just been." But his eyes still brooded on her, pleading for an answer.

She ignored them. " Shall we go, then?" she said, moving quickly to the wash basin where she splashed water on her face, then stood drying it briskly as she watched Andrew rise reluctantly from the window seat.

" I . . . I love you, Bridie. I just wanted you to know that."

She couldn't bear it. " I said, shall we go then, Andrew?"

" Yes. Yes, of course. . . ."

Her great-aunt's room with its heavy crimson hangings and ornately lacquered furniture was hushed, silent save for the busy, seemingly unstoppable ticking of the clock. By the foot of the bed old Peggy sat upon a hard wooden chair, as still as a statue. Lady Otranta too was motionless, propped up on a great mound of pillows, her breathing soundless. But her lizard eyes were open, and undimmed, and the deep lines of pain were gone from her face.

"Don't just stand there," she said, echoing her usual sharpness with gentle self-mockery. "Come on in, both of you. And sit where I can see you."

They moved forward, one to each side of the bed. Andrew stooped and kissed her cheek. "How are you feeling, Mama?"

She smiled. "What would Macnab say? 'As well as can be expected?'" Then she tossed her head and struggled herself into a more upright position. "The man's a fool—d'you know that? Bundling me up like this, just because he says I'm dying! Queen Elizabeth, now—she refused pointblank even to go to bed. . . . But then, she was a queen, so I suppose people had to give in to her. Nobody gives in to me. They never have and they never will."

Andrew straightened her sheet. "You know, Mama, I'd say you were one of the most given-in-to women in all of Scotland."

"You would, would you?" She glared at him. Suddenly her mock indignation faded. "Perhaps you're right, boy. And perhaps it would have been better otherwise. . . ." Her hands twitched convulsively. She stilled them with an effort. "You've been a good son to me, Andrew. And in return I've treated you abominably. No—don't try to deny it. You know I have, and so do I."

Down at the foot of the bed old Peggy snorted audibly. Bridie leaned forward. "You had your reasons, Great-aunt. Andrew doesn't—"

But the old lady ignored her. "How sad it is," she went on, "that we never manage to learn from the mistakes of others. I was jealous of my own son, you see, determined that he should never, *could* never take his father's place—just as the Queen had been jealous of her poor son. And I'd seen it all before, the petty indignities she heaped upon him, and the harm they did . . . yet *still* I could not help myself."

She closed her eyes, shook her head slowly from side to side. "There now—I'm sorry. And what's done can't be undone." Then she was still, her eyes open again, fixed upon him steadily. "But I'm proud of you, boy. And grateful. You never faltered. And—thank God—I think you never ceased to love me."

Andrew lowered his gaze. "Dearest Mama, you know I. . . ."

She reached for one of his hands and held it tight. "Your father was a fine brave man, Andrew. Sometimes, when I look at you, it's as if my Jamie were standing there, my Jamie with all the burden of his years lifted from him. . . . But I want to tell you this, my dear—you have something he never had. You have humility. And the strength that only true humility brings."

The room was silent. The old lady patted his hand, then released it. She turned to Bridie, a new, bright mischievousness in her eyes. "Well now, child, I've done with pretty speeches. But what about you? I take it you agree with me about this dear, idiot son of mine?"

Bridie nodded cautiously, a little uncertain as to what might come next.

"In that case, my girl, just when exactly are you going to bring yourself to marry him?"

"*Marry* . . .?" Prepared as she had been, the abruptness of the onslaught left her utterly bewildered.

"And you needn't look so shocked, young Bridie—my present situation does have certain advantages. The best of them being that I no longer have to be afraid of treading on people's toes. So what've you got to say for yourself?"

Bridie pulled herself together. She knew Lady Otranta didn't suffer timidity gladly. "To be honest, Great-aunt, the last time I talked to you about this I got the impression that—"

"Oh, I know I said you'd get hurt. And so you will. We all get hurt, one way or another. But that never stops us making fools of ourselves over the right man."

Andrew laughed. "You know, Mama, I really think—"

"And you keep out of this." His mother fixed him with a beady eye. "It's the women who decide these things. By rights you shouldn't even be present." She swung back to Bridie. " Well, child? I asked you a question."

" I—I'm not sure I can answer it, Great-aunt." She knew the answer very well. But she didn't like being rushed. And she too could be self-willed.

" Not answer it? Why not, pray? Because the foolish man drank too much at the party? That worried me too, I agree. But I've been known to do the same myself just now and then, you know." The old lady flashed a sly glance round the room. " Though not perhaps quite so often as certain people might imagine."

" I know that, Great-aunt." If this was a time for being truthful, then so be it. " I've seen that poor aspidistra in the window."

" Have you, now?" Lady Otranta regarded her great-niece through half-closed eyes. " You're shrewder even than I thought. And more discreet. . . . So much the better. You'll know how to cope with my idiot son's manifold deficiencies."

" Honestly, Mama—" Andrew's laughter was now a little forced " —you know as well as I do that I've never been drunk before in my life. You mustn't speak as if I make a habit of it."

Briefly Robert's words, instantly regretted, flashed across Bridie's mind: *He's done this before.* Which one of them, she wondered, was lying?

" Be quiet, I say!" The old lady didn't even turn in her son's direction. " Well, child? Are you going to marry him or aren't you?"

For Bridie the whole world seemed suddenly to stand still, waiting for her answer. She glanced across at Andrew, pale now and deadly serious, his eyes pleading. She could delay no longer. She took a deep breath, held it. Finally, " I am," she said quietly. " If he'll have me, that is."

Silence. Then, from Andrew, a great sigh of relief.

Her great-aunt ticked irritably. " Of course he'll have you." She sank back onto her pillows. " I always knew I'd make a good match-maker. People like to be persuaded, you know. It's all a question of who can shout the loudest."

She closed her eyes. Suddenly all the animation seemed to have ebbed from her face. Her head slumped sideways and in an instant old Peggy was at her side, pushing Andrew back out of the way. She felt the old lady's pulse, her little eyes screwed up with the effort of concentration. Then she relaxed.

" I do wish as you wouldn't do that, Madame," she chided. " Frightenin' us all so. There really ain't no need. . . ." She gestured Andrew and Bridie to the door. " But then, that's you all over," she went on, pushing at pillows and tweaking at the heavy crimson covers. " No consideration. No consideration for others at all. You always was like that, right from the start. Remember that time in Bognor, when the Perfessor. . . ."

They left the fat old dresser still in full flood. But not before Lady Otranta had opened one bright eye and winked it mockingly at them. She was biding her time. She'd go when she was good and ready. And not a moment before.

In the little octagonal room with the lancet windows Andrew stopped and pulled Bridie to him. " Did you mean it?" he said.

She looked up into his face. " Of course I meant it."

" Oh, Bridie. . . ." He held her close. But she could feel how troubled he was. When he spoke again his voice was strained. " Is it wicked to be so happy?" he murmured. " So happy, while Mama is. . . ."

She hugged him close. For a long time she didn't answer. Then at last what she hoped were the right words came to her. She lifted her head. " Your mother's happy too," she told him.

Downstairs Robert was at the organ, pounding out a thunderous toccata. He didn't stop as they went by. They found Melissa in the study. She was poring over plans of the estate.

" I've been thinking," she said. " It's high time we started replanting the south hillside. There's a lot of underbrush to be cleared, but it'll be worth it. Duncan says timber's going up in price all the time. And if there's a war. . . ."

They left her to her schemes. There could well be long and difficult hours of waiting ahead. And each member of the household must fill them as best they could.

Andrew and Bridie sat with Dr. Macnab in the library, talking a little, reading when they could. The doctor took to spending longer and longer periods upstairs with his patient. Dinner time came and went. Old Meredith had been told the family wouldn't be eating. He hovered all the same, saying cook had prepared something light to go on the sideboard just in case. The poor man was as lost as the rest of them. Andrew called him in and told him to serve what spirits they preferred to the servants below stairs. Most of them had been at the castle for many years. It was going to be a long night.

Shortly after eleven o'clock the family were all gathered in the small drawing room. A wind had got up and was pounding a loose casement somewhere. Nobody seemed to care. Bridie had just roused herself to go and fix it when the door opened and Dr. Macnab came in. All eyes turned in his direction.

" I think you should go up now."

Calmly Andrew put aside his book. " All of us?"

The doctor nodded. " Be very quiet, though."

Bridie went up the stairs last of all. Suddenly she felt an intruder. Although she had come to love her great-aunt she had only known her for such a short time, while for the others Lady Otranta had been their whole life.

She didn't know what to expect, and she was afraid. She looked up at Andrew on the gallery above, totally composed for all his deathly pallor. He'd be strong, she knew that. Perhaps she could take her strength from him.

Lady Otranta was lying back, propped up on pillows as before, her eyes closed. As they entered the room, however, she stirred, and looked about her.

" All the Tantallons," she said, her voice surprisingly strong. " That's nice."

Her children separated, Robert going to the fireplace, Melissa to the curtained window, Andrew staying by the foot of his mother's bed. Bridie lingered just inside the door. Beyond the heavy crimson curtains the wind rushed and battered. Suddenly old Peggy, who had been fussing with things on the bedside table, could stand the silence no longer. She gave a strangled sob, pressed a grubby handkerchief to her face, and stumbled from the room.

Andrew lifted his head. But his mother spoke first. " You'll look after that abominable old creature, I know."

" Of course."

" She's been with me longer than any of you. But you know that. I'd like to have made provision for her . . . she'll still need a home, you see."

" She'll never be without one, Mama. Bridie and I—"

" I hoped you'd say that. But things aren't going to be easy." She smiled wryly. " I've been a troublesome old woman. A troublesome young woman, and now a troublesome old woman. You're going to find out soon just how troublesome. . . ."

Robert stepped forward a pace. " I wish you wouldn't talk like that, Mama."

She held out a hand to him and he took it. " They do say that confession is good for the soul, Robert."

Melissa laughed briefly, somehow a reassuring sound in the airless room. " For goodness' sake, we're none of us perfect. But you, of all people, surely have precious little to reproach yourself with."

The old lady's reply was stopped by a sudden spasm that shook her whole body. When it passed she was noticeably weaker.

" Bridie? Is that you, Bridie, over by the door?"

Bridie moved to her bedside, opposite Robert. " I'm here, Great-aunt. And you mustn't tire yourself."

" What nonsense you do talk, child. There are times when to be tired is the most delightful feeling in all the world." She reached out her other hand and took Bridie's arm firmly. " The memoirs, child—I want you to listen to me carefully."

Andrew stepped round the foot of the bed. " You're confused, Mama. There are no memoirs."

" So you say, my son. But Bridie here knows better, I think." The spasm returned, and Bridie felt her great-aunt's fingers bite into her arm like claws. " Listen to me carefully, child. . . . Come along now and concentrate. I'd like to know. . . ."

She shook her head from side to side. " It's really not difficult. Not if you do your best. Just be quick, my dear. It's really not difficult. . . ."

Bewildered, Bridie looked up from the old lady's pleading face. Andrew caught her eye and shook his head infinitesimally. " I'm sure Bridie understands you, Mama. Of course it's not difficult."

" Do you, child? *Do you?*"

And suddenly Bridie did. She nodded, closing her eyes and repeating Lady Otranta's words to herself, fixing them in her memory.

" Excellent, my dear. Excellent. . . . I was sure you would. . . . They're a prickly lot, my little family. But I love them all very dearly."

The old lady's hand fell from her arm. She released Robert also.

" You know," she said, " there really are times when to be tired is the most delightful feeling in all the world. That, and an easy conscience."

She sighed then, and became still. But with a different stillness. Slowly her eyes lost their restless animation and gazed sightlessly out at the troubled world she had left behind.

For a while all was silent in the room, save for the wind and the busy, cheerful ticking of the clock. Then, softly, Melissa began to cry, the tears running unchecked down her cheeks. Andrew went to the door, called to the doctor who was waiting outside, and returned to put his arm about Melissa's shoulders. They stayed in the room while Dr. Macnab came in and removed the pillows from behind Lady Otranta's head and closed her eyes and placed two silver crowns upon them. Then Andrew led his half-sister out, Robert and Bridie following behind.

Her thoughts were in a turmoil. She felt grief certainly, but for herself and for the others, rather than for her great-aunt who was now, finally, at peace. She felt confused and uneasy also. The old lady had placed a terrible responsibility upon her. Upon her, and upon no one else. And why? With all the others in the room, why had Lady Otranta chosen her alone? Had there really been those of her closest family whom she could not trust? Robert? Melissa? Even Andrew?

They passed old Peggy, weeping uncontrollably among the bizarre furnishings of the sitting room next door. Robert would have spoken to her, but she shook him off. So they left her to grieve in her own solitary way, and went wearily downstairs. Andrew called Meredith and told him that his mistress was dead. Prepared though he had been for this moment, the old man groaned in sudden anguish, then bowed his head and shuffled wordlessly from the room.

Dr. Macnab came down soon after. He took Bridie on one side. " I think someone should go up to Peggy," he murmured. " I could get nothing out of her. But she's deeply distressed."

Bridie slipped away, mounted the stairs yet again. As she approached her great-aunt's quarters she heard sounds of terrible commotion and began to run. In the doorway to the sitting room, however, she stopped short, horrified by what she saw.

The place was in ruins. Cabinets lay on their sides, panels smashed in. Broken glass was scattered everywhere, the books torn from the bookshelves. In the midst of it all old Peggy continued her work of destruction, flailing about her with a poker taken from beside the fire, smashing at a mirrored casket. As Bridie watched she turned her attack upon the colourful, helpless little figure of Az Rah, ripping his body from the chess board and flinging it savagely onto the fire, where the silken garments flared into instant, dazzling flames.

Then she caught sight of Bridie and faced her defiantly. " Secrets as the Perfessor worked on all his life for," she cried. " Secrets as jumped-up fools like Devant would give their eye teeth for. . . . Well, they're not having 'em, see?"

She began beating at Az Rah's cabinet till the doors splintered and the mechanism within spilled out on the floor.

Bridie hesitated, appalled by such wanton destruction. The poor woman was clearly beside herself with grief. She must be stopped, her attention somehow distracted. Bridie collected her thoughts.

" Peggy," she cautiously began, " I—I wonder if you could

help me. Lady Otranta's memoirs, I think they're hidden somewhere after all, and I'm sure you could help me find them. She spoke to me, you see, and—"

"Help you?" The fat old woman paused, hands on hips, panting. "Oh, I suspected what she was up to, all right. Though I never did catch her at it. . . . But as for helping you, I'd rather die first." She returned to her battering. "All the Perfessor's secrets . . . they should of died with him . . . well, they can die with her instead. . . ."

Bridie came forward into the room, her heart pounding. She watched old Peggy, waited her opportunity, then caught the other's wrist and held on to it. For a moment they struggled together. Then, suddenly, the old woman's madness left her. She collapsed into Bridie's arms, sobbing bitterly.

"Dear Gawd, dear Gawd—what's to become o' me?"

Bridie led her to one of the few chairs remaining upright. "Hush now, Peggy. Nothing's going to become of you. You're safe enough. There'll always be a place for you, here at the castle."

Peggy sat down, sobbing still. But when she surveyed the wreckage all around her she was unrepentant. "I'd do it again, mind," she muttered. "And as for helping you—never! Them memoirs . . . I'm not daft, you know. I can add up two and two. And she never did tell me what became of that nice travelling cloak and her best straw boater. . . ."

Bridie stayed with her, scarcely listening to her meaningless ramblings, until slowly the old woman grew calmer. Then she helped her to her room. Downstairs again, she sought out Andrew and told him what had happened. He shook his head in tired sympathy. "Poor woman," he said. "In some ways tonight has been worse for her than for any of us. I'll speak to Meredith. Perhaps he can give one of the maids something to take up to her."

Dr. Macnab was staying the night at the castle. He and the others had gone to their rooms. After Andrew had departed in search of the old butler, Bridie lingered, undecided, in the huge, shadowy entrance hall. Her great-aunt had set her a task. But she was tired out and it was after midnight. Surely she could safely leave things till the morning? She collected a candle from the foot of the stairs and went up to her bedroom. Afraid that a night's sleep might drive the old lady's words clean out of her head, she sat down at once and spelled them out on the typewriter: *Listen to me carefully . . . Come along now . . . Concentrate . . . I'd like to know . . . It's really not difficult . . . Not if you do your best . . . Just be quick . . . It's really not difficult. . . .*

She stared at the words. 'Trigger phrases', her great-aunt had called them. Each one of them meant something. And the meaning was to be found in that book hidden in the glass table in the old lady's sitting room. Or wherever else it might be, after Peggy's violent depredations.

She nodded over her typewriter, then jerked her head upright. Why was she still bothering with the memoirs? Nobody wanted them, not a single soul—except possibly Mr. Pugh-Hennessy. For a moment her mind went uneasily back to the sight of him, in the rain, on Prince's Street. But she banished the vision, and its disturbing implications. She knew very well why she was bothering with the memoirs. Because it had been her great-aunt's dying wish that she should do so.

A knock came on her door, and it opened a crack. Instinctively she snatched the piece of paper from her machine and stuffed it into a drawer.

"Bridie?" Andrew stood there, candle in hand. "I was going to my room and I saw the light under your door. I don't think I'll be able to sleep much tonight. Do you mind if we talk a bit?"

At the sight of him her tiredness disappeared as if it had never been. She leapt to her feet, hurried to his side, and embraced him tenderly. His candle tilted, dripping wax onto the floor. "I'm so glad you've come. There's—there's something we can do together. One last thing for your mother. . . ."

She needed somebody to help her: somebody she could trust. And if not Andrew, then who else in the whole world?

She took the paper from the drawer and showed it to him, explaining what it was. He read the phrases over, wrinkling his brow. "I've seen Mama do her mind-reading trick with old

Peggy, of course—but I never guessed how it was worked."
He stared blankly at the paper. " If we ever get to decipher
all this, what d'you think it'll tell us?"

" I'm not sure. Where the memoirs are hidden, I expect."

" You truly believe she wrote them, then?"

Bridie nodded. He seemed so tired and bewildered. There
was so much she needed to tell him . . . about his mother's
supposed drunkenness, about Dr. Macnab's long-kept secret,
so much she needed to tell him. But not *now*—not with this
new and vital puzzle clamouring for a solution. If he could not
sleep, then neither could she. How better, then, to pass the long
hours?

They went softly through the darkened castle. In the
devastated sitting room Andrew lit a lamp, gazing around
him in sad amazement. Bridie set to work at once, trying not
to think of the thin, pathetic shape lying still and silent on the
bed in the next room. Her great-aunt's spirit, she knew, would
approve of her actions. . . . She found the glass specimen table,
surprisingly undamaged, and hunted anxiously in the hidden
compartment. His eyebrows raised, Andrew watched her bring
out the book.

" All the times I've been in this room and I never guessed
that table was other than what it appeared to be."

Together they spread out the paper with Lady Otranta's
message on the table and opened the book beside it. *Listen
to me*: Andrew found the phrase, number nineteen on M.
Houdin's alphabetical list, standing for the letter S. *Come
along now*: Bridie remembered that from her great-aunt's
explanation. It came first in the list, representing A. *Concentrate* and *I'd like to know* were easily discovered: F and E
respectively.

S-A-F-E . . . so the memoirs were undamaged. That much,
at least, was clear.

The next two phrases presented more of a problem. On the
alphabetical list they stood for R and B, numbers eighteen and
two. Andrew stared at the letters in blank perplexity. " I'll
swear there's not a single word in the dictionary that begins
RB," he said.

Bridie racked her brains, remembered the other lists Lady Otranta had mentioned, the lists of words. She flicked through the book, found list eighteen. It was a list of prepositions: inside, outside, behind, through . . . Number two on that list was *under*.

Safe under . . . it seemed a promising beginning, so they went on to the last two phrases. These turned out to represent V and R.

"Victoria Regina." Andrew closed the book. "So there we have it—Mama's memoirs are in some manner safe under the late Queen. Yet I don't really see how that helps us."

Bridie frowned. Her great-aunt would scarcely have gone to so much trouble, simply to deliver a message that was meaningless. And besides, somewhere at the back of her mind a memory lurked, something she couldn't quite call into consciousness.

"The message was for *me*," she said thoughtfully. "Your mother was referring to something she thought I'd understand. Something she knew I'd seen. . . . There's not a statue of the old Queen anywhere on the estate?"

Andrew shook his head wearily. "There's a memorial down in the village. But—"

"A portrait, perhaps?"

Distantly, somewhere in the castle, a clock struck two. The sound was bleak, infinitely lonely. Andrew sighed. "There are plenty of portraits. In the big drawing room, for example. The one done by Winterhalter."

"In the big drawing room? I'm sure that can't be right. . . ." Suddenly Bridie had it. She looked up excitedly. "*Safe under VR* . . . don't you see? She meant *the safe* under VR!"

Andrew shrugged. "I'm afraid I don't see."

But she was babbling now. "The safe, the green safe, under the portrait of Queen Victoria. The safe in the office up at the sawmill. . . ." She clutched his arm. "And that explains the other thing that was worrying me—how the memoirs got to wherever they were hidden. Duncan took them! He took them every morning, in that leather Accounts folder he always carried."

" Then Duncan helped her?"

" It makes sense, doesn't it? Someone had to help her. And who would she be more likely to turn to than Duncan?"

Andrew turned away. " That's true enough," he said bitterly.

Her heart went out to him. She couldn't explain the estate manager's long deception. All she knew was that, once the memoirs were found, everything would become clear.

She hurried to the window, pulled back the curtain, looked out. " Come on," she said. " We must find the memoirs at once. There's still a wind, but it's stopped raining."

" Do you know what time it is, my dear?"

" I don't care, Andrew. I can't rest till we've got to the bottom of this whole extraordinary business."

He didn't argue. She was afraid that he might suggest disturbing the others, but he didn't. Strangely, he seemed willing to fall in with anything that she proposed. It was activity that carried her on, activity that stopped her feeling tired, activity that dulled the night's pain and sorrow. It was her activity that carried him along also. Obediently he went downstairs to procure heavy topcoats and a lantern. He met her by a side door. The castle was hushed about them, shadows pressing in on the flickering candlelight.

" It's as black as pitch outside," he said. " Are you sure you want to go through with this?"

There was a movement behind them. A rat, perhaps. Or one of the many castle cats. Bridie took the lantern from him and lit it at her candle flame, holding it high, revealing nothing but the empty, stone-flagged corridor.

" We're going up to the sawmill," she said, quietly but firmly.

The climb through the woods in the dark was difficult. It seemed to go on for ever. Repeatedly Bridie stumbled in the muddy cart-ruts, the hem of her skirt sodden from the rain-soaked grass. But Andrew trudged stoically along beside her, his uneven stride never faltering, the lantern in one hand, the other continually supporting her.

They came to the bridge, the stream in full spate rushing

deafeningly beneath it. Then on up the last steep curve of the track. Suddenly Andrew stopped short, drew her to him, and pointed. Away among the trees a light flickered, rising and falling as the wind gusted across the hillside.

" Someone's lighted a bonfire in front of the sawmill," he whispered. Then his grip on her arm tightened. " Unless it's the mill itself that's burning—"

He left her then, and hurried forward. She ran after him and together they breasted the slope and came to the edge of the wide level clearing in the forest where the sawmill stood. The air was alive with the sound of rushing water, and of the trees tossing in the wind.

In the middle of the open space a fire was burning, pine chips that spluttered and flung up showers of sparks to be whisked instantly away. And over the fire leaned the darkly-cloaked figure of a man, his back towards them, black against the leaping flames. As Bridie watched, suddenly she realised what he was doing. In his arms there was a pile of large note-books from which he was tearing pages which he then crumpled and fed carefully, one by one, into the fire.

Uttering a low cry of protest, she started forward. At once a dog's low shape emerged from the shadows, snarling and tugging ferociously at her skirt. The man turned towards this sudden sound, the light from the fire playing redly on the heavily-bearded features of Duncan Symonds.

" Noble! Come here this instant, sir!" At once the dog released its grip and backed away. Mr. Symonds peered in their direction. " It's Mistress Bridie, is it? And Sir Andrew? So I maun apologise for the behaviour of my dog, it seems . . . though I'm thinking mebbe he did no more than his duty, warning me of intruders at this ungodly hour."

" Hardly intruders, Duncan." Andrew limped forward into the firelight. " And as to the ungodly hour, may I ask exactly what you're doing here now, man?"

" Aye. You may that." He nodded judicially. " It's your right, y'ken, now that Her Ladyship's gone." Then, stepping back a pace, he ripped decisively at the remaining pages and threw them with a sudden gesture into the centre of the fire.

Helplessly Bridie watched them blacken and shrivel, then finally burst into flame. Was this then really what all Lady Otranta's work had come to? Too late now, Andrew caught angrily at Duncan's arm. "You realise that's a criminal act you've just committed, man. And before two witnesses. Burning the property of—"

"Criminal act, is it? No disrespect, Sir Andrew, but to my way of thinking 'twas Her Ladyship who was the criminal in this wee matter."

Bridie found her voice. "But how could you, Mr. Symonds? Her memoirs—you must have seen how hard she worked at them. Yet you—"

"*Her* memoirs?" Duncan Symonds laughed comfortably. "It's clear we're talking at cross purposes. This is no Her Ladyship's work I've been setting beyond the reach of prying eyes. That's up in the office, fine and dandy. Untouched and unread, the way I made my promise—Her Ladyship will have told you of that, no doubt, seeing she's told you where to come for it."

Bridie stared at him. Then she gestured in utter bewilderment at the lowering flames. "Then what . . .?"

"Stolen property, Mistress. Stolen by Her Ladyship. . . . Stolen by myself now as well, I grant you—though I reckon you'll find that mighty hard to prove."

Andrew strode angrily across to stand over him, topping the sturdy Mr. Symonds by a good six inches. "Speak plainly, man—I don't understand you. And be careful what you're saying. My mother may be dead, but as long as I'm alive no one shall slander her good name."

Duncan stood his ground. "Aye. . . . Weel, mebbe stealing's a bit strong for what your mother did. For y'ken I've no way rightly of telling how she laid her hands upon the old Queen's papers. It wasna a thing she confided—but then, you'd no expect her to. All the same—"

"The old Queen's papers?" Suddenly Bridie thought she understood. She remembered what Robert had told her, down in the castle library. "Her diary, you mean? The one that was never published?"

233

"You've the right of it there, Mistress." Duncan held out the empty bindings to her, finely-tooled leather. "They were never published, and wi' good reason. John Brown and her. . . . She wore her heart too much on her sleeve, puir soul. Besides, there were those who said she filled her court too much wi' foreigners—Germans, that Indian secretary . . . and Scotsmen." He chuckled. "It came to Sir Henry Ponsonby to tell her so. Him and the Dean of Windsor. She didna like it. But she bowed to their superior wisdom." He paused, looking thoughtfully down at the tattered red bindings. "And Lady Otranta telling me times were different now. Weel, mebbe they are and mebbe they aren't. . . . I didna argue wi' her, mind. And I kept the diaries safe the way she said. But I'd have found a way of stopping her. If ever she'd lived, I mean." He lowered his head.

Andrew stepped back a pace. "My mother planned to publish the diaries as part of her memoirs?"

"I'm no saying that." He cleared his throat. "But she planned to use them, that's for certain. And it wouldna have been right. Not right at a'."

"So you burned them? You burned priceless historical documents?"

"You can say that, Sir Andrew. But you'll no be proving it." With a final quick movement he tossed the bindings into the fire. "Let them rest easy, her and her faithful servant. I tell you, Brown was more a gentleman than the half of her court. And the gossips may say what they like—there was never a thing between the both of them as wasna right and proper. Just a nod here, and a kind word there."

He began to walk away. Bridie looked up from the flames. "Then why burn the proof of it?" she asked.

His placid laugh came back at her out of the darkness. "Words prove nothing, nothing at a'. Words are what you make of them. And I ken weel what those wi' malice in their hearts might have made of the words of that puir wee lonely wummun. Sir Henry knew it too, y'ken. And he wasna a fool, I'm thinking."

Duncan whistled to his dog. " Good night to you, Sir Andrew. And to you, Mistress. If there's more to be said, we can say it the morn. Her Ladyship's dead, and I maun go and pay my respects."

He whistled again, then called in anger. Finally the dog came to him from the shadows, and the two of them went slowly away out of the firelight's circle.

Bridie listened as his footsteps faded down the track. Andrew sighed. " He's probably right," he said. " With King Edward on the throne the monarchy's in trouble enough. . . . Anyway, it's too late now. The diaries are gone—with no proof that they ever existed."

Bridie turned from the fire. " At least your mother's memoirs are safe."

He smiled wryly. " Safe in the safe. . . ."

Together they made their way across the sodden carpet of sawdust and shavings to the end of the mill building where a small pass-door stood open. They went in, past the silent machinery to the neat white-washed office. By the light from the lantern Bridie saw the green-painted safe gaping wide. And above it the severe portrait she remembered so well. Behind them the door to the building banged savagely in the wind, and banged again.

Bridie knelt in front of the open safe, her heart pounding, and Andrew put the lantern on the floor beside her. The interior of the safe was empty, save for an untidy stack of closely-written sheets of paper. Bridie leaned in and drew this out with trembling fingers.

She took the top sheet and held it close to the light. The writing was small and spidery, but clearly legible. *It's no use at all, sitting down to write one's memoirs,* she read, *and then trying to fudge them. One must be prepared to be utterly truthful. . . .* She lowered the paper. The effect was eerie, like listening to the sound of the dead woman's voice there in the bare, shadowy office. She shivered slightly.

Andrew touched her shoulder. " Is that what you were looking for? Is that what all the fuss has been about?"

She nodded.

" I don't think you should read it." His voice sounded strange.

" But Andrew—"

" It should be burned, Bridie. Burned along with the old Queen's diaries."

" No, Andrew. It was your mother's wish that—"

" Burn those papers, Bridie. *Please* !"

He stooped to take them from her. Instinctively she resisted. " You're wrong, Andrew. . . . What is it you're so afraid of ?"

His eyes wild, he stared wordlessly down at her. Out in the machine shop the door banged again, with renewed savagery. His gaze flickered sideways, and he backed away from her.

" Don't move," he hissed. " In a minute that door'll be off its hinges. Don't move till I get back."

He left her then, crouched on the floor by the open safe. Uneasily she riffled through the pages in her hands, holding them to the light but scarcely seeing them. A suspicion had formed in her mind. The terrible thought that perhaps, of all the people in the castle, it was Andrew who. . . . Wretchedly she shook her head from side to side. She couldn't believe it. She wouldn't believe it. Not of *Andrew*.

The door had stopped banging. She waited for Andrew to return. What was she going to say to him ? How was she going to make him see that if his mother had struggled so long and painfully to write what she believed to be the truth, then they would be wrong to suppress it ? That Lady Otranta's dying wishes *must* be respected. . . .

She waited, listening for his return, hearing only the rushing water in the mill leet above, and the restless murmur of the wind. Finally she got to her feet and, tucking the manuscript under her arm, picked up the lantern and went in search of him. She retraced her steps the length of the machine shop, shadows fleeing before her, the great blade of the saw glinting evilly as she passed it. She reached the door, found it closed.

" Andrew ?" she called. " Andrew, where are you ?"

Her voice seemed tiny in the vast enclosed spaces all around. No answer came. She tried the door. It was locked.

Up until that moment she had not been afraid, only bewildered. She knew Andrew loved her. She knew he'd do nothing to hurt her. Now, suddenly, nothing was certain, not even that.

She beat upon the door, but it didn't yield. She swung round, holding the lantern high. Somewhere, out in the surrounding darkness, a tiny movement had told her she wasn't alone. If Andrew was there, why didn't he answer? She called his name again and again. And received only silence in reply.

11

Footsteps rang out. Footsteps on iron, clicking steadily. They seemed to fill the darkness, echoing back from every direction. Bridie fell silent, and cowered back against the locked door. Abruptly, out on the gantry high above her, the footsteps ceased. A voice came down to her.

"Bridie? Bridie Tantallon? I can see you very well. Those papers under your arm—I know what they are. Are you going to give them to me?"

It took her a moment to recognise who was speaking. Then relief flooded through her. The whole thing was a joke. Some crazy joke.

"Robert?" she shouted. "Stop it—don't be silly. Come on down. You had me frightened half out of my wits."

He laughed, the sound beating back unpleasantly off the surrounding walls. "You'd be wise to be frightened, fair coz. For I mean to have those memoirs, you see."

"*Robert?*" Suddenly, horrifyingly, Bridie understood a lot of things. The car that had nearly run her down, the message in her typewriter, his ceaseless curiosity about the memoirs, always so carefully veiled. But what of his kindness, his youthful high spirits? "A joke's a joke," she said firmly. "Of course you must read what your mother's written. But—"

"Read it? I'm afraid I've no wish at all to read it. I know what she's written all too well. She's written the truth. She always said she would. I did my best to stop her—and to stop you too, when I thought you might interfere. And a fat lot of good it did me." He laughed again. "A wily old bird, the Incredible Madame Otranta. . . ."

Bridie caught her breath. Was he mad? *For God's sake, where was Andrew?* She tried to speak calmly. "What is this 'truth'," she said, "that you and Andrew are so afraid of?"

The footsteps moved, then stopped again. " I love my brother dearly, coz, but I'm afraid he's an awful fool. He's always had the crazy notion that somehow Mama contrived the death of the first Lady Tantallon. It's utter nonsense, of course. It has to be, you see, since the old witch was alive until four or five years ago. She died in Baden-Baden, I believe."

Bridie tried to back away, found herself hard up against the corner of the building, trapped. He *was* mad.

" And would you believe it, little Bridie, our noble Papa had paid her an allowance down all those years? The woman who had tried to kill him? That's how I found out all about her, you see. I picked up an old account book after his death. Payments to a Mrs. Wilkinson. A *Mrs. Wilkinson.* . . . Mama caught me at it, so I had to ask her."

He lowered his voice. " And the ridiculous thing—the really ridiculous thing is that she could have lied to me even then. She could have said this Mrs. Wilkinson was some fancy woman. I mean, Wilkinson—it sounds like some fancy woman, wouldn't you say?" His feet clanged as he moved a short distance along the gantry. Bridie could picture him, the restless pacing she knew so well. And still his voice came down to her, disembodied, out of the darkness. " But that wouldn't do for Mama, of course. No fancy woman for the noble Sir James. Anything was better than that—even the truth. The truth that the first Lady Tantallon, a murderous witch if ever there was one, had been a mill-stone round our necks down all these years. And why? All because. . . ."

Bridie was too confused, too terrified to understand much of what he was saying. But that last phrase caught her attention: *a mill-stone round our necks* . . . That, then, was what the conversation she'd overheard between Robert and his mother had been referring to. The first Lady Tantallon, and not Melissa at all. The first Lady Tantallon, who was supposed to have been dead for—

Robert was still speaking. ". . . So I'm coming down there now, and you're going to give me those memoirs. For Andrew's sake, you understand. There'll be enough of Duncan's fire left to deal with them, if we're patient. He's a man after my own heart, that Duncan. I followed you up from the castle, you see, so I had a grandstand view of your meeting. Except that that wretched dog of his nosed me out and would have chewed my leg off if I'd moved a muscle."

Bridie thought of poor Noble—if he'd been less obedient to Duncan's whistle, then—

"Well now, coz, you've been quiet a long time. What d'you say? Are you going to give me those memoirs? Or am I going to have to take them?"

His footsteps began to descend the iron ladder down from the gantry. "After all, it's in your own interest. And I did my best to warn you. Prove Andrew a bastard and that's goodbye to your hopes of living happily ever after."

He was making no sense. No sense at all. "Where *is* Andrew?" she demanded. "What have you done with him?"

The footsteps paused. "*A wee tappit tae th'haed*, as dear old Meredith would say. Nothing serious, I think. But he'll be out of the way a while yet. And you haven't answered my question."

She crept sideways, glancing fearfully around. She was quite alone. But she thought she remembered a second door out of the building, away on the far side of the machine shop. "Of course I'll give you the memoirs, Robert. If you'll just come down here quietly and—"

"You know something, coz?" Something in his tone caused her to freeze. "It may be my suspicious mind, little Bridie, but I'm afraid I don't believe you." His footsteps pattered upwards. Upwards and across. "What's needed, I think, is a small extra inducement."

There was a faint metallic scraping sound. Outside the mill building the sound of rushing water changed. She recognised the change. Desperately she made a dash across the sawdust-laden floor, needing to reach the far side before the machinery began to turn. In an instant Robert had slithered down the ladder, heading her off. With the lantern in her hand he could see her every movement. Yet without it she would scarcely dare budge an inch. She backed away from him, till brought up short against the cold metal of some massive piece of machinery.

Already the water wheel had begun to turn, and with it axles, pulleys, gear shafts within the building. In the machine behind her something stirred, a faint snatching, whining sound, and she recoiled away, screaming in sudden terror. All about her the wheels began to whisper. And Robert, visible now for the first time in the light from the lantern, on the ground, hardly ten paces away, was coming slowly, relentlessly nearer.

She turned again and ran, gathering the heavy material of her cloak closely to her. With sickening dread she recalled Andrew's words of warning: *Can't you see how dangerous it is?* She faltered, looked back over her shoulder. Robert wasn't hurrying, simply continuing slowly and carefully after her. As long as he kept her from the far door she could run where she liked. Run until she made a mistake. . . . While behind his head the blade of the circular saw spun in a steely blue arc, singing higher and higher.

" Are you ready to hand them over yet, little Bridie? Hmmm? I've often heard how wonderful it is, the way a little danger focuses the mind."

She ran again, dodging between nameless masses of equipment, each seemingly now with a life of its own, determined to snare her. She circled the big central table, putting the spinning saw-blade momentarily between her and her pursuer. If she could just dodge round the end of the table—

But Robert had guessed her intention. With a powerful thrust he set the whole table moving on its well-greased track, rolling silkily past the evil blur of the saw-blade, closing the gap between itself and the great double doors at the end of the building.

Bridie stopped short and turned, stood at bay, the lantern held limply by her side. The noise in the machine shop around her had risen till it seemed to drive all possibility of thought from her head. Pulley belts flailed shrilly, while above it all the shimmering saw-blade keened its strange, hypnotic lament. And still Robert advanced slowly, unhurriedly upon her.

Why should she not give him the memoirs? Were they worth all this? Could anything be worth all this?

It was then, when she was at the end of her resources, that a dark shape rose suddenly up behind Robert. The next moment he had reeled and fallen sideways, across the still-moving table. He lay on it stunned, inert, as the weight of its momentum carried him on towards the saw. She screamed then, and screamed again, her eyes tight shut against the horror.

Abruptly the saw's shrill keening stopped. She waited, shuddering, her mind frozen fast against all imagination. . . . It was a touch on her arm that roused her, set her shrieking again, wide-eyed back against the unyielding doors. Sense returned to her only slowly. The sight of Andrew, staggering slightly, a thin trickle of blood running down his forehead from a dark matted stain in his hair. His voice in her ear, shouting above the continuing noise of the machinery. " It's all right, Bridie. It's all right. . . ."

She clutched him to her. He stroked her hair. " I stopped the saw in time, dearest. It's all right."

Wildly, disbelievingly, she stared past him. He cast a long shadow behind, but to the left of it she saw Robert, still unsteady, heaving himself up into a sitting position. And beside him, not six inches away, the saw-blade lying still upon its bearings, the searing teeth motionless, at rest.

She wept then, safe in her lover's arms.

After a while Robert eased himself down off the table and went slowly up onto the gantry to close the flow of water outside and stop the machinery. When he had descended again he came to stand by Andrew's side.

" It seems my ' wee tappit ' wasn't quite hard enough," he murmured. " A triumph for brotherly feeling, no doubt. . . . As was yours, Andrew, when you saved my life."

He touched his brother's arm, then turned and walked away to the little pass door, inserted a key in its lock. He was about to go out through the door when he changed his mind. He came back.

" Bridie . . . fair coz . . . I would never really have let anything happen to you. Surely you believe that?"

Andrew held up a warning hand. " Later, Robert," he said. " Later, when we can look at what's happened more clearly."

Robert shrugged. " At least I did my best. And it was all for you, you know. You're the one who'll suffer most, when we're both disinherited. You're the one I really care for."

He went away then, leaving them alone. And still Bridie didn't know what in the world he was talking about. Disinherited? How could Andrew possibly be disinherited?

*   *   *

It was difficult, next morning, to slip into the sad preparations for Lady Otranta's funeral as if nothing had happened. Andrew had decided—and she agreed with him—that no mention should be made of the memoirs until it was certain exactly what they contained. Bridie had tried to read them on her return from the sawmill, but she'd stayed awake no further than the second page.

And in the morning there was Dr. Macnab to be got off to Edinburgh on the first ferry. And Robert locked in his room, incommunicado. And a note to be sent by the doctor to the Tantallon lawyers. And the authorities in Stirling to be contacted. And poor Melissa striding restlessly about the castle, alternately weeping and rejecting as hopelessly old-fashioned the idea that she might want to go into mourning. And—most difficult of all and quite unexpected by everyone—a visitor who returned in the car that had taken Dr. Macnab to the ferry. A visitor from Edinburgh.

Meredith brought his card to Andrew as he and Bridie were sitting in the study, immersed in the dismal task of wording the announcement of Lady Otranta's death for the London and Edinburgh papers. Andrew read the card, then passed it wearily to Bridie.

" Do you know anything of this, my dear? You weren't expecting him were you?"

Bridie took the card. *Benedict Pugh-Hennessy Esq. MA Cantab. 5 Cheyne Court.* The name gave her a feeling of not altogether explicable uneasiness.

" I wasn't expecting him, Andrew. Except that—" She

broke off. There were still so many things that needed to be told. And now was certainly not the time to go into her terrible visit to Edinburgh on the day of the party, when she had caught a brief glimpse of her employer. "No, I really wasn't expecting him."

She got to her feet. "But I expect it's me he wants to see. Shall I go?"

Andrew nodded absently, his mind already back on his interrupted task.

She met Mr. Pugh-Hennessy in the small drawing room. He seemed over-awed, not at all the commanding, authoritative figure she had thought him in his London office. But then, that had been more than six weeks ago. And a great deal had happened to her since that time.

"My *dear* Miss Tantallon. I come to you upon a sad day, it seems. A *sad* day indeed. . . ." He paced distractedly to the window and back. The night's wind and rain had passed over, and pale autumnal sunlight was shining on the black walls of the castle. "I only heard from Macnab a couple of days ago how *ill* your poor great-aunt was. And now—"

"You've been to see Dr. Macnab, Mr. Pugh-Hennessy?" She'd interrupted him quite without thinking. Actually interrupted him. . . .

"Certainly I have." He drew himself up, his fingers fussing with his over-long cuffs. "You *mentioned* the good doctor in your *letters*. So naturally I—"

"You wanted to see Lady Otranta?" She wouldn't chide him for saying nothing to her first about this visit. He wasn't after all under any very great obligation to keep her informed as to his plans.

"See Lady *Otranta*? Not . . . exactly." He eased his neck within its painfully stand-up collar and peered uneasily round the room. "Dear me, how *grand* it all is. I had quite forgotten. It was like this in my *own* day, of course. But that's all so *dreadfully* long ago."

The castle was indeed grand. But she realised that she no longer found it overdone or comical. Instead she had come to feel at home in its sombre magnificence. "You were here once before?" she asked, seeming to remember that Andrew had once told her the same thing.

"A visitor, you know. The *briefest* of visitors. . . . My people had rented a neighbouring estate." His gaze shifted from hers and he sucked at his ill-fitting teeth. "The . . . ah, the *memoirs*? There's no news of them, I suppose?"

Bridie temporised. "I did write to you about them, Mr. Pugh-Hennessy."

"Precisely so. Precisely so. And now the poor woman's dead. What a *tragic* circumstance." He leaned towards her, wringing his hands. "The rest of the family—how are they taking it?"

She was puzzled. So far she had been unable to discover any reason for his visit. She answered shortly. "Much as any other family that has just lost a dearly loved mother."

He wandered a pace or two away. Then he turned. "And how about *you*, my dear? I gathered from your letters that you and your great-aunt had become very close."

"I. . . ." It was a question she'd been trying not to ask herself. Well, how did she feel, now that the old lady was dead? Suddenly she knew. And suddenly everything that had been supporting her for the last twelve hours crumbled away. She felt utterly bereft. Frightened. Lost. A great source of comfort and wisdom had gone from her life.

She sank down onto a chair and covered her face with her hands. "Forgive me, Mr. Pugh-Hennessy. I . . . I. . . ."

"Nothing to apologise for, Miss Tantallon." He produced a large white handkerchief with a flourish and gave it to her. "I told myself the *moment* you came in. Too bright by *half*, I said. Something's got to give there. And soon. Don't you think?"

And there, at last, in front of Mr. Pugh-Hennessy, she allowed herself to weep. Not the fierce, horrified tears of the night before. Tears of simple sorrow rather, for a dear person, kindly, witty, sometimes cruel, always surprising, whom she would never see again. And whom she would never need to part with entirely, thank God, not so long as she had her son Andrew to love and cherish.

Slowly she grew calmer. She had cried in Mr. Pugh-Hennessy's presence once before, she remembered. After the death of her father. It was as if Mr. Pugh-Hennessy, oddly enough, was a man who encouraged such confidences.

She dried her eyes. "I must ring for Meredith. You'll be staying at the castle, of course?"

If he thought it strange that such an invitation should come from her, he made no comment. He was, in fact, far too busy protesting. "Not at all, Miss Tantallon. Not in the least. I wouldn't *think* of it." He hurried to the door and opened it, almost as if afraid he might be kept on the premises against his will. "I must return to London tonight. That's why I came really—this being my last day. But I must leave *at once*. The firm needs me. Don't you think? It does *need* me?"

His plea was so pathetic that she reassured him. And besides, the firm probably did need him. By what she could judge from her brief acquaintance with his chief clerk, Mr. Thwaite, the entire staff would have resigned as one man if left to his tender mercies.

"You'll take lunch with us, surely, before you go?"

Again the protestations. He wouldn't for the life of him intrude.

She gave in. "I'll have the car brought round to the door, then," she said. "There'll be a ferry back to Edinburgh in about an hour."

They waited in the pale sunlight on the steps outside the massive entrance porch. She recalled her earlier puzzlement. "Mr. Pugh-Hennessy—you still haven't told me your real reason for coming all this way."

He flapped embarrassedly at the long skirts of his travelling cloak. At once she regretted having pressed him. He was such a confused person. "Forgive me," she said quickly. "That was impertinent, I think."

"Not at *all*, Miss Tantallon. Why else should I come, except on account of the *memoirs*? I'm a *publisher*, my dear. A publisher will go anywhere, do anything for the sake of a *book*."

She didn't wholly believe his answer. It had a cobbled-up,

over-vehement air about it. But it made her feel guilty all the same.

"Perhaps they'll turn up after all?" she suggested tentatively. Wouldn't it be nice, she thought, if in a couple of days she could astonish the old man.

His embarrassment seemed to increase. "I . . . I don't suppose your great-aunt talked much about the *first* Lady Tantallon?" he said at last.

"I don't think she ever mentioned her."

"No. . . . Well, it's all a long time ago. Don't you think? But I never *quite* understood the *extraordinary* circumstances of Lady Margaret's death."

"They were odd, weren't they?" Bridie only knew what her cousin Andrew had told her. Wisely she refused to be drawn, however.

Mr. Pugh-Hennessy fiddled with his tall, old-fashioned hat. "I was acquainted with the first Lady Tantallon, you see. Only *slightly*, of course. . . . They were quite wrong for each other. Quite, quite wrong. It was very sad, really. . . ."

The motor car arrived, Duncan at the wheel.

Mr. Pugh-Hennessy turned to her and held out his hand. "Well, Miss Tantallon, I'm really *most* grateful to you for all your efforts."

She blushed as they shook hands. "I'm sorry they weren't more successful," she stammered.

"You did your best. No one can do more. . . . I'll instruct Mr. Thwaite to settle with you to the end of the week."

He left her then. She knew she shouldn't accept his money. But she could think of no convincing way of refusing it.

As he was climbing laboriously into the Argyll Melissa emerged from the stables and pedalled sombrely by, wheeling away down the drive in the direction away from the village. He waited till she was past, then beckoned Bridie out to him.

"Tell me, my dear, would that have been Miss *Melissa* Tantallon, by any chance?"

Bridie nodded. "She's very upset today. I expect she's gone out just to be on her own."

"Yes, indeed. Poor thing." He rammed his hat firmly down

247

on his head and beat with the knob of his stick on the outside of the car door, as if alerting a coachman. " You may drive on now, my man," he commanded.

Bridie caught Duncan's basilisk eye and had to smother a giggle. He went round the car and climbed in. It started with an unusually severe jolt, and rattled precipitately away down across the drawbridge. Still puzzled, Bridie went indoors. She was glad she hadn't told Mr. Pugh-Hennessy about spotting him on Prince's Street five days earlier. It would have embarrassed him beyond belief. He really was the most extraordinary person. Extraordinary, but quite without malice.

It wasn't until the early afternoon that she was at last able to settle down quietly with the closely-written pages of her great-aunt's manuscript. Andrew had been obliged to go and see the minister down in Kincardine, Melissa was still away from the castle, and Robert was understandably keeping to his room. Once she had settled to them in the library, the memoirs didn't take Bridie very long. As she read them it was as if the old lady were sitting beside her, telling the story. But this was no longer a disquieting experience. Rather it was a tribute to her great-aunt's frankness and directness of style. So that even the most shocking parts were somehow bearable.

When she had finished she sat for a long time, staring at the last page where it lay upon her lap. The words ended in mid-sentence. Slowly Bridie's eyes filled again with tears as she imagined, tried not to imagine, the agonising moment when Lady Otranta's pen would move no further. Not a phrase, not a single word more to round off the meaning. And strange, faithful Duncan taking even this incomplete fragment and depositing it, punctiliously unread, with the rest. . . .

Time had run out. Life itself. And every single page, Bridie saw now, part of a race against death. Her great-aunt would have known the truth about her condition, guessed it no doubt even before the doctor's reluctant confirmation. That, certainly, was what had decided her, what had driven her on down all the long months of increasing pain and infirmity, to put into words this, the final testament, the guilt of a life-time, the happiness and the love.

And time had run out—but not before the first, and most important part was finished. Was it in fact mere chance, Bridie wondered, that had brought the writing to end when it did? Or had not her great-aunt's determination, her incredible fixity of purpose, only been sustainable that long? The rest, the evidence of the old Queen's diaries, might well have ensured the memoirs' success—indeed, the promise of it was undoubtedly what had attracted Mr. Pugh-Hennessy—but it was not what mattered, and never had been. Not to Lady Otranta.

She'd held out against death. She'd held out against human opposition also. Old Peggy's—the family's—Robert's in particular. The hints were there in the text, clear enough for all to see. Yet the fears that had driven her even to the bizarre pretence of drunkenness—Bridie felt sure they'd been overblown, the exaggerated anxieties of a mortally sick old woman. Nobody would have harmed her, certainly not Robert. He might bully her, frighten her even, but he'd do no more than that. Not even for his brother's sake.

No, it could only be that her years with the conjurer Salvador had left their mark. She had become so fascinated by the dangerous magic of lies and illusion that in the end it had quite distorted her reason.

Bridie riffled back through the pages. There were in truth pathetically few of them. Each one, however, written in blood —for all the pervading tone of cheerfulness and wry good humour. She sighed. What with the story's shortness, and its unfinished state, there was surely nothing there fit for publication. She could say that with an easy conscience, and thankfully, needing to fear no conflict of interest between Mr. Pugh-Hennessy and the Tantallon family. She had no idea what the legal situation might now be. Obviously, for Melissa's sake, the truth must be made known. But only—at first, at any rate—to the dusty world of solicitors, discreetly, decently. The public scandal that the memoirs' publication would have caused—perhaps somehow that could be avoided.

Poor Robert. She might not excuse what he had done, but at least now she understood. He'd said it had been for his brother's sake, and she believed him. It was Andrew who had the most to lose: the title, the estate, everything. And even when Robert had tried to prevent her marriage he had only, she supposed, been acting in what he thought was her interest. A penniless husband and—to use his own ugly word—a bastard: he might well have thought it best to try to save her from that.

His mother had known better, of course. In the end their marriage had been what even she had wanted. Something— the telling of her own story, perhaps—had reminded her that when two young people were in love, nothing else mattered. Neither parentage nor poverty were of the smallest account. They would face the future together come what may, Andrew and she.

Bridie laid down the manuscript and got slowly to her feet. When Andrew returned from the village she was waiting for him in the courtyard. Melissa had arrived back at the castle a short time before, slinging her bicycle into one of the stables and striding wordlessly in past Bridie where she stood on the steps. Bridie had followed her in—just in time to see the last of her cousin's retreating figure up on the gallery overhead. A moment later a bedroom door had banged. She'd contemplated going up after Melissa, but had decided against it. Melissa would come down when she was ready. It would be time enough for her to learn the truth about her new situation then.

Andrew looked pale and wretched. If she could have spared him further distress that day she would gladly have done so. But the memoirs were waiting. So she kissed him lightly on the cheek, then led him through into the library.

She indicated the neat pile of his mother's manuscript. " I love you," she said. " Whatever you read, just remember that. I love you for what you are. For *yourself*. Nothing your mother says makes the slightest difference."

He picked up the papers without a word. She kissed him again, the mere brushing of her lips on his unresponsive cheek, then left him and sought refuge in the quiet of the sunlit garden. She wandered for a while up and down the paths between the rose beds, pausing by the lily pond to watch rainbows flickering in the fine jets of the fountain. Later she turned her footsteps in the direction of the arcaded terrace.

Old Peggy was there, hunched on one of the far benches. For a moment Bridie hesitated, came near to turning away. But the old woman looked so desolate that Bridie took pity on her, walked on down the terrace and seated herself beside her. She wanted to help.

Peggy pulled her shapeless dress more closely about her, and said not a word.

Bridie folded her hands in her lap. " You were quite right about the memoirs," she said gently. " Lady Otranta *was* secretly writing them."

When this gained no response, she went on, " I think you ought to know, Peggy, that there are going to be changes here at the castle. But none of them is going to affect *you*. It was one of Lady Otranta's last wishes that you should be made welcome here for just as long as you care to stay."

A few hours before she'd have suggested that Peggy remain at the castle to look after the children that would surely be born, hers and Andrew's. Now all that was changed. The castle was Melissa's now, and she might have her own plans for it. Or, more probably, Andrew might prefer to make his home somewhere else. He would have to find a job, for one thing.

Still old Peggy didn't react. Bridie cleared her throat. "Of course, you'd have been welcome here anyway. Perhaps it's not for me to say this, but I know how grateful the family is for everything you did for Lady Otranta."

The old woman's shoulders shuddered. " I did nothink at all," she muttered. " Nothink at all."

" You did *everything*." Bridie leaned forward and took her hands in hers. " Everything in the world."

Suddenly Peggy began to cry. " I was proud to, Miss. Proud to. . . ." She groped for a handkerchief. " Folks thought as it was the drink, y'see. But it was them drops, the laudanum that doctor give her for the pain—that was what really got to her. The poor soul. Oh, the poor soul. . . ."

Bridie stared at the old woman, remembering her great-aunt's graceless, snoring figure, and Peggy's fierce, protective gentleness. *Laudanum*—at last the final piece of the puzzle had slipped into place.

All at once another voice, a man's voice, harsh and self-condemning, broke in on Peggy's strangled sobs. " Laudanum's like that. We all saw what it did to my poor brother."

Bridie looked quickly up, saw Robert standing over them. " It was easy enough for me to scrounge some," he went on bitterly, " and slip it into his wine at the party. A last, ridiculous attempt to discredit him, you see, and stop the marriage."

Peggy dried her eyes. " That was downright wicked of you, Master Robert."

He sighed. " More than that, I fear. It hastened my mother's end, I swear it did. The shock of seeing poor Andrew. . . ." He choked, turned briefly away. Then he lifted his head and met Bridie's gaze. " There's a saying, though, that to understand is to forgive. You understand me, I think. As to the second part, well, I can only live in hope. . . ."

Bridie remained silent. Forgiveness was going to take time. The agony of mind he had put her through—had put them all through, especially his mother—would not easily be forgiven.

Robert sighed again, then shrugged and did a sad little soft shoe shuffle on the paving stones. " *Nobody loves me,*" he chanted, " *Everybody hates me. I'm going down the garden to eat worms. . . .*"

He looked so comically pathetic that she couldn't help laughing. It was a verse she hadn't heard since she was very little. As he went on with it she joined in.

" *Big fat juicy ones, little squiggly niggly ones, going down the garden to eat WORMS!*"

It was no use. One couldn't go on being angry with Robert. One just couldn't.

" Shame on you both," said Peggy, rising tearfully to her feet. " And Madame lying dead on her bed this very minute!"

Robert stood suddenly very still. " It was she who taught that to me," he said quietly. " And I honestly don't think it's such a bad thing to remember her by. . . ." He turned to Bridie. "You know, coz, Mama was always such *fun*."

Bridie nodded. Andrew had said the same thing. And surely there was indeed nothing better to be remembered by.

They left Peggy then, and went slowly away together between the fragrant roses. There was an autumnal chill in the air, but the pale sunlight lay golden on banks of tousled chrysanthemums against the towering walls of the castle.

At the garden door Robert stopped. "I truly am sorry," he said earnestly. "The motor car, the horrible note I left you, my childish cruelty up at the mill . . . most of all, though, I'm sorry for what I wanted to do to poor 'Lissa. To keep her for ever from her inheritance." He frowned unhappily. "The thing is, it was her or Andy. And he's my *brother*. . . . My judgement got twisted somehow. It wasn't for myself, you understand. I'll get by well enough. But it still wasn't right."

Bridie looked up into his troubled face. It was weak, perhaps, but not wicked. A younger brother, spoiled, hero-worshipping his bigger, older, stronger brother. . . .

"Melissa needn't ever know," she suggested.

Robert smiled wryly. "Bless you, little coz. But I think I'd better tell her all the same. As Mama herself said, confession is good for the soul. I'll tell her in a few days' time, when things have settled down a bit."

She didn't think he would, not when the time came, not as long as some sort of excuse could be found for putting it off. Not that she blamed him. Blame—like forgiveness—didn't really come in to it. He turned then, and they moved away through the door, into the castle. She remembered that she'd left Andrew reading the memoirs, so they went to join him in the library.

He was sitting where she'd last seen him. His mother's manuscript was face down on his knee, the last page turned and finished with. He was staring blankly into space.

When he heard them enter the room he lifted his eyes. "Robert?" he said. "All this—would you really have tried to conceal it?"

Bridie crossed quickly to his side. " For your sake, Andrew —not his own."

" I know that." He shuddered slightly. Then he got to his feet. He took a deep breath. " Naturally our engagement is at an end, my dear. You'll want to leave for London in the morning, no doubt."

She stared at him incredulously. " But I *told* you—"

" I know what you told me. You could say nothing else. You're loyal, Bridie, and of course you had to—"

" Loyal? I'm not loyal, Andrew. I *love* you. . . . And I won't let our engagement be over." She checked. " Unless *you* want it to be, of course."

" But Bridie—"

Behind her the door burst open. Melissa stood there, steadying herself against the jamb, her breathing fast, her pale face strangely set and determined.

" I'm sorry to barge in like this," she blurted out, " but I've a confession to make." She squared her shoulders. " And don't any of you try to stop me. I've been gathering up my courage to do this all day."

Her arrival had been so dramatic that it was hard to take seriously. Except that everything about her demeanour showed that she was in deadly earnest. She strode forward into the room. It is doubtful whether she even saw the stack of papers on the table beside Andrew's chair. Certainly she exhibited no interest in it.

" I know very well," she said abruptly, " that dirty linen's best washed in private. But now, with Mama's will to be thought of, and me supposed to be her step-daughter, I frankly don't see how it—"

Andrew interrupted her. " Mama didn't make a will," he said. " She always refused—I thought you knew that. It seemed inexplicable at the time, but you'll see her reasons clearly enough if you read this."

He stooped and picked up the manuscript. Melissa watched him uncertainly. " Will or not," she insisted, " there's still something I want to get straightened out. I've made up my mind, you see. And not before time, either."

She flung herself down in one of the library's huge leather chairs. Almost immediately she got up again and moved away to the large terrestrial globe in its mahogany frame by the window. She spun the globe slowly and for a full minute watched it turn. Then she began. " That wretched shooting accident—"

Andrew allowed her to get no further. " I won't let you dig that up, 'Lissa. It's all over and done with long ago."

" But it's *not*. Can't you see? For God's sake, Andrew, you've covered up for me long enough!"

Andrew glanced anxiously round at the others. " You—you were overwrought, 'Lissa. I simply did what was necessary, that's all."

" Overwrought? Of course I was overwrought. But did you never think to ask me why?

" That was your business." Andrew's glance was wary. " You'd just come back from visiting that lawyer. I thought you were. . . . Look, do you really want to bring all this out now, of all times?"

" Dear Andrew. . . ." She smiled at him with unnatural brightness. " Yes, I do. I must. There's really no alternative."

She turned to Bridie and Robert, her hands tightly clenched and her eyes closed momentarily beneath their steeply sloping brows while she gathered her strength. Then she relaxed, opened her eyes again, and looked directly from one to the other.

" Andrew says I was overwrought. He's quite right. I was so overwrought that I wanted to kill myself. I went to the gun-room. He followed me in just in time to stop me. We struggled with the gun. It went off. . . ." She squared her shoulders and pointed down at Andrew's injured foot. " I've lived with that reminder of my wickedness ever since. He saved my life—and crippled himself in the process."

The room was suddenly utterly silent. Bridie looked away, appalled; Andrew, her Andrew, would have kept the secret all his days.

Melissa leaned forward over the globe. " I fetched his mother. Typically, they both insisted that the whole thing be hushed up. An accident, they said. An unfortunate accident. . . . And, bless them, they never demanded to know my reasons. The visit to the lawyer, they told themselves. A foolish, hysterical girl—and tactfully left it at that. And I, for my sins, let them."

She lowered her voice. " It was my eighteenth birthday, you see. The day when I inherited a small trust fund from my mother. Not very much, but I had to go in to Edinburgh to sign some papers. . . . And the lawyer had a letter for me. A letter from my mother. A letter from the first Lady Tantallon."

She spoke the words with sudden venom. Bridie took a pace forward, thinking that she knew what had been in that letter. But Melissa waved her back and, with an effort, calmed herself.

" It was a horrible letter. She'd written it soon after my birth, and it was full of the vilest things about her husband. Wicked things that I knew from my life-time with him must be untrue. One thing, however, was true enough. Not even she, not even my *mother*, would have been brazen enough to invent that—"

Her voice broke, and she bent her head. For a moment her attention appeared to be on the globe, still spinning slowly beneath her. When she spoke again it was in scarcely more than a whisper.

" Whatever happened, she said, I wasn't to worry. For reasons she didn't explain she seemed to think that Sir James would soon be dead. But even if he wasn't, and if he lived to show himself to me in his true colours—*her* true colours, I still wasn't to worry. She'd paid him out. He was a monster, and cruel and unfeeling, but he wasn't my father. She wrote it with pride. The man she had married was not my father."

She paused, then lifted her gaze. " In the event, of course, it was she who died. And he who lived—to be the best father in the world to me." She pushed her long dark hair back from her face. " Is it any wonder," she asked, " that I wanted to kill myself? When I learned that I had no right, no right whatsoever to his love? No right to his generosity? No right to *anything*? And is it any wonder that I should be ashamed to this very day? Accepting so much, and myself not even a Tantallon?"

It was Robert who broke the silence, laughter spilling out of him in a helpless, shocking, unsuitable torrent. " It's . . . it's a catching complaint," he gasped. "Would . . . would you believe it, dearest 'Lissa, if I told you the only true Tantallon in this room is little Bridie?"

*   *   *

It was a situation close to farce yet, for those involved, utterly, painfully serious. Explanations followed, lasting well into the evening. Explanations not as distressing as Bridie might have feared—not with Melissa long inured to the bitter, twisted reasoning of her mother. Not even the planning of murder could surprise or shock Melissa now.

Who her real father had been, the first Lady Tantallon had never disclosed—except that he was a nonentity; a passable enough agent for her scorn of Sir James, but a harmless, indifferently well-connected nonentity all the same.

Bridie, however, could make a good guess as to his identity. So many things added up. The dark hair and sloping eyebrows . . . the enthusiasm for Lady Otranta's memoirs, nothing to do with the old Queen at all . . . the ' personal reasons ' for coming to Edinburgh . . . and the final, wistful visit to the castle that could not be resisted, with its cautious questions as to the real manner of the first Lady Tantallon's death and the eager interest, quickly hidden, in her daughter. . . .

Mr. Pugh-Hennessy, she knew, had never married. Possibly he carried in his heart to this very day a romantic picture of that woman long ago who had beguiled him, no doubt flattered him, finally used him. The truth would hardly help him. Certainly not the knowledge that he had been regarded as a harmless, indifferently well-connected nonentity.

Neither, Bridie decided, would the truth help Melissa. The shy, engagingly eccentric old man who had left the castle only a few hours ago was a father no one need feel ashamed of. But the advantages to either side in acknowledging him were doubtful. For Melissa he would be tainted by her judge-

ment of the woman who had used him. And for himself—
well, he'd been a bachelor, a solitary far too long. He knew
this himself: witness the firm determination of his departure.

Eventually the discussion in the library was interrupted by
the sound of the gong for dinner. Melissa had been dipping
incredulously into sections of Lady Otranta's memoirs. Now
she looked up at Bridie. Her face was pale, but she was
smiling.

"Lucky old you," she said, quite without rancour. "Little
did the old lady know what she was landing in your lap."

"In *my* lap?" Bridie gaped at her.

"Of course. Don't you see? Castle Tantallon, the estate—
it's all yours now, every stick and stone of it."

Bridie was aghast. The thought simply hadn't entered her
head. "But—"

Andrew stepped forward. "'Lissa's quite right. I expect
there'll be all sorts of legal difficulties. But we'll get them
sorted out, I promise you."

Robert spread his arms theatrically. "And it couldn't happen to a nicer person," he cried.

Slowly Bridie crossed to the fireplace, where a low log
fire was smouldering. She needed time to think. "Your father
left the Tantallon estate to you, Andrew," she said.

Andrew nodded. "With a substantial legacy for Mama. But
he had no right. They were never married. I couldn't possibly
be his legitimate heir."

"I see." Bridie contemplated the flames. "And since Lady
Otranta left no will, her inheritance would usually be divided
among her family?"

"I . . . I believe so. But it wasn't legally hers in the first
place, you see."

Bridie made up her mind. She turned to Melissa. "Did
you keep that letter from your mother?"

Melissa shifted unhappily in her seat. "It's . . . it's locked
away at the back of the bureau in my bedroom."

"Would you fetch it, please?"

Her cousin seemed about to protest, then changed her mind,
rose to her feet and hurried from the room.

Robert scratched his head. "Poor old 'Lissa. I'm sure she'd rather not have that letter pored over by—"

Bridie cut him short. "I know that. But that letter's the only proof we have of her story."

"Come now, coz. She'd hardly have invented a thing like that, would she?"

Bridie didn't answer. They waited in uneasy silence. While Melissa was upstairs the gong sounded again out in the entrance hall, loudly and urgently. Nobody seemed to hear it.

Soon afterwards Melissa returned, a smudged and tattered envelope in her hand. She gave it to Bridie without a word and stood, her arms behind her back, scuffing the carpet. Bridie went to the chair where her cousin had been sitting, and picked up Lady Otranta's memoirs. Then she faced the three others in the shadowed, leather-smelling room.

"This letter and these papers—you don't mind my keeping them?"

"Of course not," Andrew answered, a little sharply.

"Then you'd say they're mine? By rights my property?"

"I . . . I suppose so."

"Good."

In one quick moment Bridie had gone to the fire and flung the letter and the first half dozen or so sheets of paper into the flames. If Duncan Symonds could burn unwanted evidence, she thought, then so could she.

Behind her no one moved. The paper burned sluggishly at first, but soon began to flare. She added more of her great-aunt's manuscript. The light of its burning cast brightly flickering shadows round the room, on the shocked, spellbound faces of her cousins.

She stacked the last of the memoirs in the fire's centre, watched the blackened husk of Melissa's envelope rise and dance away up the chimney, then straightened her back.

"Two of the most improbable stories I've ever heard," she said. "And without one single scrap of evidence to support them." She looked fondly round the group. "The law," she said, quoting Mr. Dickens, " is an idiot. But we're sensible people—we don't have to share in the idiocy. It's not bits of paper that make a family. It's what people *are* that counts."

An agitated tap came upon the library door. She glanced at Andrew, but he didn't appear to have noticed it. " Bridie, dearest. . . ."

" Yes, Andrew?"

He opened his arms and she went to him, welcoming the gentle warmth of his embrace. He would never, she knew, burden her with his gratitude. Gratitude wasn't for lovers.

Behind them the door had opened unbidden, to admit a distracted Meredith. " Sir Andrew, please . . . if you're no wanting your dinner, then mebbe you'd be good enough to break the news to cook. Meself, I daresn't."

It was Robert who roused himself first. " Of course we're wanting our dinner. And please apologise to cook on our behalf for keeping her waiting." He moved to Meredith's side. " And you can tell her too, with no disrespect to Mama's memory, that life at the castle has just taken a sudden turn for the better."

The old man looked from him to Andrew and Bridie, still locked in one another's arms, and then back again. " I'll tell her that, Master Robert. She'll be gey pleased, I'm thinking. We all will."

He held the door open and Robert stalked grandly through. Melissa followed him, then darted back. Awkwardly she pecked at Bridie's cheek. " You're a trump," she muttered. " An out-and-out trump."

And a moment later she was gone.

A tearful smile on Bridie's lips, she looked tenderly up into Andrew's face. " D'you think your mother'd say I was a trump, too?"

" I . . . doubt it. She never approved of slang expressions. But she'd agree with the sentiments."

She dried her eyes. " I do love you, Andrew."

" And I you, my dear."

He released her. With grave formality he offered her his arm. She took it and together they walked slowly out past the shyly delighted Meredith, across the entrance hall to a dining table slantingly lit with the last golden light of the setting sun. To a dinner, hardly the first and certainly not the last she would eat at Castle Tantallon, of oatmeal in all its richest and most Scottish permutations.